HALLUCINATIONS

DW Hohlbein

For Visala and our children and their children

Prelude

Whenever she wakes from a dream, Iris tries to capture the images—she wants to remember—but the pictures in her mind that linger for a moment are like sparks in the night air: brief lights blinking out. She is there in a dream, and then she is there no longer. She is her dream self, and then her eyes open, and she is her waking self, thinking about her agenda for the day, whatever she was dreaming forgotten forever.

She wonders if the people who report on their dreams as if they are short stories they just finished writing actually remember everything they claim to remember, or do they embellish for dramatic effect?

If they do remember, she imagines them lying in their beds, warm under their blankets, not having to get up just yet, enjoying replays of their dreams while luxuriating in the lingering bliss of a deep sleep. How pleasant that would be!

She envies them.

Iris is pretty sure the dream tellers fabricate details and fill in gaps just as everyone does with stories about waking life. Why should the temptation to make a story better be resisted when telling dream tales? If they really can remember their dreams so well, those people must be blessed with some special channel in their minds, something genetic she didn't inherit.

The dreams she does remember are almost always the same: she is driving on a fog-shrouded bridge that is impossibly high, seemingly endless, and the higher she gets,

1

the more frightened she becomes; or she is wandering around an ancient mansion in which a malevolent being lurks, unseen but sensed. She plays the part of one of those hapless characters in a horror movie who, instead of leaving the house and fleeing from danger, continues to explore, no matter how terrified she becomes—or should become—as if she has been captured by some supernatural force that is reeling her in. Eventually she comes to the door behind which the evil lies in wait, opens it, and engulfed in the terror created by a formless monster she can only feel, not see, her body flooded with fear, she screams the silent, tongue-less scream of dreams, and wakes herself up.

She supposes that the dreams of most people these days are just such byproducts of anxiety as these dreams she remembers, since, when awake, she and everyone else is living through a terrifying and unsettling time, the Anthropocene, the mass extinction of life on earth.

Terrifying only for those who believe it's happening, she thinks bitterly. Everyone else continues to sleep the sleep of undisturbed ignorance. Her mother believes the reason so many people choose denial is that the reality is too terrible for them to face. Humans can cope with only so much stress before they overload and defend themselves. Fight or flight, and they choose to flee into denial rather than try to fight against impossible odds.

There are too many problems, they rationalize. *They're too big, and it's too late. I'm only one powerless person; what can I do?*

Her mom points out that most people don't take responsibility for anything, so it shouldn't be surprising they aren't willing to take responsibility for their part in killing the planet.

But, Mom, she argues, *no one can be excused any longer. Refusing to accept reality is killing everything. We're committing suicide in slow motion.*

Sure, that's true, but so what if it is? The economy takes priority over all, including life on earth. Extinction is nothing but the cost of doing business. No one can question the sanctity of the economy. If thousands of species must die out to make a profit, so be it.

***

The dream Iris has just awakened from this morning resembles the dreams she sometimes remembers, but only in small part.

She has never had a dream as vivid and strange as this. She not only remembers every detail, she doubts she will ever forget a single one.

In her dream she walks up a flight of stairs to the wide covered porch of an old manor built in an earlier century. The imposing, ornate front door, equipped with a heavy silver knocker, is open, and crossing the threshold, she enters a sitting room, empty except for a woven bassinet mounted on wheels occupying the center.

The room is windowless and dark. Next to the crib, a lamp with an antique stained glass shade directs a single bulb of light toward a tin ceiling. She can see that the walls are wainscotted and wallpapered, though she can't make out the pattern of the wallpaper in the dim light. As she approaches the crib, the only sound is the echoes her boots make as she walks.

She bends over the crib and for a moment can't comprehend what she's seeing, because what she sees is too strange: lying on its back, looking up at her through eyes that are completely black, like two onyx marbles, is a hairless, milky-white baby with no arms or legs and no facial features except the two bottomless onyx eyes.

The creature lies motionless on its back staring up at her. She holds its unwavering gaze, feeling simultaneously fascinated and repulsed.

The baby—if that's what it is—makes her extremely uncomfortable, and after staring into its fathomless black eyes for some time, she turns away, frightened, and starts walking away. She feels as though she might somehow be captured by those eyes, that if she stares into them any longer, she will not be able to break away from its lidless stare.

The creature, though mouthless, says something to her as she is leaving. She thinks it might be, *I didn't think you would come*, or maybe *I hope you will come again*. Whatever it somehow communicated telepathically carried a feeling of sadness and regret.

Then she is awake in her bed, the image of the baby, she is sure, forever etched in her mind.

Iris wonders if the dream could have something to do with how old her mother is, so old it seems possible she might return full circle to whatever primal, formless state human beings exist in before birth. Her unconscious might have unleashed the anxiety she feels about her mother eventually becoming senile, helpless, and incoherent. Iris dreads the thought of bearing witness to any of those states her mom could enter.

She doubts, however, her mom will ever become *that* old. Helen wouldn't abide any of those awful states.

The feeling of sad regret must be her own. Sad that her mom would die soon—she had to, didn't she?—and regret that she had not spent much time with her since she had moved to the barn 20 years ago.

Because she has neglected her mom, her daughter, Persephone, barely knows her grandmother, and that is something Iris truly regrets.

She leaves the visits to check on Mom up to her siblings, excusing herself because she doesn't have a convenient way to get to the property. Raven has his electric bike after all, and Ursula actually has a car. All she has is the antique one-speed Schwinn that her brother reconstructed for her.

Not only that, she tells herself, the library is a big responsibility. Whenever I leave for more than a day, something goes wrong.

She knows her excuses are lame. Was her unconscious urging her to deal with her guilt?

Iris gets out of bed and in bare feet makes her way to the bathroom between the tall, closed stacks of the library basement. The library, where she and Persephone live, is where Helen Banis, her mom, worked for 30 years until she retired. Iris inherited the job of the librarian when she and fellow neighborhood citizens occupied the building to prevent it from being torn down by developers.

The occupiers were able to enter the building using her mom's keys. Since taking that stand, their ZeroG neighborhood has evolved, the library a symbol of their resistance to the billionaires who have taken control of the country, and who since the late 20s remorselessly pillage the earth for every last resource they can profit from regardless of the consequences.

After brushing her teeth, she heads to the kitchen, the former break room for library staff. Persephone is there, eating one of the scones left by a neighbor at the circulation desk.

"Thanks for making coffee, Percy."

"Sure, Mom."

"I just had a dream I'll never forget."

Iris recounts the bizarre encounter with the black-eyed albino baby who somehow talked to her even though it had no mouth.

"Jeez, I'll never forget that either, Mom. I'm not sure I appreciate you putting the image of that creepy baby in my head. But, hey, if you're feeling guilty about not getting out to see grandma, I'm up for visiting anytime. Maybe we can get Aunt Ursula to take us."

"Maybe."

"So...mom...I was wondering...is the circulation desk covered today? I'm not in the mood for checking books out and making small talk, and Diosa has some newborn chicks for us. There are a lot of coops still waiting for hens."

Percy and her partner Tristan build chicken coops for the neighborhood. They hope every home in the Library neighborhood has chickens one day. The protein they provide is important, but even more important is the chickens are fun and comforting.

"Are you ever in the mood, Percy?" Iris says, responding to her daughter's question, keeping disappointment out of her tone. She knows it isn't fair to expect her daughter to take on too much responsibility for the library. Percy doesn't have the same attachment to printed books that she and her grandmother have. She has other priorities.

By the time Iris was in high school, years before Percy was born, books were becoming dust-collecting relics. If her mother had not been a librarian and passionate about reading—actual reading, not scrolling, not listening—Iris and her siblings could have easily gone through life never opening a book, much less reading it, and Iris suspects that neither Raven nor Ursula have ever read a book from start to finish. They may have listened to one or two when they were still commuting to work, but that didn't count as reading as far as their mom was concerned.

Iris, though, fell under the spell of books early on, hanging around the old Carnegie library with her mom at work behind the giant desk in the middle of the open stacks where patrons came to check out and return books.

Built back in the 1920s, the wide steps leading up from the street were said to symbolize the mind *rising out of the depths of ignorance to the heights of knowledge.* Now the building is a sentinel of past ideals considered quaint, ideals long superseded by amoral market forces for which ideals have nothing but sentimental value. Money became the sole ideal, the means and the ends. The value of everything. In 2053, a public lending library where books can be borrowed for free by anybody is an anachronism kept alive only by Iris' dedication and the help she receives from her neighbors.

Persephone has read her share of books, but she would choose building a chicken coop over reading a book 100 out of 100 times, and she sometimes teases her mom about her zealotry for the perfect bound printed word.

I thought we were ZG, Mom. Couldn't the space used to store the books and the energy used to keep them from getting moldy be used for something more important?

Like what, Percy? What's more important than preserving books, especially now! History doesn't exist anymore except in books.

But we don't need history, Mom! We need a new consciousness. We need to stop everything we're doing for as long as it takes. ZeroG, right? We need miracles! The capitalists have already ended history, and they're going to end the future, too.

***

Iris smiles at her daughter and answers her question.

"OK...no problem. Don't worry about covering the desk today, Percy. Can't have too many chickens. Or eggs."

"The little chicks are so cute! They make everyone happy." Persephone rinses out her coffee cup.

"Our neighbors aren't going to ransack the place if there's nobody there to check out books."

"Thanks, mom.....The thing is, Dad just told me about some patriot trouble yesterday, and to tell the truth, sometimes I'm a little scared working the desk. Some random yahoo might wander into the neighborhood looking for something or someone to fuck up. They're always out there cleaning their guns, complaining about their miserable lives and who's to blame and who they hate...and they especially hate librarians."

"Your dad told me. They drove around dumping bags of to-go containers filled with rotten food and empty beer cans on the street, chanting, *Gas, guns, and garbage!* making fun of our new 'Zero G(as), G(uns), or G(arbage)' sign, yelling *Fuck you, you fucking communists!* at folks on the street. I don't think these idiots would bother with the library, though. They would have to get out of their car."

9

Iris laughed. "Dad thought it was funny that they totally whiffed on the garbage. The to-go containers were compostable, and the cans recyclable, so they actually dumped zero garbage, and left us some compost."

PART ONE

SEARCHING FOR HELEN

Knowledge-Holding Deities; lead me on the Path, out of your great love.
Tibetan Buddhist prayer

1.1

Raven lifted his bike onto the wide cement porch of the old horse barn, grateful for the shade provided by the porch roof. Even though it was late September, it was still too hot to be riding his bike 60 miles, electric or not. He had been hoping while he rode that his mom was expecting him and would be there waiting in one of the two Adirondack chairs where they would always sit, but she wasn't. The cold herbal tea on the little table between the chairs that he was hoping for wasn't there either. He surveyed the field where horses used to graze looking for his mother and called out to her. Getting no answer, Raven poked around inside the barn, peering into the stalls which now served as bedrooms. He thought she could be napping.

She wasn't there.

He tried her phone. Dead as usual. Needing rest from the long ride, he sat down in one of the porch chairs, closed his eyes, and tried to relax, though anxiety had started to flare up.

Why was he anxious? If she had received one of several texts, she would have known he would show up that afternoon, but he knew very well that there was a very good chance she had not. Despite her age and her living alone miles away from her children, his mother was notorious for ignoring her phone. There was no longer any point in admonishing her about it; she ignored all admonishment from them and from anyone else for that matter.

There was no note on the door or inside on the weathered picnic table telling him where she was. This did not trouble him. What made him nervous was not sensing her presence. The barn felt abandoned.

He got up from the chair and started pacing the length of the porch, panning the grassy expanse that stretched a half-mile to either side of the barn, looking for her sun hat or a waving arm, listening for a shout.

Why should today be different from any other day? There were still hours of light left; she must be out on the property somewhere digging, planting, foraging, gathering wood, or just sitting by the pond meditating, keeping the ducks company. His mother defied age. Though 100 years old, she only stayed indoors when it was too hot or too cold or too wet to be outside. It was hot today, but not like July and August. Double digits, not triple.

He would just go out to find her, despite being exhausted from his trip. Better than waiting on the porch for her to return.

He had a bad feeling, though. Something was wrong. He could feel it, and over the many years of his life and its lessons, he had learned to trust his feelings.

He set out, water bottle in hand, and searched for the rest of a waning afternoon, crisscrossing and circling the acres of grass, wildflowers, and shrubs, as well as hiking up the forested hill that rose above the meadow.

He would stop, cup his hands around his mouth, and yell her name, then stand there motionless, waiting to hear something other than the cries of the circling raptors or the squawking of ducks on their way to the pond, trying to hear a human cry, not a bird's, no matter how faint. After he held his laboring breath as long as he could, trying to hear his mother's voice, he would take deep breaths and keep moving through the tall grass, stepping carefully over the uneven ground, constantly tripped by low-lying vines, disturbing the voles, getting surprised by a snake.

The sun descended as he searched, gradually dimming the light to the point that he decided to head back. He hoped she would be there waiting on the porch, looking for him as he had looked for her when he had first arrived. Seeing his bike leaning against the barn wall, she would know he was there.

As he walked, still calling out for her along the way, he began praying she would be there. His mom had often tried to convince him and his sisters about the power of thought, that visualizing something can make it happen, so he visualized her sitting in one of the chairs on the porch. He imagined her standing up and waving at him as he made his way across the field. He saw her smiling while she waved. He could feel her hugging him once he reached the porch.

Despite his fervent wish, she wasn't there. Standing on the porch in the deepening twilight, he kept his eyes focused on the field and the hillside, still hoping to see her. He watched intently, his eyes barely blinking, as the sun dropped out of sight behind the trees that lined the ridge of the hill, creating slants of light and slowly lengthening shadows.

Night was coming, and he didn't know what to do. What *could* he do? Search with a flashlight? He's 70 years old and exhausted. He doubted he had the stamina to keep looking much longer. What if she showed up, and instead of finding him there waiting for her, he was wandering around the property in the dark?

He would wait and try to stay calm. Try to sleep. If she didn't come back sometime in the night, at daybreak, he would hike up the hill to search for her there again. He would walk farther along the trails than he already had. He would walk down all the trails he skipped in his search that afternoon, afraid if he followed them, he might have trouble getting back before nightfall.

Peering into his mom's bedroom stall, he noticed that her bed was unmade.

She always makes her bed. This is not good.

The ashes in the stove were damp from condensation. There was no food on the table. There was always food on the picnic table in the middle of the alley between the stalls— apples, squash, carrots, berries, mushrooms, something.

Where were the half-filled cups of tea?

She wasn't there, and it felt like she hadn't been there for a long time.

He tried her phone again. Nothing.

His mother hated cell phones. She would rant that our alien overlords had created the perfect weapon to render humanity stupid and helpless. Except they weren't aliens, they were worse: they were greedy humans who enthralled us with evil algorithms, who kept us chained to invisible cyber leashes, which they jerked on incessantly with vibrations and beeps, making us look.

Then we stare at the screen, and it gathers the information it needs to keep us in a state of permanent distraction, to render our consciousness null and void. We are prisoners of the phone: we don't talk to each other; we don't look at each other; we don't do anything that doesn't in some way involve a phone.

When her phone died, she usually didn't bother to recharge it unless she needed to call her kids for some reason, usually a request for some supplies, or when she remembered, on their birthdays. He was reassured. Of course, she hadn't checked her phone. She didn't know he was coming. She must have gone somewhere and would be back.

Still, he nagged himself, even if she wasn't expecting him, where would she go? Who would she go with? She never goes anywhere, and she doesn't have any friends left who might take her somewhere.

He occupied himself with starting a fire in the stove next to the table. He needed to eat something, and if his mom did show up in the middle of the night, at least the barn would be warm. The nights out on the property still get cold, and she would be cold.

While searching that day, his thoughts had ping-ponged between imagining her lying dead in the field to the slightly comforting thought that injury was more likely. While heating up the potato soup he found in the refrigerator, he worked on convincing himself that rather than dead, she was probably injured and unable to walk. It would be easy enough for her to have sprained her ankle, and somehow he missed her on his search. She could be unconscious and unable to hear him yelling her name. She could be somewhere off the property, somewhere she goes that he doesn't know about. She would not just wander off and get lost... *unless she has finally been overtaken by age and is losing her mind.*

It was true that it had been too long since any of them had visited. In that time, she might have finally deteriorated mentally. He and his sisters had been expecting her to show signs of dementia for years...

Helen: I know what you're thinking: when is your old mom going to lose it? But I have already! Who but a demented person would live like this?

Ursula: You *are* really old, Mom, older than anyone. People half your age start to forget things, get confused. It's not like we're expecting you to become senile. We just won't be able to believe it if you do.

Helen: Do you really think you're not going to be able to tell when my mind is gone?

Iris: Of course not. This is a stupid conversation. I have no idea what Ursula is saying...What *are* you saying?

Ursula: I'm saying that it's possible that we might have a hard time being objective when it comes to Mom's health. You know she'll never admit she needs our help, and we might hesitate when she really needs it.

Helen: I will definitely ask for help. How proud do you think I am? Then again, if I'm truly demented, I won't know to ask for help, will I? It's going to be up to you all to figure it out.

Ursula: It's natural that we would worry, Mom. How many people do you know who have lived for 100 years? How many people do you know, even 20 years younger than you, who could live out here by themselves?

Helen: I don't know anyone anymore. Everyone I used to know died, so take care of yourselves and don't die before me, OK? I really couldn't live with that! Ha, ha. When I've gone dotty, I won't hesitate to ask you to take care of me. Bundle me off to Birnam Wood, where I can rest in peace, safe, and sound behind your neighborhood's impressive wall.

Ursula (obviously stung): No need to get snarky, Mom.

Iris: *Dotty*, Mom?

Helen: You don't know that word, Iris? It means you've lost your mind, but in an endearing way. That's how I hope to be at the end—no worse than endearingly dotty.

Raven remembered this conversation and others like it as he considered all possible reasons for his mother not being there with him sharing the soup he had just warmed up. Maybe it was not that farfetched to think she had wandered off and got lost. In the morning, he might find her on one of the many forest paths she has made and maintains, physically no worse for wear after a night in the woods, just bewildered, not knowing how she happens to be there or why Raven is there, or worse: not knowing she is encountering her own son.

No matter how hard he tried *not* to imagine the worst, he kept having to admit to himself that her absence might mean what it clearly suggested: she lay dead somewhere on the property, having been felled at last by age. He did not let himself imagine finding her body. He could not imagine that.

Suddenly, he felt a chill, his t-shirt clammy with sweat after searching all day, hiking for miles, so he opened the cedar chest he had made for her years ago, looking for a blanket. He took out a wool comforter and wrapped it around his shoulders. Under the blanket, filling the rest of the chest, he was surprised to find a dozen or so notebooks—journals—of various sizes and colors. He stared at the jumble for several moments, wondering what he was looking at until he realized that he had discovered where his mother was hiding her writing.

***

When he or one of his sisters, or on special occasions when all of them came to visit, they would often walk in the door and find her at the picnic table frantically hiding what she was doing. Her desperate efforts were comical as it was obvious she had been writing. Still on the table were pencils and crumpled pages torn out of a notebook.

"Mom," one of them would say, "there's no point in trying to keep your writing a secret from us. Can't we read it?"

"Not yet. It's not ready."

After years witnessing this same scene, and then asking again if they could read what she was writing, they gave up. She would never believe it was good enough for them, her precious children, for whom nothing was ever good enough, even though they were hardly children—they were old enough to be grandparents. They came to believe that the most likely fate of her work was it would be destroyed before they ever saw it. One night under a full moon, Helen would build a fire and chant a mantra as she tossed each notebook into the flames rather than risk offending any of them by what she wrote, or hurting their feelings, or, worse, disappointing them.

Feeling a little guilty for not asking his mom's permission, Raven chose a notebook and started to read.

She had written with a pencil. Seeing actual writing on a page, in his mother's hand, took him out of the present and the nagging fear about what might have happened to her. He was, instead, in a time and place that had manuscripts, that had people writing by candlelight, that had chronicles, history. What he was reading was not cast in a digital typeface displayed on a back-lit screen; it was actual writing, marks made by hand on actual paper. Sentences and paragraphs had been erased and rewritten. There were pages with rips where the erasing had been furious. He was experiencing reading as people had once experienced reading before computers and cell phones, before printing presses and typewriters. The experience was immersive and meditative; his senses shut down almost completely.

All he needed were his eyes, and as he read, the only sound he heard was his breathing.

I am 8 or 9, maybe younger, maybe 7, which would be second grade, the year of Miss Quasdorf. She was old, her white hair always in a bun, her voice always quavering. With straws stolen from the cafeteria, we would fire spit wads at her back as she faced the blackboard. She couldn't feel the tiny balls of paper and spit as they struck, and while most of them fell harmlessly to the floor, some would stick to the woolly sweater she wore, which was the goal. No matter how many stuck and how funny it became, we had to keep from laughing, or she would turn around and start a classroom sweep for straws and suspicious pieces of torn paper. If caught with incriminating evidence, it was off to see the principal.

I can't remember her name, the principal, but I can conjure up her image. She was a big woman, tall and wide, with short grayish hair that looked painted on. Definitely intimidating. No one wanted to be sent down the hall to visit her, so while we gently pelted Miss Quasdorf, we kept our laughter to ourselves, flashing undercover grins to each other if a wad clung to her back. This was before the overhead projector came into use, putting blackboards out of business. Teachers didn't have to turn their backs to the students to write on the board, so this kind of fun was no longer possible.

Do you remember spit wads? If you do remember, then you remember in those days you raised your hand in the classroom to speak, or you were in danger of verbal humiliation, if not physical abuse. Even then, in the middle of the 20th century, not long before JFK was assassinated and we landed men on the moon, kids were still being punished in public schools. They might be ordered to sit in the corner by themselves at the back of the class, or they might get a glancing whack on the head or some other form of minor assault. For what? For not raising their hand to speak. For disobeying the rules.

We followed the rules when we had to, when we could be seen, when we could be heard, fearing shame and punishment. Otherwise, we were kids and gave no thought to rules. We were seen and heard most diligently in the cafeteria by the roaming lunchroom monitors who forced us to eat all of the awful cafeteria food presented on beige plastic trays that had compartments for the protein (often canned), the starch, the soggy frozen vegetable, and the little dessert square. Eat it all, or no recess! Instead, lunchroom cleanup.

No talking, no touching, no running. Definitely no hitting. Line up against the wall and walk silently in a single file. No shoving, no sniggering. To start the school day, the principal would actually remind us over the PA system, her voice echoing from a speaker mounted on a wall in every classroom, that we should only say nice things to each other or say nothing at all. Then we would stand, put our hands over our hearts, and following the principal's lead, recite America's pledge together, the whole school chanting as one their allegiance to the flag and to the nation for which it stands, one nation, under God, with liberty and justice for all.

At the time, we didn't give a second thought to what we were pledging or what it meant. 'Liberty?' 'Justice?' Those words meant nothing to us. We were Americans, and Americans pledge allegiance. That's all we knew and all we needed to know. Funny, how that era, a century ago, is what the patriots say they want to resurrect—you know, the good old days before the 60s happened and America went to hell—except principals in patriot schools would never remind children every morning to be nice. The patriot prosperity gospel doesn't mention being nice. Being nice is what leads to your living outside your prosperous gated neighborhood, outside the safety of its walls. Being nice is for losers.

Even though I remember almost nothing else from childhood, I do remember a few of my elementary school teachers. In third grade, I had Mrs. Walters. I was her papergirl every morning—daily and Sunday. Imagine that: a girl on a bike early in the morning delivering actual newspapers, rolled up, rubberbanded, and tossed door to door. Everybody got the paper then. The few who didn't were always suspect. You know, suspected of being different, subversive, weird, perverted or whatever. Everybody was getting their news from the same sources. Everybody believed what they read and what they heard on the radio or on TV. There was no reason not to believe.

I think I might have also mowed Mrs. Walters lawn.

In fourth grade, I was lucky enough to have handsome Mr. Corcoran, a spiffy dresser with beautiful wavy black hair, natural, not greased up, who read the Narnia books to us at the end of every school day. Those books endured: I read them to my kids, and Iris read them to her daughter, and Persephone still has a chance to read them to her kids.

I don't think that's happening, and for good reason.

I remember the school playground being an asphalt expanse where we would line up next to each on our bikes and then on GO ride as fast as we could until we got to the monkey bars; then, passing under, we let go of the handlebars and with both hands grabbed the steel bars above us, letting the bikes go riderless until they crashed. The winner was whose bike crashed last. It didn't have to go farther, just crash last. What fun it was: the exhilaration of speed, the adrenaline rush of danger as you had to time the grabbing of the monkey bar just right or risk serious injury, and the anxious anticipation as you hung from the bar watching your bike moving without you, straight and true for a while, then wobbling, then falling down drunk.

I don't remember teachers on the playground supervising. They were probably all having a smoke in their classrooms. That was when everyone smoked all the time anywhere they liked. Kids were considered indestructible, I guess—or maybe just replaceable. It was every kid for herself out on the playground. Kids would get hurt because they were just kids and needed to learn the lessons of the school of hard knocks.

Seven seems the right age for this memory. Second grade. I'm lying on my back in the middle of a field of canary grass taller than me, variegated grass with edges that sliced your fingers if you weren't careful. Like getting a paper cut. The shoots had a smooth side and a rough one, sort of like velcro, which had not yet been invented, or if it had, I was not aware. This is the late 50s or early 60s, a century ago, but velcro seems like something that was probably around then. This was the kind of grass that waves as one in the wind and gets matted down into temporary nests for animals. The kind of grass that I and other kids and adults, too, would snap off and fashion into kazoos, putting a splintered end in the mouth and humming. This was before I knew what a kazoo was.

When does anything, like the kazoo, begin? When does anything end? In a mysterious mist where past and future don't exist. In the eternal present of becoming and ending. Shit happens and continues to happen. Take dinosaurs, or rather take the human race: no one knows, and no one will ever know when human beings began, and no one will ever know when human beings end despite all the talk of our impending extinction, which is not just idle talk. The extinction of our

24

short-lived (on the geological time scale) insanely self-destructive species is certainly becoming more probable as the earth continues to heat up to unlivable temperatures, the web-of-life continues to unravel, and the earthquakes, floods, and fires keep coming, along with the viruses and their unceasing mutations and everything else which threatens our survival and the survival of all living things.

Why should we be exempt from the mass extinction of the Anthropocene when it's our fault? We are the eponymous species after all. Why should we get to wipe out thousands of species of life and be spared? As always in nature, all must adapt or die, but thanks to our death-dealing technology, there is not enough time left to adapt. Code Blue is blaring throughout the world. Will some of us humans manage to adapt as necessary? Will the adaptation be sufficient to keep our species extant? Will there be anyone left to bear witness? And at what stage of the adaptation will resilient survivors not be 'human' anymore? If the obscenely rich orbiting in their habitats above the earth after it becomes uninhabitable end up downloading their neurons into some sort of cyber existence, they are certainly 'being' something, but is it human? If they are nothing but quantum bits encased in a hard drive, are they alive?

There's been talk my entire long life about how the planet is threatened, but the planet is capable of defending itself and will do what's necessary and sufficient to survive, which may very well mean our extinction. So be it. We came out of nowhere and will disappear into nowhere in the blink of an eye, as far as earth time is concerned. From the void to the void as go all. From nothingness to nothingness. There go all the precious egos. And really, looking back, what will any witness be able to say was gained during our brief attempt at dominion over nature? Nothing really. Nothing real. We made up stories about ourselves. And what was lost? A chance. An opportunity to know who we are and why we were given the opportunity to know who we are.

Not too many humans are concerned anymore with the opportunity provided by our self-consciousness. They live their entire lives completely oblivious to our great blessing. We've been pushed down Maslow's hierarchy to the bottom level of physiological needs: water, food, shelter, and sleep, in that order, with what passes for entertainment thrown in. Who has the luxury or, more importantly, the motivation to consider metaphysical questions?

Actually, I do. I do have that luxury and tremendous motivation. I am and have been very concerned with the opportunity provided by my consciousness, and shouldn't I be? I'm going to have to die here pretty soon. Any day now. I want to know what to expect. I want to be prepared.

Just seven years old, but being a little animal myself, I instinctively knew how to make a cozy nest in the middle of the field of grass that lay just across the street from the house where I grew up. It was one of the first houses built in the area, which at the time was on the outskirts of our small town. It was gradually surrounded by other houses and eventually far from the outskirts. There was the cul-de-sac developed behind the house that subsumed the other lonely farmhouse nearby and the houses that one-by-one occupied the undeveloped space across the street, one of which replaced the field where I spent many hours lying in my nest looking up at the sky, observing the shapes and movement of clouds and listening to the sound of wind-ruffled grass, the flitter flutter of small birds, and the background buzz of insects. So many crickets then would jump up like jacks-in-the-box as you walked through the field on a summer afternoon. And there were dragonflies, of course, and butterflies. The field was full of butterflies. I can't see them anymore in my mind, but I know I once could see them with my eyes, in the wild, so to speak. I know that I had friends with butterfly collections. I can't remember any of the friends, but I can remember the glassed cases in which they pinned up butterflies for display, each with a neat, typed label.

I was there in the field one summer afternoon, a little girl lying on her back in the matted grass under a sky like a gigantic deep blue plate, when, for whatever reason, I started thinking about death and about how I would die someday. I remember this clearly. Distinctly. The realization filled me with dread. I thought, 'I will end someday. I will cease to be. This voice in my head will be gone. Where will I be when the voice is gone?' I'm almost positive this was the first time an awareness of my mortality came upon me if for no other reason than why would I, even now, a lifetime later, be so sure I remember this? Why would I make up such a memory? I do believe it's an actual memory. I think it is my earliest memory, the beginning point of my self-conscious life, and how poetically convenient to make this the start of the story of my life! How literary. How dramatic. How perfectly symmetrical to start with a realization of the inevitable end.

Then again, I have every reason to doubt the truth of this memory, because the truth of a memory can always be questioned, but I accept it as true as a memory can possibly be, all things considered.

And is this going to be the story of my life?

I don't know yet. I'm still alive.

Raven returned the journal he'd been reading to the chest. He remembered his mom describing this childhood scene to him, telling him about realizing she would die someday, realizing that death was certain, and how unnerved she had been by this revelation.

"Or is it..." she had asked, not him directly, but rhetorically, to herself, looking up at the beams supporting the barn roof... "Certain? I mean, no one really knows anything about death. The heart stops. The brain fizzles out. The body stops moving, but then what? We're not just a body. I know I'm more than just a body." She continued looking up at the ceiling, allowing what she said she knew to sink down and settle. After some moments, she added, still not addressing him but interrogating herself, "No one knows why we are born only to die, and no one will ever know. That's the great mystery."

He was sure he remembered her saying this to him while he sat on the chest he was sitting on now. *I found her journals for a reason,* he thought.

If there is one thing his mom believes, it is there are no coincidences. Reading about his mother's premonition of mortality was not a happenstance. He could hear her voice in his head telling him it was an omen. *The Greeks believed birds to be omens, and the world is filled with birds.*

He had no doubt that it was an omen, but was it a good one or a bad one?

He finished eating and considered reading more, but something stopped him. Her work was all there below him, begging him to discover what he and his sisters had for so long wondered about. He could stay up all night reading, and the mystery would be revealed. He won't be able to sleep, so why not?

But there was a reason why not. He could feel it, and he knew by now, having lived 70 years, that when his inner voice told him 'no,' ignoring it was not an option. At least not a wise option. *I don't have her permission,* the voice said. *Anyway, my sisters would not appreciate being left out.* He was sure he wouldn't be able to sleep, but he needed to sleep, even if he lay in bed for hours just trying. He needed to rest before continuing to search in the morning.

He got up from the table and moved to the stall where he always sleeps when visiting. The bed, a foam mattress on plywood supported by cinder blocks, was familiar and comforting, a bed he had slept in so many times before that it invited him, siren-like, to sleep. Raven didn't have to labor at subduing his mind: sleep just came to him as soon as he lay down, as if his mother was asleep and snoring in her own bedroom stall next to his, as if everything was as it had always been.

1.2

Anxious about his mom, Raven kept waking up throughout the night. Each time he woke, he went outside on the porch and strained to see something in the moonlight. Helen might be out in the field trying to limp home, feebly calling for him. There was nothing to see, but he heard owls hooting. It was a full moon, a perfect, fogless night for raptors to hunt, and the field was stocked with prey.

It was barely dawn, when he was up once more. Wispy fog clung to the grass. He stoked the fire in the stove to boil water for coffee, and after the water filtered through the grounds, he went out on the porch to get caffeinated while waiting for the sun to appear.

His mom had not shown up overnight. Sitting in his porch chair, sipping coffee, he fought against the feeling that searching for her again was useless, because if he did convince himself that searching was useless, he had no idea what to do then. Just leave? What if... there were too many what ifs. Just search again. And again? Better just to stop thinking about it.

The sun was an LED bulb warming up, gradually illuminating the field in front of him. Through two cups of coffee, he had grown more and more frustrated by the situation. He had no theories and no obvious course of action. Searching was the only thing that felt like control. He didn't want to keep searching compulsively because he had no idea what else to do, but he really did have no other idea. He wished in weaker moments to find her body, and that would be the end of it. Except it wouldn't, of course. There would be painful grief to cope with and difficult decisions to make.

His inner voice kept whispering to him over the static of frustration and confusion, *You're going to have to call your sisters*, but he doesn't want to call them. Calling them is the last resort, and he is not yet close to the last resort.

Why a last resort? They're your sisters, your mom's daughters. You can't not call them.

Because I don't want to deal with the shit between my sisters. Because what could they do anyway? Because they will bring everyone with them—Zephyr, Tristan, Persephone... even Dion.

Fucking Dion, the bagman. It might come to that, though, having to call on him. Probably it would. Seemed like it often did, which accounts for Raven's resentment, which just makes him more resentful. The thought of all of them congregated there on the property, disrupting the peace, the vibrations getting all whacked out by everyone's personalities and agendas, was disturbing.

He was already feeling disturbed; the last thing he needed was more disturbance. Dion and Ursula might even bring Birnum Wood security lackeys with them. Talk about upsetting Mom! No, he really didn't want to bring any of them onto the scene. Not yet.

Raven packed a couple of apples, some sourdough crackers, and water, and set off from the porch to find his mom. Fully awake, his mind resolved for the moment, he felt optimistic. He would find her. He must. He hadn't had that much time to look the day before. Of course, it was entirely possible that he had missed finding her. She should be OK. It hadn't been that cold overnight. No frost. He just kept telling himself that she was probably injured, that he would find her, and that she would be fine.

He retraced his steps from the day before, calling out as he did then, holding his breath and waiting to hear a response, however faint. He circled the perimeter of the field bordered by impenetrable blackberry thickets. He zigzagged across the meadow, creating a symmetrical geometry of paths through the tall weeds, making many more diagonal slashes than the day before. After completing multiple passes, he was satisfied she was not lying there hidden in the tall grass.

Raven returned to the barn and followed the well-worn dirt path to the pond, the first place he had looked yesterday afternoon. Maybe she had left the path, foraging for something, and been hurt.

He thoroughly scoured the area on either side of the trail without finding her and returned to join the resident ducks. He sat in the green plastic chair by the edge of the water to rest. *This is where she should be*, he thought, crunching the apple he had packed, *her favorite spot*.

The pond was what convinced his parents to buy the property. His father, Kaspar Banis, thought the family needed a place to escape to if and when civilization disintegrated into chaos, something which his father believed was more likely than not.

"I'm not a prepper!" he protested when Helen teased him. "You can hardly call the barn a bug-out cabin."

"Why not?"

"I'm just worried. The kids might need the place after we're gone."

"So, a bug-out barn, then."

There was a spring feeding the pond. They would have clean water. All they needed were solar panels on the roof of the barn, which fortunately happened to be south facing in a large clearing, and a lot of batteries.

You had to put in some work to get to the property—not that hard, it was only a mile up the trail—but you would have to get out of your car and hike. His dad thought that would discourage most people who might be nosing around.

They took possession in 2020, the year his niece, Persephone, was born and the first pandemic hit. People were getting nervous then about the state of everything. The billionaires were assuming political control of the country, pledging to extract every last drop of oil in the ground and to hell with the planet, a promise that appealed to a horrifying number of people.

There was fear in the air, and his dad was susceptible to anything in the air. He said he felt tremors of violence. He feared there would be an eruption of rage, and he was not entirely wrong. His father claimed that pent-up anger brought to the surface by social media was overwhelming the collective psyche. Social media is designed to attract crazy people, because it's the crazy people who compulsively click on bait, which means profit for the owners of the bait. The crazies were going to start doing the terrible things they fantasize about, enact the violent fantasies they share on their phones, and the people with the most rage to release have all the guns.

This is the kind of stuff he would mutter about, and the family recognized the irony of the pot calling the kettle, but still, he was feeling something, and they empathized. A worldwide pandemic threatening the global economy and the rise of fascist rhetoric in the US was definitely unsettling. On top of that, there was an ongoing environmental crisis threatening the planet. Everything did seem to be going to hell, everyone seemed to be afraid of something, and maybe it wouldn't be a bad idea to have someplace to go where they could possibly live off the grid in peaceful anonymity. For a while, at least.

Raven finished his apple and tossed the core into the shrubs that circled the pond. The ducks scrambled out of the water, looking for it.

There was only one more area to search thoroughly: the forested hill. This would take some time. He walked on the myriad paths Helen had made through the firs, oaks, maples, and madrones and ventured off the trails into the thorny underbrush on either side, looking for any signs she may have left—a footprint, a piece of clothing, food scraps. He found no evidence or clues. The forest was silent and empty, except for a deer he startled and a few scrub jays.

At some point in the search, his optimism was left behind on the trail, gradually replaced by despair as he walked, and at some point, he stopped calling out her name. He was compelled to keep searching as long as possible, but he didn't believe he would find her. She was gone. Somewhere. When it grew too dark to keep looking, he gave himself permission to walk back to the barn, still looking, but resigned to having to decide what to do next.

He fell into one of the chairs on the porch. Slumped there, unable to think, his mind went blank. No ideas popped up, just a thought train to nowhere.

… She must be dead …

… But it sure doesn't feel like she's dead …

… So why haven't I found her body?…

… This sucks!

After finishing the rest of the soup he had found the night before, he sat at the table, staring at the fire in the stove, stalling, telling himself he had to come up with something to say to his sisters that would not immediately result in some kind of drama, knowing there was no way to phrase 'Mom's disappeared' that wouldn't upset them.

If I don't call them now, they're really going to get on my case for not calling earlier, like yesterday. They'll be here tomorrow. Actually, Ursula will probably drive here tonight.

It occurred to him that his mom's journals were there. Didn't it make sense to look in them for clues? This time his inner voice did not try to stop him.

Raven held an open hand face-down over the journals, as if the pile of notebooks was a Ouija board, trying to sense which one to read next. He closed his eyes and picked.

This year is my personal centennial. I will have lived through the last half of one century and the first half of another. As I've aged, I remember more and more of the first half-century, less and less of the second, as if time is going in reverse, rewinding back to the beginning, which, actually, it may be doing, considering how everything goes in cycles.

At least, I think I'm remembering. What I mean is I believe I really am remembering what I did, what I experienced, thought, and felt, but one thing I've learned over a century is that memory is slippery. Slimy, even. It has a thin wet film over it, distorting it and making it difficult to hold on to. It's hard to know whether or not to truly believe in a memory. We're always making shit up about ourselves, every day, every moment, trying to make ourselves look good, feel good, trying so hard to be someone, a remarkable, wonderful character in a story.

Astrid and I have talked often about memory, and I've been experimenting with remembering, as she has urged me to do. I meditate, and when a memory surfaces, instead of letting it slip away in order to reach the silence meditators hope to reach, I concentrate as hard as I can on that memory, trying to make it resolve into a kind of high-def memory, like a vivid dream, something I can virtually re-live. At times, I have felt that it might be possible to fully enter my memory and actually re-live it, as if traveling back in time. I stick with the memory as long as I can. It's an interesting, at times scary exercise. The longer I stay fixed on the memory, the deeper I go, so deep I might as well be dreaming, and I wonder, am I dreaming? Where is the boundary between remembering and dreaming and what we call reality? That world we awake to and wander in day after day, fully conscious, or so we assume.

I think this is what Astrid wants me to experience and eventually be able to navigate: the permeable membranes of our consciousness. She wants to make me aware of how we can move from one state to another without too much effort if we practice enough. I think she wants me to understand there is only one state of consciousness despite our experience of waking, dreaming, and remembering as different, our consciousness being like one of those light bulbs that has three different settings: no matter what setting, it's the same light. I suppose that Astrid is trying to help me prepare for what's to come. Right? But, how about you let me know, Astrid? You are as slippery as memory in your purpose, in your motivations. Why did you enter my life at the point it would end? I know there is a reason. There is always a reason.

I keep thinking it must be time to shuffle off this mortal coil, but every day I keep hanging on, and the thing is, I wake up and feel good. I feel pretty damn good for a 100-year-old lady, or so I believe. I still get around, slow but steady. I still swim (float) in the pond. I still have an appetite.

Life is good. Life is always good. Being alive is good. Why do so many people not get that?

YOU KNOW WHY

Raven stopped reading. He felt light-headed as questions piled up causing his mind to gridlock. The last line of his mom's journal entry was written in dark ink, not pencil, in a strange archaic font. It looked as if it had been imprinted on the page—stamped, not written.

Why would his mother do that? How would she do it? Having conversations with herself in these notebooks—is this why she didn't want to share them? And who the hell was Astrid? She had never told him about Astrid, and his sisters had never mentioned her. He had never met her over the years. She had been living like a hermit since Kaspar had died. Was she so lonely that she needed to create an imaginary friend? How well did he or his sisters actually know their mother? She was eccentric, but just how far removed from convention had his mom become in her solitude?

Exiting his momentary state of shock, he thought, maybe writing **you know why** to herself was not that strange. Maybe he was just spooked by the experience of encountering his mom's writing voice.

He didn't want to read anymore while he was there alone. It was time to contact his sisters.

1.3

Ursula was surprised to get a text from Raven asking her to call him. Since she had married Dion and moved to Birnum Wood, she and her brother were more or less estranged. Neither of them was in the habit of contacting each other just to chat. She knew it was petty, but she couldn't stop herself from thinking that money was the only thing Raven ever called her about. He and Iris relied on her and Dion to bail them out financially more often than they would ever admit. The arrangement they had was like a microcosm of the economic arrangement between their ZG neighborhood and hers.

Raven had told her he was going to visit Mom. None of them had been out to see her in weeks, so it wouldn't be surprising if there was a problem, and potentially a big problem considering their mother's age. This might explain the text.

Though she and her siblings live in the same town in Northern California, they are effectively living in two different towns, each representing a faction in the ongoing American civil war, now sometimes cynically referred to as the '100 years war.' Raven and Iris live in 'The Library,' one of the first ZeroG neighborhoods. Ursula and her husband live in Birnam Wood, a gated enclave surrounded by high cement walls in which people still drive gas-powered cars, eat fast food, cut down trees for the view, and use leaf blowers.

Since marrying Dion, Ursula has been forced to navigate the minefield that family relations became because of what her family saw as a defection to the enemy side: the party of carbon-burning kleptocrats, the billionaires' party. The family tries to mask their disappointment in Ursula's choice to marry an unapologetic capitalist—a crypto-miner at that—and live in a gated community, but their best fails. Disdain for Ursula's lifestyle leaks out like water from the Dutch boy's dike.

Iris and Ursula especially have struggled with disappointment in how their lives have diverged. They might have been co-librarians after the occupation. They could have gardened together and talked about the books they had read. Instead, they were wary of even visiting each other's neighborhoods. Their family, like many families in America, was another minor battlefield in the war.

Curious and worried, she called her brother.

"What's going on, Rav? Is Mom OK?"

"I don't know if she's OK or not; that's the problem. She's not here."

"What do you mean she's not there?"

"I mean, she is not here. Anywhere. I've been searching the property since I got here two days ago."

"You're not making sense. Help me understand what you're telling me: you're saying she's not there at the barn or anywhere on the property, and two days later you decide to let me know?!"

"Ursula, I know I probably should have called yesterday, but I wanted to search for one more day to make sure, and now I'm sure. She's not here. I didn't want to upset you until I was certain."

"And you know for sure she's gone how? Because she can't just be gone. She's one hundred fucking years old, Rav. Where the hell would she go on her own? She has no car. Who would take her somewhere?"

"I don't know, Ursula! That's why I texted you."

"Are you saying she's been kidnapped?"

"Kidnapped? What? I'm not saying that. I'm not saying anything. She's just not here, and there's no note, and her bed is not made."

"Her bed is not made?"

"She always makes her bed first thing when she gets up. It's an OCD thing. It's like she left in a hurry, but kidnapped? That doesn't make sense."

Mom has disappeared? She was having a hard time accepting what he was saying.

"There has to be something going on we're just not aware of. She was expecting you, right?"

"Well, you know how she is about the phone..."

"So she didn't know you were coming, then."

"Her phone is lying around somewhere, completely dead."

"Sure, yeah, so where would she go?"

"I don't know, but she must have gone somewhere. I've looked everywhere for her phone. It's not here. I called her multiple times, and it's not ringing. Just drive up here, will you? I have a bad feeling about this."

"Of course I'm coming, and I'm bringing Iris, Dion and Zephyr with me. We can all search for her.

"There's something else, Ursula: I found what Mom has been writing and hiding from us. A bunch of journals. I read a few entries. One thing I read is pretty crazy. Disturbing, actually."

"You found her writing but not her. Great."

"Can you *not* bring Dion into this yet? He'll want to get your neighborhood security goons involved, as if they could do anything, and he'll pretend he knows what needs to be done. He's not going to be able to help, trust me. Just you and Iris, OK?"

"What about Percy?"

"If she wants to come, sure."

After ending the call, Raven felt better and worse.

He was relieved not to be solely responsible any longer. His sisters would come, and they would make decisions together as a family.

He was also completely drained and incapable of doing anything except flopping into a porch chair and waiting.

***

Raven opened his eyes. He must have fallen asleep in the chair, which was not surprising, considering he'd had more exercise in the last two days than he'd had in months—years, if he were honest with himself. He was active, always working, the neighborhood's DIY person, someone with a lot of tools and the determination to figure out how to make anything not working work again. Every ZG neighborhood needed someone like him, since throwing anything away was not acceptable. If it couldn't be fixed, it had to be re-purposed. His usual work didn't tax his cardiovascular system, though, just his imagination and patience.

It was the hour of gloaming, the long shadow from the hill having covered the pasture, and his sisters had not arrived yet. Raven got to his feet, stretched his arms, and surveyed the field, as he had done obsessively since arriving. He thought since they would be showing up soon, he should probably get a fire going in the stove, but instead, abandoning that thought as if he had never had it, he stepped off the porch and walked out into the tall grass. He stopped about 50 yards from the barn and stood there as twilight sank into night.

He was barely breathing, trying to be quiet, listening, though he had no idea or image of what it was he was listening for. Maybe it was just habit after two days of listening for his mother's voice with such intent to listen for the slightest sound, the tiniest hint of something. Anything.

Ground fog developed as he stood there, swirling over his boots. He could hear a breeze whisper through the field. For a reason unknown, he was convinced if he stood there quietly enough, long enough, something was going to happen. Something would break through from somewhere, from some other dimension, and he would see something, hear something, realize something. Something or someone was trying to reach him.

Suddenly, Ursula's flashlight was blinding him. The entire field was illuminated as if an alien spaceship was hovering overhead preparing to abduct him. He put up a hand to shield his face. She and Iris were standing on the porch.

"We're finally here," Iris said, puzzled by why her brother was standing out in the field in the dark. He looked dazed.

"Are you OK? What are you doing out there?"

"I have no idea."

"Hmm, OK. Well, we're here," Ursula said. "Shouldn't we go inside? It's late. You can fill us in."

Raven was disoriented.

Fill them in? Why were his sisters here? Why was he standing out in the field in the dark?

His memory came back. He had fallen asleep in his chair on the porch, waiting for them, and now they were here.

He didn't remember why he left the porch to walk out into the meadow. It had not been dark when he woke up; now, it was well into the night.

"I was waiting for something," he told his sisters still standing on the barn porch, wondering what the hell was wrong with their brother.

"There was something out here in the field. I must have heard something. I don't know. I fell asleep in the chair for a while."

Raven took a breath, waiting for his memory to resolve completely.

"When I woke up, you weren't here."

It was all he could say for the moment.

"Are you sure you're OK, Raven?" Iris asked again, worried now. Her brother was barely coherent.

"I'm fine." He walked back toward them. "Just really tired and stressed out."

Iris and Ursula took turns hugging him when he stepped up onto the porch. They stood together awkwardly for a moment, not knowing what to do next. There were no precedents to guide them.

Per her role in the family, Ursula got the next step in motion. "Let's go inside and make some tea. We brought food."

"I have to get a fire going," Raven replied, remembering. "I should have done that knowing you were coming."

"I'll do it, Rav," Iris said, looking at her brother with concern.

"Take it easy. You must have been really freaking out since you got here. Try to relax. We'll figure out what happened to Mom. She must have gone somewhere. We just don't know where."

That's it, Raven thought. *Now I remember.*

"Why wouldn't she leave a note then, Iris?" Ursula said with the slight undertone of condescension that annoyed both her siblings.

"We already talked about all this in the car," Iris snapped, her back turned to her sister as she arranged the kindling in the stove. "She let her phone go dead or lost it, or didn't check it. As usual. She didn't know Raven was coming. She had no reason to leave a note."

Iris got a fire in the stove started, and Ursula put the tea kettle on. She brought out egg salad sandwiches Iris had made and laid them out on the table with some apples.

Raven ate steadily, barely pausing to take a breath, enjoying Iris's olive bread. The water boiled, and Ursula made tea from chamomile Helen had gathered and dried. Hopefully, the herb would calm Raven's mind, as it seemed to need it.

They all took a break from talking to eat and sip the tea until Iris got the conversation going again.

"When has Mom ever told us her plans? She has lived out here by herself for 20 years. She's not in the habit of telling us her plans or anything else. The only time she calls is on our birthday."

"When she remembers," Ursula said under her breath.

Raven nodded agreement, while chewing steadily.

Iris continued, "So, how long do we wait for her to return?"

"Like we talked about in the car, Iris, we need to search the property again tomorrow."

Raven grunted, his mouth full of bread.

"She's not out there," he mumbled. "You won't find her."

"We still have to see for ourselves," Ursula said. "You know you would feel the same way, Rav."

Done eating, Raven suddenly got up, animated and excited.

"Remember, Ursula, that I told you I found what she's been writing?"

He walked over to the cedar chest and opened it.

"Come and look.

His sisters gathered around and looked down at the cache of notebooks.

"I took one out and read it, hoping to find out something, and I did."

He picked up the notebook he had read the night before and handed it to Ursula.

"She seems to have a friend named Astrid. I'm not sure if Astrid is real, though. Read it."

Ursula held the notebook open and started reading where Raven pointed. Iris read along over her shoulder.

She finished before Ursula and looked up at her brother, her green eyes wide. Ursula closed the notebook and held it with both hands on her lap, her head bowed over it, thinking. They were both processing as Raven had when he first read their mother's writing. He understood that encountering her writing voice was a strangely moving experience. It was a different her speaking, a distant authorial her, their mother talking to them, but not just them, talking to everyone, talking to herself.

"Well...?"

"We're going to have to read them all," Ursula said, looking up.

Iris nodded. For once, there was nothing for them to argue about.

1.4

After dinner, the three siblings moved from the confines of the barn to the porch, hoping fresh air and wide open space would generate insight.

It didn't. There had been little conversation while eating sandwiches, and now, on the porch, there was none. They sat together in the dark, tired and worried, observing autumn's silvery fog materializing in front of them as if blown in by a machine off-stage, each of them haunted by the last line of their mother's journal: **You Know Why**. That sentence had imprinted itself on their consciousness just as it seemed imprinted on the page of the notebook.

"So...Astrid..." Raven ventured, "any theories?"

"What's yours?" Ursula said brusquely.

"I have one or some."

He thought that Helen might be writing to herself, or her selves, exploring the possibilities that writing offered. Instead of creating a fictional world with different characters, she was exploring the selves that inhabited her interior world and conversing with them. Astrid could be one of many different selves. They might meet other characters as they read more.

"Developing her own form of solo psychotherapy would be so Mom," he concluded. "Another thought I had was she could be experimenting with automatic writing."

"Raven, why is it so hard for you to believe the simplest and most likely explanation, which is that Astrid is a real person? A friend," Iris said impatiently.

Ursula nodded with a strained expression on her face. This was how Raven thinks—obtusely, the opposite of how she thinks.

"Your ideas are stretches," Iris continued, "especially automatic writing. That's just bizarre. Do you even know what automatic writing is?"

"It's not crazy to believe Mom could be trying to communicate with the spirits. Why is it so hard for you to imagine she might be trying—and even succeeding at—automatic writing? Have you ever heard of Astrid? Did Mom ever mention someone named Astrid to you? Ever?"

"No....So? Do you know everyone that Mom knows or has ever known? Maybe she just met her. How is this not a reasonable explanation? She might have a new neighbor we don't know about."

"It seems reasonable, but it doesn't feel true. I don't know why, but it doesn't. Tell me honestly if it feels true to you or if you're just hoping it's true."

Iris conceded his point by just looking at him without responding.

Ursula broke in to have the last word.

"Don't senile people live in the past? They don't recognize you and believe you're some person they used to know. She's not immortal. We've been wondering for years when she would lose it. The mind goes along with the rest of the body. It's inevitable. You don't want to believe it, but Mom probably has dementia. Astrid must be someone from her past she imagines is alive and hanging out with her."

Getting no blowback, she pressed on.

"She took a walk into the woods or up to the road and got lost. We have to stop making up ridiculous theories and accept the most likely explanation for her not being here."

She had her story and would stick to it. There was no use arguing with her; she had a point.

"So, what is it that you're really wanting to say, Ursula?" Iris asked, resigned, knowing already what her sister would push for, having known since she got in the car with her. She knew this was why Raven had waited too long to contact them. He didn't want to have a confrontation with Ursula about getting help from the outside, specifically from Dion and authorities from Birnum Wood.

"I'm saying that I don't have much hope we'll find her. Raven has already searched the property for two days. I'm saying that we need to accept that Mom is probably demented. I mean, think about what we just read: she's either writing about an imaginary person or about someone she used to know in her past who is probably dead, and she believes that person is out here on the property talking to her, advising her to practice re-living her memories in order to what? Prepare for death? Who would think that? She's going to the trouble to write about her, for God's sake! What I'm saying is we have to ask for help and extend the search so we can find her, wherever she is. She could be hurt, or ..."

She didn't need to say the last part out loud.

While his sister was talking, Raven visualized the search parties, the 4WD vehicles smashing through the field, the furious texting, the phone conferences, the cops from Birnam Wood issuing orders, and then, inevitably, the postings on social media, the cascade of false tips, countless bloggers chiming in with their opinions, their theories, their moralizing, their speculations about the lost 100-year-old woman, the former librarian turned recluse and her eccentric family, the founders of The Library, and the worst part of his vision, the nightmare that he would not allow to happen: the property exposed, the barn, the field, the pond, their parents' place, their place, a sacred place, ruined forever, infiltrated from every possible angle in every possible way, corrupted, the harmony lost, the peace gone.

If the mystery was made public, their family's property would be constantly circled by vultures who would try to find a way to profit from the story. The story would become a product for sale, just like everything else.

Raven vowed to himself that this was not going to happen. The vultures would not be alerted. Wherever his mom was, she was counting on him not to let that happen.

"Before we make any decisions about what to do, we should read more of what Mom wrote," Iris suggested. "Shouldn't her journals tell us something?"

"There's a lot to read, and there's no more time," Ursula said. "Every hour is important."

She looked at Raven.

"You should have let us know two days ago. Mom could be anywhere by now."

Yes, he knew that. He had his reasons not to let them know, and she knew what they were.

"I think we should take turns reading each of these journals aloud," Iris said.

She didn't want to call in search parties any more than Raven. She knew that was the last thing her mom would want, senile or not.

Not waiting for agreement from her sibs, she took out a journal and read to them, buying some time.

Today would have been Denny's 102nd birthday. Sometimes I wake up on one of the kid's birthdays and don't remember it until later in the day, and then, oh yeah, it's whoever's birthday. I've even forgotten all day, which I know hurts Ursula's feelings. I don't think Iris or Raven care. When I wake up on my brother's birthday, though, I always remember. It's my first thought. I see him in my mind's eye so clearly, the young man, Dennis, my older brother. I feel his energy. I miss it, and I miss him. There was so much drama in those last days we had together, drama I've never experienced again with anyone else, drama that seems unimaginable now, even with the end of the world looming.

We were together for the days of rage in Chicago, our hometown, half-listening to the speeches in Lincoln Park, getting all hopped up on illegal substances and passionate rhetoric along with everyone else gathered there to express their righteous fury. He had a lot more to be raging about than me because he had just been drafted and ordered to report to an induction center. From there, once he passed his physical, he'd board a bus to get his basic training in killing, and once trained and equipped, he'd take a plane to Vietnam filled with other teenage conscripts, 18-year-old boys like him. But there was no way he would ever go to the induction center or get on that plane.

We malingered in the park with the crowd, which was in the hundreds, not the expected thousands, waiting for the signal to raise hell in the streets—as if throwing rocks through windows and setting cars on fire was going to accomplish anything, but hey, our anger was justified, no matter how pointless the expression of it. While we waited for our orders, the Weather Underground leaders were reciting the radical screeds of the day concerning the sins of imperialist Amerika with a 'k' and the crimes against the people perpetrated by racist, fascist icons—Nixon, Hoover, Kissinger, et al—and their hypocritical gaslighting about how America had to stop communism wherever it rears its evil head, no matter the means as long as the means meant the end of communism, when as always the powers that be were just protecting the interests of wealthy capitalists, the same people in charge of our country now, who like those men who waged war on Vietnam and orchestrated coups in Latin America have never given a shit about ideologies, who only care about their access to natural and political resources that will make them more money and keep them in power. Who cared how many Vietnamese died? How dare the communists in the North claim to be fighting for the Vietnamese people, as if their cause was just? They were communists! Bomb them. Raze their jungles with Agent Orange. Spray their villages with Napalm. Smoke them out of their tunnels. We were saving the world from the evil communist scourge.

It's so ridiculous how nearly a century later the patriots, who are living in what has become an ideology-free world completely devoted to the private accumulation of capital, still call people communists. There is no communism anymore, and there are no communists. The capitalist neoliberal Trojan horse ridden in by Ronald Reagan crushed communism—the evil empire—and conquered the world back in the 80s. Nobody is a communist anymore. The patriots need to do better if they want to be insulting, but their imaginations aren't up to the task, if they even have imaginations, which is debatable. ZeroGeers are hippies, if anything, not communists, but I guess calling people hippies doesn't have the same zing as far as insults go. Or maybe it's because they know in their hearts that the hippies were right about everything, especially money.

While Denny and I waited for the signal to move, he lit up his draft card. Everyone around us was entranced by the flame as he held the card up high, its ashes floating to the ground. Those watching nodded their approval, smiled, laughed, and clapped. He had just committed a felony, something akin to treason in a lot of eyes, and we were just about to start a riot, another felony, and when we eventually did, the helmeted, armored, baton-wielding police were ready, outnumbering us 5 to 1. It didn't take more than 15 or 20 minutes for us all to be scattered, choking on tear gas, running from their snarling dogs.

Denny and I were separated in the melee. I ran away, not throwing anything anymore, just running as fast as I could to get as far away as possible. Getting teargassed is horrible. Denny, though, was arrested with brick in hand, charged with conspiracy to riot, and if the prosecutors had been given the opportunity at a trial, in their discovery they would have found out he had burned his draft card.

Out on the bail we raised, he told us he would go underground and keep fighting, and if necessary, he would seek political asylum in another country. We never saw him or heard from him again. It's possible he took part in the Weather Underground's bombing of the Capitol and the Pentagon a few years later, but we don't know. Mom and Dad stayed in Chicago, but I left to go to school in Oregon, to become a librarian. The FBI visited all of us, but Denny had made sure by disappearing without saying a word that we knew nothing. We tried to forgive him, telling ourselves he wanted to protect us.

Considering his status as a domestic terrorist, he might have been right not to let us know where he was, but I don't believe it was right. By the turn of the century, the days of rage were ancient history that no one remembered or cared about. The events of the 60s had been reduced to popular mythology and coopted by the capitalist marketing machine. There was always money to be made. He might have been a celebrity if he had returned! He could have written a best-selling book while in jail and, once released, gone on tour, been invited to late-night shows, and made a cameo appearance in a movie based on his story. Not that my brother would have ever taken that path, but he could have at least texted us on a burner phone to let us know he was OK.

I think he must have died not long after he fled. Actually, I don't really believe that; I just want to believe it rather than believe he lived a long life somewhere without ever looking back, just letting us go without another thought.

What a heartless thing to write. I guess I have to admit I never forgave him.

He was 18. I was 16. It was 1969, the year Nixon began the not-secret bombing of Laos and Cambodia, the beginning of the end of the war, though it dragged on for another three years until we helicoptered away in shame, defeated by the communists of Vietnam, the last true communists.

"Did Mom ever talk to you about her brother?" Iris asked once they had had time to process their mom's story. "I remember Dad saying he was a casualty of the 60s. I didn't know he meant that literally."

"It must have been Uncle Denny's birthday," Ursula said, remembering. "Dad explained to us why Mom was so upset that day. What about you, Mom's darling boy? Did she tell you about her brother?"

"I can't help if I'm the only son," Raven retorted, "and the oldest. Wasn't given a choice."

Ursula's bitterness about feeling as if she was the least loved child was something she wore on her sleeve. She judged herself not as creative and sensitive as Raven, not as intellectually curious as Iris, just competent and responsible. In other words, mediocre. She self-soothed by believing that in every family there must be at least one person like her, and that person is never appreciated but always needed.

"Seems like Mom would have confided in you, Raven, at some point."

"Well, she didn't. All she ever told me was he had to leave the country to escape the draft, and they never heard from him again."

"So she never told you he was in the Weather Underground?" Iris asked. "They were terrorists trying to overthrow the government. They actually bombed the Capitol!"

"No. She never said anything about that. I've never heard of the Weather Underground or the Days of Rage."

"It's hard to imagine Mom and her brother in a riot, getting chased by the police," Ursula said. "They were still in high school."

"People were really angry about the Vietnam war. Just as angry as we are now about the billionaires killing the planet," Iris pronounced from an invisible soapbox. "It's the same anger about the same thing. Killing people and trashing the environment for money and power."

"It's sad," Raven said. "Mom lost her brother, and we never got to meet our uncle."

"You need to keep reading, Iris," Ursula said, resigned to what she believed was a waste of precious time.

Even though she was interested in what her mom wrote, she couldn't relax enough to really take it in. Her mind was preoccupied with trying to figure out what they should do to find her. Reading her journals was not going to help. Not like getting a lot of people out looking for her would help. She could accept their hanging around the barn reading only because it was too late for searching that night.

"Me again? Give me another one, then."

Raven held his hand over the journals as he had the night before, trying to sense which one held a clue.

"Any time, Rav."

"It's ridiculous that these journals are not dated," Ursula said. "For a librarian, Mom sure wasn't organized."

"When did Mom start writing these, anyway?" Iris asked, interrupting Raven's ritual. "Do either of you remember when we started catching her hiding this stuff?"

"Maybe ten years ago?" Raven offered. "Definitely some years after she moved here."

"That seems about right to me, but I really don't remember," Ursula said.

"At least the notebooks are small," Iris added, and began to read the one Raven handed to her.

Will there be a day when I don't wonder if my living out here by myself like a hermit is the right thing to do? Kaspar would know, or at least help me answer that question, but I can't ask him. After being married to me for 50 years, he knew me better than anyone else. I suppose I may have known him just as well as he knew me, but I wonder what it means to say to someone I know you, or you know me? No one can really know another person's experience.

I think we came close sometimes.

Maybe writing is my way of keeping him with me. He should be here with me, but whatever we think should be is irrelevant. Karma decides these things. Unlike our human laws, the law of the universe is eternal and immutable, unchangeable and unbreakable. There's no going around it, no loopholes, no way to bullshit your way out, nothing to bribe with, and no one to bribe. Karma just is. Every thought, every act, has a consequence. The law is simple, elegant, and brutal.

When the kids ask me why I live out here all alone, I give them the reasons they expect, so they—mainly Ursula—won't get all concerned and start questioning what I'm doing. I tell them what they will understand: that I want to spend the last years of my life in peace, away from the world and its problems, especially the violence. I've had it with the violence, the guns that so many own, and why? So if they have to, they will kill someone? What kind of reason is that?

I've done what I can to live a good life, tried to do as little harm as possible, and tried to help. I risked a lot when I gave the library keys to the occupiers to keep it from becoming another retail outlet. To preserve something valuable rather than destroy it. I could have been arrested, but the billionaires had more important things to do. I was a nobody librarian in a little town of no consequence far off the freeway. My civil disobedience was inconsequential, hardly worth a blogger's time. They weren't going to make any real money selling whatnots out of the library. Might as well let the hippies live in their squalid ZeroG community trading hand-me-downs and riding bikes. Who cares?

Yes, I say, responding to what I imagine would be Persephone's lecture, I'm escaping. It's all too true that the privilege I was born with made my escape possible. Go ahead and tack on more accusations, prove my complicity, establish my guilt. I own it, but this is what I'm doing, and it feels OK. Kaspar and I bought the place, and I want to live here while I can. He would want me to. I welcome the solitude and being close to nature. I am happy, not lonely. Of course, you kids are welcome to visit any time. Please come!

And so on and so on, and despite their protests about my being old and needing help and we won't be able to see you all the time, they seem to accept my vague explanation for leaving the world.

I don't tell the kids the real reason, which is I'm escaping the world to prepare for my death, which should come any year now, shouldn't it? That's probably why I ask myself every day what I'm doing living out here, because every day I ask myself, really? Do I honestly, deep down, believe I am here to prepare myself for death?

I still need to convince myself. It's not like I'm a yogi who's been meditating for years in a Himalayan cave trying to attain enlightenment. I was a librarian for 30 years. I meditate, though. I have so much more time. I always had time, but I also had a lot of convenient excuses. No excuses now.

As part of my preparation to journey to the undiscovered country, I tell myself that I'm here to explore consciousness, because everything is one eternal consciousness, which is not just something I believe—it's something I know. I have experienced connecting with the eternal consciousness, and I don't see why the experience of oneness with the universe induced by a barrel of orange sunshine or a tab of windowpane somehow invalidates the experience.

There was one night I lay on my back somewhere in the wilderness, looking up at the sky, and found myself speeding through the galaxy, faster and faster, the stars becoming blurred as I raced past them. I pulled myself back, afraid I would eclipse the speed of light and never return.

One afternoon, hiking along a ridge, I stopped to rest in a spot with a clear view of a mountain which rose above the valley below. While I stared at it, cracks began to form, spidering in every direction as they do in a windshield. An intense white light shone through every crack. The cracks widened to the point that the mountain was breaking apart. The light was too bright to look at. I felt certain if I didn't look away, if I didn't stop what was happening, the entire world would disappear, along with me, and all would become that light. The light was what the world was made of; I didn't want to surrender to it. I wanted to keep being me, so I looked away.

We are an electro-chemical contraption made almost entirely of water. Our bodies run on chemicals. Our natural chemicals alter our consciousness all the time, and we don't say, 'hey, I was under the influence of my hormones, so whatever I just experienced was not real.' Consciousness is chemical. Introducing another chemical that causes a chemical reaction doesn't disqualify the reaction from being 'real.' Accepting that logic means that none of our experiences are 'real,' which billions of Hindus and Buddhists believe, so there's that.

I digress. As always. One thought leads to another, and I slipslide into the stream of consciousness, happy to have it carry me away to wherever, but I need to get control over all those thoughts flowing through my mind. I want to be able to make my mind one-pointed on command. I want to have an anchor that I can throw into the stream when needed. This is the preparation I need before I die, or so I tell myself, so I believe.

I don't think the kids would want to hear any of this. They definitely would react in unhelpful ways to my saying to them point blank: kids, I am preparing for death. Maybe they're different, being raised by Kaspar and me. Maybe they're not death-averse as most are, but I don't think they would want to hear me say it out loud. I could be wrong. I might ask them, Raven first. He wouldn't protest. He'd listen, interested, sympathetic. I would explain to him that it's important to get as familiar as possible with my consciousness before I die, because in the bardo I will be confronted with the projections of my mind.

Buddhists say the moment of death, when your consciousness leaves your body, is like the moment of birth in reverse. Just like we don't remember our birth, we don't remember our death. Life after life, we don't remember those transitions from one state of consciousness to another and back again. The Buddhists say be prepared for the moment of death because if you can maintain a clear mind and somehow realize you are no body, no thing, not separate, that the 'I' you thought was your self is not your self, that you are one with the eternal consciousness, you may not get seduced into returning to another body and assuming another personality. You just have to have the presence of mind to recognize the clear light of reality, and you might be able to stay in Nirvana.

Shouldn't I want eternal bliss?

As if I will have a clear head when face to face with the clear light of the void.

As if I will be ready to realize what is real.

As if I'm ready for enlightenment. Funny. Ha, ha.

Where's my faith? Where will it be at the moment of death? I can't be on the fence that I'm on now, where I don't really believe, but I really do believe, but in my intellect, not my heart. I have to believe in my heart and leave my intellect in the dust with my body. At the very least, I hope not to fall into a pitiful state of terror when confronted with my demons. At the very least, I hope to be able to make a good choice for a womb in which to be reborn.

The Buddhists say that it is possible to choose. I don't want to choose out of fear. I want to choose out of love. I want to at least take a step toward liberation.

Iris looked up from the notebook. No one spoke as they absorbed what she had just read. None of them knew their mom believed in karma and reincarnation with such conviction, that moving out to the property to live out the last years of her life was not her way of dealing with the grief of suddenly losing her husband to a stroke, to avoid family obligations, or cope with a culture gone mad. She had moved to the property to prepare for her death.

"Not just preparing to die, but to be reborn in the proper womb," Ursula scoffed out loud, breaking the spell cast by what Iris had just read. "One chosen with love, like picking out a coffin, except in reverse."

"You think it's silly, but what do you know?" Raven sputtered angrily. "What does anyone know about what happens when we die? Nothing."

His sister's attitude was so typical: don't believe in anything, because if you profess your belief in something, you risk looking like a fool, and what could be worse than looking like a fool? There's nothing worse than being someone not in the know, not clued in, and not cool. The chorus of one of his dad's favorite songs started playing in his head; one Kaspar would sing along to while working on some project:

I heard it was you...
...talkin' 'bout a world where all is free.
It just couldn't be.
Only a fool would say that.

Ursula ignored her brother's outburst. "Why didn't we know she believed so strongly in all of this? I knew her interest, obviously, but I never thought she would follow through on it like this."

"Like she wrote: she thought we wouldn't want to know why she moved out here. She probably thought we— especially you, Ursula—would try to stop her."

Raven gave Ursula a sideways glance, then addressed both his sisters: "Don't either of you ever think about dying? We're not close to being as old as Mom, but we're old. I'm 70, for God's sake. I think about death all the time."

"So what do you believe, Rav? We were all given darshan by the guru when we were kids. We went to the retreats...you kept going long after we stopped. We heard the satsangs. Did anything stick?"

"I don't know what I believe, Iris. Everything... nothing... I wish I could talk to Mom about it now, though."

"Me, too."

Silence again as they thought about what they believed, as they imagined her death, their own deaths.

"Enough reading," Ursula pronounced. "None of it is going to tell us where she is. Tomorrow we will find her alive and well, and she can read the rest to us."

Iris couldn't sleep, not only anxious about the next day but disoriented by the dark quiet of the cabin and the heat of her sister's body under the wool blankets.

Lying next to each other in their mom's bed was not something they had done since they were little girls. She could barely see Ursula, but she could sense her every movement, however slight. She heard Ursula breathing as if she were wearing headphones and listening to a recording. Her mind, overly stimulated by everything she had experienced that day, seemed to be transmitting and receiving thoughts and feelings across the narrow alley between their bodies, thoughts and feelings that had accumulated over the years, and it seemed as if they were now confessing to each other.

What they were communicating silently brought them closer together. An understanding was reached that was long overdue. They were sisters who needed each other, and there was no reason to defend against that need. By the time light began to filter through the walls of the barn, she had relaxed enough to fall asleep, side by side with Ursula, facing her, sharing breaths.

1.5

Raven was awake most of the night, trying to come up with a plan that would somehow derail the inevitable incursion from the outside world. Ursula's grand search was not acceptable, but doing nothing was not an option. Helen was somewhere, dead or alive, and they would have to keep trying to find her until they had exhausted all avenues, until faced with either knowing what had happened or not knowing. Not knowing was an awful thing to have to live with. He would even agree to call in the Birnum Wood cavalry if it came to that.

He was up at first light, as he had been since he arrived, his circadian clock now totally in sync with the sun. While waiting for his sisters, he stoked the fire, boiled water, and made coffee, which he left on the stove to keep warm.

He went out on the porch to drink his coffee while watching the sun slowly make its way across the field. The dew-soaked pasture steamed as it heated up. On the porch of the barn where his mom had come to die, in a chair he always sat in whenever he visited, still half-asleep, he felt outside of time as if he had entered a dimension in which he and his sisters would debate forever unanswerable questions, and would for eternity wonder what had happened to their mom.

"Thanks for making coffee, Rav. How long have you been up?"

Looking closely at her brother, trying to get a feeling for how he was doing after his third night in the barn, Iris was reminded by his distracted look of how they had found him the evening before.

"So, Rav," Iris said tentatively, worried she might somehow be broaching a sensitive subject, "when we showed up last night, you were standing out in the field looking stoned. You said you were waiting for something."

"I remember."

"You said you didn't know what you were waiting for."

"I didn't. I don't know why I was standing out there in the dark or what I thought I was waiting for."

"You have the same look now as you did then."

"What I have is the look of a mind that has been reduced to rehearsing an endless loop of questions: Is Mom really dead? What if we can't find her? What are we supposed to do? Back to: Is Mom dead? And so on and on and on until I get my mind to stop. That doesn't last long, though. So, yeah, I probably look lost. I feel lost. I don't know what to do. What is the right thing to do? You don't know. Ursula doesn't know. Who *would* know?"

Raven looked up at the rosy dawn sky.

"What am I waiting for? For something to change. I'm waiting for direction." He laughed. "From Mom, maybe."

"No one likes to feel out of control," Iris said.

"What choice do we have? I stare into the night sky, trying to see choices floating out there because there aren't any in my head. All I have in my head are these pointless questions repeating themselves over and over."

Her brother looked like he was about to cry, or scream, so Ursula broke in, trying to break the mood.

"I think if we had been here for three days looking for Mom, we would be feeling lost, too. This situation is stressful enough without reading the crazy stuff she wrote. It's really disturbing to hear that she moved out here to die when we are all here trying to find her, hoping she is still alive. We should get on with the search."

"Shit!" Raven suddenly blurted out, apparently rescued from despair, "the chickens! Eggs!"

***

The 'colony,' as Helen had dubbed it, is far enough from the barn that the crowing of the roosters can barely be heard in the morning. You have to be awake listening for it.

When constructing the coop, Raven and his father devised a safe way for the chickens to get in and out. They step on a trigger-plate that opens a small trap door, and once through, it automatically closes with the help of a hydraulic spring. They were worried their invention wouldn't stop a determined predator, but over the years, it kept the chickens safe enough, and they had multiplied. No one knows how many chickens now reside in the colony because an unknown number have gone feral, establishing roosts outside the coop. Raven thought it was likely that predators were kept satisfied by the wild chickens they could poach, so they ignored the ones in the coop, never giving the door a real stress test.

On the path to the colony, the sisters ventured into the brush on both sides, looking in all directions, calling out for Helen. For Raven, listening to them calling her name was painful. He had done the same thing for two days, and listening to their cries only reminded him of the futility of the search. She was not going to answer and not going to be found. He wanted to ask them to stop, but he understood they needed to feel satisfied that they had done what they could.

When they reached the coop, the chickens foraging outside ran over, greeting them with excited muttering, pecking madly at their feet. The ones inside crowded by the door, pushing each other around, trying to be the first to get out. They were all hoping the visitors had brought some food scraps, which Raven had: old bread that he tore apart and tossed to the clamorous crowd.

He went inside the coop and collected the eggs while the colony residents were preoccupied with finding every last crumb. He emerged with a bucketful. He could have filled more buckets.

They all knew that Helen normally visited the colony every day. Eggs were a main staple. She claimed her long life was due to them. He didn't have to explain to his sisters that the large number of eggs he had found meant she had been gone for a long time.

On their way back to the barn to cook breakfast, Iris and Ursula were subdued. Being confronted by evidence that

Helen hadn't been around for weeks, not days, the optimism they had felt when they woke up evaporated.

"Should we even bother looking for her?" Iris asked while they ate fried eggs on toast. "Seems like the only point of searching again is so we can feel like we did something."

"We have to search. We won't feel right if we don't."

"You don't have to go with us today, Rav. Why don't you stay and read the journals?"

Ursula agreed with her sister. Raven looked worn out, and she hoped he could get through the rest of the notebooks while they were searching. She didn't expect there would be anything in what Helen wrote that would help, and if she and Iris didn't find her, she was going to insist on getting more people involved and widening the search.

She understood Raven's misgivings about this plan, but she didn't share them. The property, for her, was not a sacred space; it was a nice place for a picnic on a sunny day, nothing much more than that. Her plan was to ask Dion to drive out with Zephyr, and then in their two cars, they could both start contacting neighbors in the surrounding area.

Raven didn't say anything, but when his sisters got up from the deck chairs, he didn't move. He had dreaded having to walk the property again that day and was glad for Ursula's suggestion. He asked them to wait and then described all of the places he had searched and the trails he had followed. He tried to rally their spirits by saying that since there were two of them, there would be two voices instead of one and four eyes and ears instead of two. Their extrasensory teamwork might discover a clue he had missed.

His sisters stepped off the porch, and after walking out into the field a few yards, they turned and waved. Once out in the pasture, as they had discussed, they split off in opposite directions. They would walk in concentric circles until they reached each other in the middle, like walking a labyrinth in opposite directions until meeting at the end. If they didn't find Helen in the field, they would head up the hill and follow the paths through the woods.

Raven watched them for a while, wishing he couldn't hear them yelling, '*Maw...Umm*.' He was done with the searching and the yelling. All he wanted to know was if his mom was alive or dead. He didn't think that was too much to ask.

So, karma, Mom, why is this happening?

What actions of hers, his, or theirs led to this? In what lifetime? How is this situation balancing out the karmic scales?

Once his sisters were out of sight, swallowed up by the towering canary grass that hadn't been cut since the 20th century ended, he went inside to pick out another notebook to read, hoping his mom would explain everything so that he could rest.

Is it morbid to honor Kaspar's death day? Why not celebrate it like we do birthdays? We have one birthday and one death day per lifetime. They should have equal weight. I can imagine the kids reading this someday thinking, 'Wow, Mom is really obsessed.' Maybe I am, but death needs to be acknowledged, not ignored, as it is in our culture. Pathologically so. I understand why people who believe in Christian dogma don't want to dwell on death. Everyone is a sinner, and unless you are sociopathic, you are aware of your sins, no matter how successfully you manage to rationalize them to soothe your conscience. Judgement day—when you find out if you're going to heaven or hell for eternity—is the last thing you want to think about. I get that.

Americans, especially, are not keen on getting old, on hanging out with old people, and being reminded of their mortality. As soon as you're born, the programming from advertising kicks in. Celebrate your youth and stay young as long as you can. Though it's not possible to stay young forever, you can at least try to look young as long as possible because only the young have fun, only the young feel good, and only the young are happy, so stay young, at least at heart, or forget about enjoying life, because being old sucks. You might as well be dead once you're old. Do the world a favor and die peacefully in your sleep once your hair turns white and your skin gets spots. Do all the things you did in your 20s until you're in your 70s. Who knows? You may live indefinitely. You may defy death itself. You owe it to yourself to try. If you follow the program, everyone will love you: They will say, 'you look the same as you did 20 years ago!' the best compliment an old person could ever hope to get. You will be greeted with a cheery 'you look so young!' You will receive endless kudos for running that marathon and climbing that mountain. You look so fit, they will say, and you will smile humbly on the outside, but inside, you will feel smugly gratified.

The stay-young-forever program is especially important for the economy. So many products and only so much time, so don't waste it. Anticipating your death is a drag for everyone. Spending your last days preparing for it is anti-social, depressing, and unhealthy. Only a deranged person dwells on death unless he or she is terminally ill. Then it's understandable. Then it goes without saying that financial affairs must be put into order, goodbyes said, regrets voiced, and amends made. Otherwise, if you still have your health, why would you jinx it by thinking about death? It's your patriotic duty to keep buying stuff as long as you're alive to keep the sacred economy growing. Thinking about death does not motivate you to shop for anything, except a coffin, or an urn to house your ashes. Why would you want to bring your loved ones down by talking about death? Are you really that selfish, that self-absorbed?

My answer to that is yes and no. I am no more selfish or self-absorbed than normal, but I do believe in karma and reincarnation, as do billions of people around the world who do not live in America, and for those billions, including me, who believe in reincarnation, preparing for death is not distasteful or morbid—in fact, it is socially appropriate and encouraged—it's necessary in order to insure a desirable rebirth, if not escape the endless karmic cycle.

I'm imagining the kids reading this and questioning my beliefs. They are wondering how strong is my faith in these things. Well, I wonder too! Every day. And so did Kaspar, but he didn't have a chance to do what I'm trying to do. His death was too random and unexpected, but even so, if he were alive, I don't think he would have been as comfortable as I am in following my faith.

Honestly, kids, I ask you, and I ask you because you're the only people who will ever read this: what is easier to believe? Would a loving, omniscient God sentence his creation to eternal hell for any reason? No do-overs, no takebacks? Karma and reincarnation just make more sense: every action causes a reaction; every cause has an effect, just as in nature. It's physics. It's natural law. We can observe it every day. Your fate is in your hands. It's free will. Do good, and good will follow; do bad, and bad will follow. You reincarnate as many times as necessary to eliminate the bad and become the good. It's not up to God to decide what you deserve. Why would God even make judgement his responsibility? He's omniscient. He knows his creation has a lot to learn and that mistakes will be made. A God of love and forgiveness can't also be the God of wrath and damnation. It doesn't add up. And as for those who proudly claim that there is no such thing as God, that religious dogma is superstitious nonsense, stories to ease existential fears, that consciousness is nothing more than a byproduct of mechanical brain activity, that the universe is a random event that occurred for no reason and when it's momentum runs out will collapse into a black hole, that there is no such thing as a soul, that we are born just once and die when our body expires, as it must, as everything must in the end...

... to you hopeless cynics, I have to say I am not impressed by your courage. Your fear of being considered fools for believing in your own divinity makes you foolish. You are profoundly ignorant of who you are, and that is nothing to be proud of.

Getting carried away.

I just want to say that even if the agnostics are right, so what? Who wants to live in a lawless, incoherent, meaningless, mechanical universe? We should at least have the imagination and the guts to believe in something grand, something good, something magical. I can't believe that deep down, the materialists actually believe what they say they believe. They're just afraid if they say they believe in something that can't be 'proved,' they might be proven wrong. Oh no! Not that!

The ego is the first, the last, and everything-in-between problem.

I WILL HELP YOU

***

So, last night, 'I will help you' just appeared on the page of my journal, like a mirage coming into focus. I was deciding if I had more to write or if it was time to stop when those four words materialized on the page. I was not high, but I was pretty tired, so I thought I'd just go to bed and look at it in the morning. Maybe it will be gone.

In the morning, it was still there, imprinted, stamped, undeniably there. I stared at the words thinking that might lead to an insight, a theory explaining how that sentence got there. Whoever or whatever it is, offered to help me. With what?

76

My writing? My dying? It had to be my ego. The last line I wrote had to do with the ego.

Silently I prayed: Please, anonymous thing, help me with my ego. I welcome your help. I promise that I, it, my ego will not oppose you. I consent to your interference in my life.

I waited for it to write something again.

Nothing appeared. I closed the book and went away for several hours and then looked again.

Nothing.

I wondered if I was having a psychotic break. Was this magic really happening? I have had other supernatural experiences. Years ago, in my twenties, camped in the Ventana wilderness east of Big Sur, I was sitting on a rock next to a mountain creek, high on LSD. Across the creek, I saw a naked woman with silver hair down to her waist riding bareback on a white horse—Lady Godiva, I know! She was coming toward me.

I swear this is true. She rode across the creek no more than 10 yards away from where I was sitting without saying a word. I was splashed by her horse. She didn't look my way. It was as if I did not exist in whatever dimension she existed. She cantered on into the forest and disappeared.

Why did I see Lady Godiva? I still wonder about that. Something manifesting out of my unconscious mind? But why the hell that, of all things? I don't even know the story of Lady Godiva. Was she a denizen of the forest that I was able to see at that moment of expanded consciousness? Was she a woman who just liked playing Lady Godiva riding her horse?

At the time, she was as real as anything else. Actually, she seemed more real, hyper-real. She had an energetic aura that made the air around her crackle. I admit I was peaking at the time, but so what? She was not a hallucination, or I should say she was no more a hallucination than anything else. Everything we perceive, on drugs or not, could be called a hallucination. The stuff dreams are made on.

I'm not scared; I'm intrigued. I want whatever this messaging is to keep happening—who wouldn't want supernatural help?—but I am cautious. I believe in elemental beings; everything in nature is alive and conscious. Out here in the field, in the woods, I'm surrounded by spirits. Anyone who spends time alone in nature feels them. I just have to sit still, slow my breathing, empty my mind, and my sixth sense apprehends them. The barriers between the dimensions are not impermeable. They are thinner than our neurotically protective ego wants us to believe. Despite the friendly message, though, whoever or whatever made those words appear might not be kind and benevolent. He, she, or it could be messing with me. A bored trickster looking for a laugh. Who or what wants to help me? How? Why?

I couldn't think of anything else to do but go outside and look around.

It was mid-afternoon. I stood on the porch for several minutes. I was literally holding my breath, trying to be as quiet as possible while scanning the field. Didn't see anything, but I felt something. The air was prickly. I thought I might see sparks. Finally, I got tired of standing still, looking around and seeing nothing, and getting spooked when a slight puff of wind ruffled the grass, so I walked to the pond. I felt compelled to do something.

I sat in my spot, a green plastic chair set in a small opening I cut out of the cattails that ring the pond. This is where I meditate most often. The wind sloughs through the cattails and ripples the water. The nearness of water and the sound of nature breathing draws me down deep until I don't hear the sound any longer, until I can hear the silence that underlies everything. This spot is where the barrier between what I imagine is me and what I imagine is everything else disintegrates, and I lose the sense of time. I thought I might meet the mystery writer here.

I sat there for a long time. It was a pleasant afternoon; the hot season had passed, and the cold one had not yet arrived. Ozzie and Harriet, the resident duck couple, were swimming around as they always do, eating whatever ducks eat, which is not something I've ever identified, no matter how many hours I've spent watching them. How do they eat anything with those beaks? Dragonflies bombed around from every angle. I asked the universe, 'Am I expected to write something back? Should I write down my questions and wait for a reply?' I was anticipating some sign. I believed that whoever or whatever made those words appear had to be aware of me, had to be interested in my reaction, and had to know I was sitting there by the pond waiting. At least I was sending that expectation out to the universe. Actually, it was more of a demand: 'I know you're out there,' I was thinking, 'show yourself!'

I kept sitting there, not knowing what else to do. Then I saw something I had never seen before: a fox. Not a coyote, I see packs of those regularly, and I hear them yipping all the time. It was a fox with a bushy tail. It was across the pond in the midst of the cattails, looking directly at me. I looked back into its black, unblinking eyes. 'Of course, a trickster,' I thought. 'I have conjured it up.' I wasn't sure the fox was real. I had just jerked awake after nodding off in the chair, and there it was. Maybe I was dreaming. While I thought these things, I swear I saw it smile, and then it just disappeared. I mean, it was suddenly not there, and the cattails did not move.

I decided that was what I was waiting for, and it was time to go back, even though I had no idea what it meant to see the fox, or if the fox had actually been real, or if I had been in some sort of half-dream state or what, but I got out of the chair and walked back to the barn.

An understatement: today was not my usual day.

When I got back, there was a woman standing on the porch. When she noticed me approaching, she waved and called out, 'hi.' I joined her on the porch; she apologized with great sincerity for trespassing. I said in a measured tone, 'Yes, you are trespassing. What are you doing here?' She told me she was a neighbor who often rode by on her bike. She said she felt drawn to the meadow and had followed the trail. 'I had no idea someone was living here,' she said. 'All you can see from the road is this beautiful field.' It's true. It is beautiful in its wildness. She told me her name was Astrid.

We made brief small talk about what plants grew in the meadow. Yes, I make tea with some of them, and no, I said, I've never seen a bear. I was not in the mood to do more than be polite. I had other things on my mind and wanted her to leave. She got the message. I told her it would be fine to drop by again if she felt like it.

80

She seemed OK. She was a young woman, maybe early thirties, dressed hippie style like Persephone. Very pleasant, but I wondered if, after meeting me, the old crone who lived in the horse barn, she would ever stop for a visit again.

The fox haunts me. Is it somehow connected to the magic words? And then finding Astrid on the porch: Is everything that happened today my imagination? Am I finally losing it, as Ursula believes is inevitable?

No, I'm not.

Right, anonymous?

Keep your word. Help me.

Raven put down the journal. There was too much to process. Was she taking psychedelic drugs? There were plenty of psilocybin mushrooms growing in the former animal pasture. She could have friends who supplied her, and Astrid might be one of them. Taking psychoactive drugs could be a way to become familiar with the projections of her mind before encountering them after death.

He stared at the last page he'd read, transfixed by the words **I will help you**. They looked like they had been jetted onto the page by an old laser printer, like they were embossed. He kept staring at the sentence, and it kept confounding him by its presence. It wasn't going away, no matter how hard he willed it to disappear. It was real. Someone or something put it there, just like the other sentence, **you know why**, and it wasn't his mom. She believed someone or something was sending messages to her. Observing her, reading what she writes, and writing back to her. He was sure his mom didn't write the messages. He wasn't sure about anything else.

He knew that Ursula would have a simple explanation. She insisted on the sensible, the empirical...on proof, like most people. Her imagination did not improvise wildly as his was doing at the moment. He was always willing to believe in the supernatural. He wanted to believe. He had always believed.

He didn't understand why so many settled for the mundane, why they so fiercely defended against mystery. Raven was not interested in the explanations that satisfied his sister. He felt something emanating from the messages in the journals, and he could sense his mother urging him to follow his feelings, to listen to his inner voice, to go deeper. She didn't want him to flee from or fight his intuitions; she wanted him to get out of his head and open his heart, experience the moment, and let what was happening happen. She was not interested in explaining away anything either and hadn't been for years. She was asking him to accept that the property was a magical place where magical things happen. She and Kaspar had made it so with their thoughts, beliefs, and affirmations. They had supplicated themselves, asking nature to reveal its secrets, and nature had responded, or so he was feeling, and so she seemed to be communicating to him. He turned his head away from the journal, breaking the spell cast by the sentence, **I will help you**.

He knew what to do: walk to the pond, sit in his mom's green chair, and wait for the fox.

1.6

For several hours Raven scanned the cattails surrounding the pond, but no fox appeared, only the ducks, who swam close by in case he might throw them a treat. He thought he should probably give up the vigil and get back to the barn, as the afternoon was waning and his sisters would be returning from their search. He was sure they would come back without having found Helen or any clue as to why she had disappeared—or evidence that she had actually disappeared—and they would feel forced to take the inevitable next step: call Dion, who would round up Zephyr, and possibly Persephone, to join them.

At the moment he was about to get on his feet to walk back, he realized there was a woman sitting lotus style on the ground next to the chair, looking across the pond as he had been doing.

How had he not heard her? Had he been that focused on watching for the fox?

She was 30-something and tiny, *childlike*, he thought, wearing a tie-dyed T-shirt, baggy cotton pants, and tennis shoes. Her auburn hair was tied back in a ponytail.

She looked up and smiled.

"I didn't want to disturb you. You were concentrating so hard. What were you looking for over there?"

"A fox."

"I don't think there are foxes around here."

"I didn't think so either, but my mom said she saw one."

"Well, if Helen saw one, there must be one."

Raven was flummoxed. How did he not notice her when she sat down next to him?

"You must be Astrid."

"I am, and you must be Raven." She laughed. "I guess we already know each other. No introductions needed."

"My mom has been writing about you, so..."

Astrid laughed again, interrupting Raven.

"She wasn't too happy when she found me on her front porch."

"She wrote about that. It sounds like you're good friends now."

"Your mom is amazing."

Raven wanted to interrogate Astrid about the nature of their friendship and how was it that no one in the family had ever heard of her, but he was distracted by Astrid's luminous hazel eyes, which held his own without blinking.

He suddenly felt an impossible intimacy with her.

Astrid looked away, breaking the spell. It took Raven several moments to reorient himself after being overcome by what he could only think was bliss or something like it.

He looked down at the ground, shaking his head back and forth to clear out the confusion of thoughts and emotions. Then with some effort, he regained the ability to speak and asked Astrid if she knew where Helen was.

"I was just coming by to say hello when I found you sitting in her chair. Is she not here?"

"I came three days ago. She's not here. I've searched the property, and now my two sisters are searching again. We don't know what else to do."

"That's odd. Was she expecting you?"

"That depends on whether or not she looked at her phone. I'd say the chances are 50-50."

"So you're worried."

"Very worried. Even if she wasn't expecting me, why isn't she here? Why hasn't she returned from wherever she went? She doesn't have a car. Where would she go?"

Raven looked at her, expecting her to say something, but she just looked back and smiled.

"Where do you live, anyway? I have never met a neighbor from around here."

"Around. Nowhere. I'm a vagabond."

"You live in a tent? Like a gypsy or what?"

"Sometimes...or I live in something else, whatever opportunities the universe offers. I'm cabin-sitting right now, taking care of a friend's donkeys."

"And this cabin is where?"

Raven was spitting out his questions now, obviously suspicious, though of what he didn't know. *A vagabond?* She had said it as if he should know what she meant, as if it were a new social designation he should be aware of.

Apparently reading his mind, Astrid explained: "I don't have a home, a job, or money. I suppose you could say

I'm a bum, but times have changed, or at least the language has. A lot of people are vagabonds these days, by choice or not. You know how things are. But I'm happy to be a vagabond. How can I be homeless when I've never wanted a home? And I have no use for money. I definitely wouldn't want to spend precious hours of my life working for money just so I could rent some boxy prison cell in the city."

Raven looked down at Astrid, who was still sitting on the ground in the same pose. She captured his eyes as she had before and said emphatically, with a soothing warmth in her voice, "I'm sure she's OK, Raven. Your mom will always be OK. She's doing something she needs to do, that's all. She didn't know you were coming."

The ease with which Astrid could command his attention and her confident tone confused Raven. Why was she so sure there was nothing to worry about? How can she presume to know that his mom will *always* be OK? Where did that come from? What is it that his mom needs to do, and why would Astrid know this? Her assurance, though, calmed his agitated mind. He felt some welcome relief from the constant anxiety he'd been suffering from since he had arrived.

"So, this cabin? Where is it?"

"Over the hill," Astrid pointed. "There's a trail to and from your field, though it's not traveled much except by deer. You have to know the way."

"When was the last time you visited Mom?"

"I don't know. A month ago? She was fine. In high spirits, as always."

Raven winced at Astrid's choice of words, remembering what he'd just read. "So are there other neighbors? Anyone who also visits?"

"There are other people around here, but I don't really know anyone except your mom and my friend who lives in the cabin. I don't think they know each other. Actually, I say he's a friend, but it's just by chance. I was roughing it in the woods, and he came across my camp. He needed someone to watch his donkeys, and I said sure."

"The universe providing."

"Exactly, and it's providing for Helen, too. What good is it to worry and imagine the worst? How does that help her? How does it help you?"

"She's not your mom, Astrid!" Raven sputtered. "She's really old. She might be lying somewhere seriously injured. She might be dead. I can't help imagining these things. I have to worry!" He was shouting now.

"I understand. Sorry."

Raven was losing patience with Astrid's platitudes, and making it worse, she seemed to have no helpful information at all, only the mysterious confidence that his mom was fine.

"Look, Astrid, I need to get back to the barn. My sisters should be there. They'll be wondering where I am."

"I saw them on my way here."

"Really?"

"It must have been them, two women walking around the meadow."

For a moment, Raven thought the polite thing would be to invite Astrid to come with him and meet his sisters, but then he thought it was not the time to be entertaining a guest and getting to know one of his mom's friends. He and his sisters had a lot to talk about. He had already asked Astrid all of the questions that needed to be asked, and she didn't have any answers. All she had to contribute was her absurd confidence in his mother's well-being. He got up to leave. Astrid stayed seated on the ground in her yoga pose.

"I'm going to hang around here for a while if you don't mind. If I see the fox, should I come and tell you?"

"I guess so."

"Your mom is going to be fine, Raven."

Irritated, he snapped, *you don't know that*, and started walking back to the barn. After taking a few steps, he stopped. He felt compelled to look back. He wanted to confirm she was real.

It was actually more than that: he realized as soon as he walked away that he wanted her to come with him, that he wanted to feel bliss again.

She was gone.

1.7

As the sun was setting, Ursula and Iris came up on the porch, their arms scratched and field debris clinging to their clothes. Raven was sitting in his chair. He offered them water and dried pears, which they accepted without a word, each of them dropping gratefully into the weather-beaten deck chairs which furnished the barn's outdoor living room. After drinking their fill of water, they moved onto tea Raven had made, quietly sipping it, looking spent and discouraged.

Ursula's report on the day did not take long. They had traversed the field multiple times and hiked the full length of all of the trails meandering along the forested ridge and had found nothing that could be considered a clue. She and Iris agreed: they should contact Dion and Zephyr and ask them to come—that night, if possible.

"Can you live with that, Raven?" Ursula asked.

"What about the Birnam Wood cops?" Raven replied bitterly. "You thinking of hiring them?"

"That's a last resort. Let's talk to the neighbors first."

Raven sighed. The inevitable was happening, as it does.

"So that's it, then? You both believe that our senile mom took a walk and got lost?"

"What else is there to believe?" Ursula retorted.

"I don't know what else, but I know I don't believe that. What I know is Mom was—no, sorry—*is* involved with something bizarre. Look at this." He handed the journal to Ursula and pointed to the mysterious offer of help that ended the entry.

She glanced at what Raven was pointing at but didn't take time to comprehend what he was showing her.

"I have to call Dion" is all she said.

***

After Dion groused for a while about being asked to join them on such short notice—he had plans for the next day—*business*—he agreed to drive over with Zephyr first thing in the morning. It made no sense to come until then. They couldn't knock on strangers' doors in the middle of the night asking if they had seen Helen.

"I don't think anyone around there knows her," Dion protested. "I get the plan, but I'm not optimistic."

"They might not know her or what she looks like, but they will remember seeing an old woman with long white hair wandering around alone. At least we'll know she's alive."

While her sister was on the phone with Dion, Iris called Zephyr. He knew Helen well and immediately questioned the urgent need for such a full-scale intervention.

"Iris, c'mon; this is your mom. What are the chances she had no idea Raven was coming? Better than 50/50. More like 70/30 or 80/20. She must have gone somewhere with someone. Took a little trip. Does she run everything she has planned by you? When does she ever consult with you about anything?"

"Who would she take a trip with and to where? It looks like she's been gone a long time."

"If you don't know, how would I know?"

"Look, Zeph, we've found a bunch of stuff she's been writing; it's pretty crazy. She actually says that she moved out to the barn to prepare for her death."

"Seems sensible, considering."

"Jesus, Zephyr, stop with this shit!" Iris shouted. "We have every right to be worried! We have to do something, and we're asking for your help. I'm asking for your help!"

Iris took a moment to let her anger register.

"Ursula has already called Dion, and he says he'll pick you up at seven, all right?"

"I'm sorry, Iris. I didn't mean to upset you. Of course, I'll come, but I think you and your sibs are working each other into a frenzy for no good reason. I'm sure your mom is fine."

"Wow, you're lucky Percy isn't on this call with us. Imagine what she would have to say about your mansplaining. You're just trying to calm the hysterical women, right? Really, Zeph? You have no idea what's going on around here! I know the last thing you want to do is drive out here with Dion, but too bad. We need your help."

After a brief post-spat silence, Zephyr said he thought Persephone should come with them. The patriots who had dumped garbage in front of the library had escalated their harassment, driving through the pedestrian-only streets of the neighborhood in mini-convoys of gas-guzzling cars and trucks, honking non-stop, American flags flapping from their vehicles, yelling FUCK YOU ZERO FREAKS at the people they drove by and throwing half-eaten cheeseburgers in foil wrappers at them. They shot up the neighborhood's new

ZeroG sign until nothing was left of it but a heap of splintered wood.

Neighborhood citizens followed the protocol for patriot incursions, clearing off the streets and waiting for the invaders to get tired of performing to an audience that has disappeared. When no one is watching, their motivation is gone.

Like every other ZG neighborhood anywhere in the country, they had endured these displays of unconscious rage for years. Patriot outbreaks flare up and eventually die down, so long as the citizens of The Library don't react. Any reaction encourages more trouble and increased violence. If the patriots believe they have pissed off their enemies, disturbed their peace, caused the people they have been brainwashed to hate to feel the way they feel—victimized and disrespected—they take that as a victory in the 100-years war. No matter how inconsequential and meaningless the victory, they are motivated to keep up their incursions, hoping for another rush of vindication.

Zephyr was worried about Persephone's safety because the library was a trigger, a symbol of the liberal values the patriots despise, an edifice built over a century ago for the educated elites they believe look down on people like them, the people who consider them stupid and ignorant, the godless atheists who want to take away their guns and make them drink beer out of compostable containers.

"So, what did Zephyr have to say?"

"He said he was sure that Mom is fine. He thinks she must have gone somewhere with a friend."

"But he's coming?"

"Yes, with Percy. Since we left, the patriots have been roaming the neighborhood. He doesn't think she's safe being the substitute librarian and all."

Raven smiled and laughed quietly to himself.

"What's funny about that?"

"That's just what Astrid said."

"What are you talking about? I was saying that Zephyr is worried about the patriots shooting up the neighborhood and Percy catching a stray bullet."

"Yeah, what *are* you talking about, Raven?" Ursula chimed in. "Are you OK? I think maybe being here for four days is getting to you."

"You just need to read the journal."

"Raven!" Iris said loudly enough to fix his attention on her. "Listen. You just said *that's what Astrid said*. Are you in touch with Mom's imaginary friend or what?"

"I met her while I was sitting by the pond."

Angry glares from his two sisters.

"When were you going to tell us this?"

"When did I have a chance, Ursula? Anyway, it's not important. She doesn't know anything. She came by to visit and found me sitting in Mom's chair, that's all."

"So she's real?"

"She's real, and just like Zephyr did on the phone with you, Iris, she did her best to convince me that Mom was fine and there was nothing to worry about. That's why I laughed. Astrid told me *your mom will always be fine*, which was a weird way of putting it, but that's her, I guess. She has an eerie way of getting close to you, as if you've been friends for a long time. It's hard to explain. She's Percy's age and dresses like a hippie from the 70s, Mom style. By the way, after reading the journal, I think it's possible they're taking psychedelic drugs together, and not in micro-doses, either."

Raven's sisters were staring at him, waiting for him to drop more surprising revelations about their mother and her friend, but he didn't continue. He knew they wanted all the details, and he eventually shared what she had to say. She was cabin-sitting for someone, taking care of his animals. She claimed not to know anyone in the area and had no idea where Helen could be. She called herself a vagabond, someone just roaming around relying on what the universe provides.

"How ZG is that?" Ursula couldn't help saying. "No wonder they're great friends."

"The thing is, she doesn't know where Mom is, and she's no kidnapper. We should be happy that Mom has a friend out here."

Impatient, he added, "Will you just read this journal, Iris? You're the designated reader. There's another message."

"Now, what are you talking about?"

"There's another note stamped at the end of the entry. It looks like the other one we saw."

Raven opened the notebook and stabbed at the sentence with his forefinger several times, trying to focus their attention.

"Same black ink, same weird font, same cryptic message from the unknown."

"Shit," Iris said, looking at what her brother was pointing to.

Ursula glanced at what Raven was so excited about but said nothing.

***

After everyone finished the rice and vegetables Raven cooked to feed the hungry searchers, Iris began to read. Almost immediately, she stopped to say something, but Raven urged her just to keep reading all the way to the end. They would talk when she was done. Ursula nodded. There was a lot to get through.

When she had finished and put down the journal, though, no one spoke. Raven had had time to process the latest musings from their mom, but his sisters had not

Eventually, in the matter-of-fact tone of someone commenting on the weather, Iris announced: "We saw the fox, too."

"Of course you did," Raven muttered to himself, loud enough for his sisters to hear.

"Why do you say that?" Iris asked, irritated. "You need to let us know what's going on, Rav."

Instead of responding, he lowered his head and stared at the cement slab under his feet, noticing where cracks had formed and the patterns they made. Ants emerged from and retreated into them, creating a dynamic, incoherent pattern.

That is a picture of my mind. What did I mean by saying, 'of course you did'? Nothing. It just came out. A meaningless, throw-away remark. How can I explain what's going on with me when I can't explain it to myself? How do I know Mom has not wandered off somewhere and gotten lost? I just know. I believe what she says she believes, that someone or something is communicating with her because I have felt something trying to communicate with me since I arrived. I was waiting in the field for a message from that someone or something.

Iris cleared her throat and tried again to get something useful out of Raven.

"When we first got here, Rav, you didn't seem to be aware of us, even though we were standing on the porch under the light not that far from you. You didn't acknowledge us at all until Ursula shined her flashlight in your face. I asked you what you were doing, and you said, '*I'm waiting for something.*' What were you waiting for?"

Raven looked at her blankly. "Why are you asking me this again? What are you trying to get me to say?"

"Like I said, I want—we want—to understand what's going on with you. You have been acting strange since we arrived. You say stuff under your breath that doesn't make sense. You look at us as if we're a nuisance you will be glad to be rid of. It's not OK. We're your sisters. We are just as worried about Mom as you are. You have no right to shut us out."

"And like I said when you asked the first time and the second, I don't know what I was waiting for. I guess since I got here, I feel like I've been waiting for something. For Mom to appear, maybe, or for something else. A sign."

"Like Astrid?"

"Like her or the fox, I don't know. How would I know? How do we know anything? What I know is what I already told you. I was sitting in Mom's chair at the pond, hoping to see the fox she wrote about. I was sure I would see the fox there, but then Astrid suddenly showed up out of nowhere. I mean that literally: she was sitting on the ground next to me, but I didn't hear her or see her coming. I told her we were here looking for Mom, and she assured me that Mom was OK and that I had no reason to worry, and for some reason, I *was* assured, at least for a while. We waited for the fox, but it didn't appear. I got up to leave, and she said she would stay there for a while, and if she saw the fox, she would come and tell me. I turned around after taking only a couple of steps toward the barn and looked back at her. I was thinking of asking her to come and meet the family, but she was gone, like she'd never been there. That's everything that happened and everything I know."

"Do you think it's possible she actually wasn't there, Raven?" Ursula asked, in the tone of someone talking to a client in therapy. "Could you have fallen asleep? Been dreaming?"

"Sure, I could have been dreaming, or we could all be dreaming. The mysterious correspondent writing to Mom may be a powerful magician, and Astrid is his familiar. Anything is possible around here right now. What I want to know is why it is so easy for you to dismiss what Mom has written."

"Nobody's dismissing anything, Rav!" Iris exclaimed.

"What is this anonymous going to help her with?" Ursula sputtered, annoyed by Raven's insistence on his fantasies. "Help her die? Help her choose a place for her remains?"

Her parents and her brother's belief in the metaphysical had always bothered her. Where did their faith come from? She saw no reason for faith in the unseen and unknowable. All the evil shit in the world, and where was the divine intervention? It never comes, and now, it seemed, the world was going to end with the faithful still clinging to their desperate hopes. Seems like the devil is in charge, not God.

She resented how she was cast as the heretic of the family merely for having material things, for having money, for driving a car, and for marrying a banker. What right did they have to assume moral superiority? Why despise her for enjoying what comforts she might have in life? The one and only life she would ever have?

"Sure, help her die. Why not?"

Ursula ignored his comeback.

"We did see a fox while we were searching. It was not far off a trail in the forest, looking at us. We stared back at it, and I swear it smiled before it ran into the woods. But so what?

We want to know why you said *of course you did* when Iris told you we saw it."

"Because I am not surprised."

"Why?"

"I'm going to quote anonymous here: You know why."

Ursula muttered, "for fuck's sake."

Iris said, "that's not helpful."

Raven was not concerned about his sisters being so exasperated with him. He thought it was just a matter of time spent on the property; a few more days and they would start feeling the presence he felt. After reading more of the journals, they would understand that Helen was trying to communicate something to them, something important. Given enough time, they would come to know what he knew, that their mother was exploring realms they had no knowledge of, that she was in touch with something completely unfamiliar, something outside of their experience, and if they really wanted to help her, they needed to open their minds and let her, him, it or whatever it was in. They needed to try to understand, not control and fix. He couldn't communicate these thoughts to them because they weren't even intelligible thoughts, just vague inklings leaking into his mind from an unidentifiable source, and he was at a loss for words to explain.

"I'm sorry. I don't think I can help you understand what I'm experiencing."

"Try," Iris said.

"OK, then. I sense Mom, and I sense other things, but I don't know what they are. I can't identify them. I can't name them. I guess that's what I meant when I said *I'm waiting for something*. Emphasis on *some* thing. I'm waiting for whatever it is to appear, to make itself known."

His sisters looked at him expectantly, waiting for more. "I told you I can't explain. It's something I'm experiencing. That's why I'm not surprised you saw the fox and that it smiled at you. Nothing is going to surprise me while we're here."

"So you say you sense Mom," Iris said softly.

"Yes. More every day. I think if you stay a few more days, you will too."

"I think Astrid got to you, Raven," Ursula sniffed. "Her saying that Mom is OK..."

"Will always be OK."

"Exactly. You and Mom are close, and that's what you needed to hear; you're clinging to it like a life ring. You believe you're feeling her presence, that she's letting you know she's fine, because you're the sensitive, intuitive one, while we're the what? The dull, unimaginative ones? The ones incapable of sensing anything, including Mom?"

"Ursula, stop," Iris pleaded. "This is not the time."

"I think Raven is stressed out and might be losing it."

"Astrid is real, Ursula. I wasn't asleep. I didn't dream of her."

"And you are not making a lot of sense, Raven."

"Explain those two sentences you saw with your own eyes, then."

"Easy. Mom has a pen with black ink and wrote them."

"To herself?"

"Yes, to herself. She's 100 years old. She lives out here alone, eating nothing but roots and berries. And now it seems she has a history of drug use and may be picking mushrooms from the field and making a tea out of them."

Ursula looked at Raven and smiled.

"I imagine you've picked your share over the years...."

"Actually, no," Raven said quietly. "I wouldn't know which ones to pick."

"I don't know what's going on," Ursula continued, "but I do know there is no mysterious being from another dimension communicating with Mom. She is writing some weird stuff that old people taking drugs or just plain out of their minds might write. I'm worried that she's lying somewhere injured or dead right now, and I want to find her, and I'm sure we *are* going to find her tomorrow once Dion and Zephyr get here, and we can drive around this area and talk to people who might have seen her or might even know where she is. I'm really at a loss trying to figure out why this plan is somehow not the right one. Do you not want to find Mom? Are you satisfied with pretending you feel her presence? I'm not."

Raven turned away from his sister. He wasn't angry or hurt. He knew that Ursula, especially, would reject any way he tried to explain what he was feeling and his claim to know anything about Helen.

He was just resigned to what was inevitable as soon as he contacted his sisters. Dion and Zephyr would come, and everything would change. The energy they brought with them from the outside world would prevent him from sensing anything. He would be shut down. Helen and anonymous would disappear until they left. They would not find her by driving around in their cars. She would never be found by them. She would come home when she was done with whatever she was doing, as Astrid had said.

"We're all pretty frayed," Iris said, trying to make peace.

"I'm definitely stressed out," Ursula admitted. "Mom's bizarre writing, not finding her, seeing the fox and then coming back to read about it, Raven meeting Astrid—it's all piling up and making me feel crazy. I don't like feeling crazy."

"I understand, Ursula, believe me. Just don't think I'm losing my mind because I'm not."

Iris started rummaging through the pile of notebooks in the chest.

"It's not too late. I want to read some more. There are still a few left that we haven't looked at. Why don't I scan these for Astrid's name and read that one? She seems important now that you've actually met her."

Ursula, subdued and tired, agreed.

"Good idea," Raven said.

Iris looked through the notebooks they had not read yet. It didn't take long to find Astrid's name.

Since Astrid showed up that day on my porch, she continued to visit me. It's always a surprise. She doesn't have a phone, and even if she did, it wouldn't matter since I don't use mine. She seems to show up when I am thinking of her, wanting her company. The more I see of her, the more I look forward to it and think it would be nice if she came by, so apparently, by my wish, she is visiting more frequently.

When she comes, I never see from which direction. She suddenly appears next to me, and I am always a little startled. She says sorry and laughs. I'm used to it now and expect it, but I am still surprised every time. When she leaves, she walks into the field and disappears into the grass. I don't know where she goes after I have lost sight of her. I don't ask, and she never says.

It's been over a year since we met, and she has dropped in at least a dozen times, but we've never talked about the things that people normally talk about. From the beginning, there was no small talk. She has never asked me what I'm doing, such an old woman, living out here alone. She has never asked about my family, where I'm from, what I used to do for a living, etc., and I have never asked her any of these things that people normally ask either.

We do talk about the weather, though. When you live close to nature, the weather is not just a topic of conversation.

Astrid is not the typical human being looking for a transaction, a quid pro quo, and neither am I. Neither of us is looking for anything at all. Somehow we know this about each other. When she visits, we often don't talk much at all. We sit in silence, meditating, sometimes in the middle of the field, beside the pond, or on the hillside under a tree. She keeps me company, and I guess I keep her company. We are comfortable being silent. When we do talk, we share our observations of nature, about what sort of bees are out and what they're pollinating, what plants are blooming or about to bloom, scents on the breeze, what raptor is circling above us. From there, we may move on to talk about the actual act of observing, about how our minds work, how we perceive, what we choose to attend to, and what we decide to ignore and why, and invariably we seem to arrive at questions of who we are, what we are, what is our purpose on earth, what is consciousness and why do we have it, and on to speculations about the nature of reality, of time, and what happens after death.

My favorite topics!

I wonder how our relationship can feel so intimate when we don't know anything about each other, but there's the paradox: the usual details we know about a person reveals nothing about them. Those details we so diligently mine in getting to 'know' someone, as we say, do not reveal anything essential. They do not reveal who the person really is. What we discover in our interrogations are just the trappings of personality that accrue over time.

Maybe that's why the social protocol is set up the way it is. We maintain superficial, transactional relationships so who we really are won't feel vulnerable. We will feel safe from hurt, and perhaps joy as well, but still, safe. We will be safe from feeling and from knowing. We will remain ignorant of the mysteries of life and death. We will be sheltered from change.

I feel like Astrid and I reveal our true selves to each other and have become truly intimate, despite only seeing each other now and then, but I would never ask her if she feels the same way. There should be no need to ask, and there is no need. I know she feels the same because I feel it. I don't need to ask her to prove it to me.

She is so unlike anyone I've ever known that sometimes I wonder if she is something other than human, though I have no idea what that could be. When I'm with her, I never feel anxious. I feel loved. When we're together, we're just together in the moment with no expectations, and that is all there needs to be. We're not looking toward the future and our next encounter or looking back at the past, dwelling on some upsetting remark or imagined slight, we're just together, and that's all there is and ever will be.

She comforts me. I don't know how or why, but she comforts me. When she leaves, her comfort stays with me, within me. I feel it securely lodged in my heart. I have never felt this way about anyone, not even dear Kaspar, who always comforted me, but I would need to ask for his comfort again and again. It was not something I carried with me. I don't know how it is possible for me to feel this way about Astrid, but I do, and I'm grateful because no matter how I try to prepare for death, I am still afraid, so I am glad for her comfort.

Iris put the notebook down, signaling she was done. The atmosphere in the barn was charged by Helen's words as if she had been the one reading. Raven and Ursula sighed, letting out the breath they had been holding. Hearing about

Astrid in their mom's words just after Raven had told them about their meeting made her very real.

"Like I said, Astrid has an uncanny emotional effect."

"You said that Astrid had no idea where Mom is. Do you still think that's true after hearing what she wrote about her?"

Ursula's voice was rising with every word.

"How can you have any doubt now that she is somehow involved in Mom's disappearance, if not entirely responsible for it? It sounds like she could have easily manipulated Mom. It seems like if anyone would know what happened to Mom, it would be her. I think the first thing we need to do when the men get here is to find this cabin where she is supposed to be staying. I wonder if it even exists."

"Astrid was not lying. She cares for Mom, and for me, too, which is just another thing I can't explain. I felt it, though."

"You said she assured you that Mom is OK, that Mom *will always* be OK."

Ursula was worked up imagining the power that Astrid might hold over Helen.

"You said she made you feel relaxed, like she hypnotized you. Some people can do that. Look at how Mom described her feelings for Astrid. I think she hypnotized Mom and made her follow her somewhere."

"I wasn't hypnotized."

"How about seduced, then?"

Suddenly, a ringtone blared, shattering the escalating tension, and they all twitched in their seats, searching for their phones. Iris pulled the ringing phone out of her pocket and answered. It was Persephone.

"Mom, something crazy just happened. I got a strange text. I think it must have been meant for you because I don't have a brother... but you do, and you're with Uncle Rav, so I thought it must be for you so..."

"Percy, slow down! What are you saying?"

"I got a text from someone, but I think it's for you."

"Why? What does it say?"

"All it says is, *listen to your brother.*"

Iris gasped and almost dropped the phone. Ursula and Raven stared intently at her, waiting anxiously to hear what their niece had said that clearly upset Iris. She regained her composure and held up her hand to ask her siblings for a moment of patience.

"That's what it says, Mom: *listen to your brother.* You're the one with a brother, and you're with him right now, so why was this sent to me? Who sent it?"

Iris was breathing raggedly into the phone, as if she had suddenly contracted asthma.

"Mom, what's going on? This is bizarre. Say something."

"Percy, don't delete it. We need to look at it. I have no idea who sent it or why. I wish I could be more clear, but I can't. It's getting harder and harder to understand what's going on here."

"Mom, it's pretty crazy around here right now, too. The patriots are shooting up the neighborhood."

"I know. Dad told me. We'll talk tomorrow when you get here. Bring your phone."

"Why are you supposed to listen to Uncle Rav? And why *aren't* you listening?"

"Don't worry. We'll be together tomorrow, and we'll figure it all out."

"Mom, are you OK? I can hear how fast you're breathing. Take some deep breaths."

Iris did as her daughter suggested and got her breathing under control. She reassured Persephone that she was fine, that they were all fine, and ended the call, advising her daughter to get some sleep.

"Uncle Dee is picking you up early. I'm glad you're coming."

"Me, too, Mom. I'm worried about you."

Iris put her phone down and stared into space, not saying a word.

"Iris, what the hell? What did she say?" Ursula's nerves were shot. She was shouting at her sister.

"Percy said she got a text." Iris reported slowly. "You're not going to believe..."

Ursula and Raven looked at her, their eyes urging her to get on with it.

"We're not going to believe what, Iris?" Raven said, knowing that whatever it was, he would not have any trouble believing it.

"Percy called because she just got a text that said *listen to your brother*. She thought it must have been meant for me."

Her siblings kept looking at her, expecting her to say more. They weren't grasping yet what she had told them.

"She's going to bring her phone. We can look at the text tomorrow."

Iris was trembling and had a hard time getting the phone back in her pocket. She was scared.

Ursula finally registered what Iris had told them.

"Astrid sent it! She knows where Mom is! She probably has her in that cabin!"

She was pacing up and down the alleyway between the stalls of the barn, ranting angrily, convinced that Astrid was guilty.

"The next text will probably be her ransom demand! This is how the universe provides for her."

1.8

From the backseat of Dion's sleek solar-powered car, Persephone handed her phone up to her dad so he could take a look at the mysterious message. Zephyr studied it for a moment and then pointed out the absence of any identification.

"I know," Percy said. "It came out of nowhere from nobody."

Without looking at it, Dion claimed it would be easy to figure out who sent it. He knew people.

"Why it was sent is the question. Why order them to listen to Raven? Is the message a threat? It sounds like directions from a kidnapper. Ursula thinks the person who sent it is this Astrid, your grandma's mysterious friend. Why would a young woman your age get friendly with someone old enough to be her grandma? You know, old people get preyed on like this all the time."

Aside from the text, their conversation on the way to the property revolved around what could have upset the siblings enough that they had been called in to help. Everyone in the car knew that it must be serious if Raven had actually agreed it was OK for them to come.

The men couldn't fathom why Helen not being home was a reason to assume tragic or nefarious events. Why jump to terrible conclusions? Why the paranoia? Sure, she was old, but she was able in body and mind as far as they knew. Why couldn't she have just gone somewhere? If she wasn't expecting any of them to visit, why would she leave a note?

"Mom was hyperventilating after I told her about the text. I had to calm her down so we could talk," Persephone offered.

She was worried about her mom. Whatever was upsetting her was something real, not imagined. Something to be taken seriously. But she kept her feelings to herself. Also kept to herself was her annoyance with the men she was riding with. She listened without comment as her Uncle Dion and her dad confidently expressed, as men do, that once they arrived, they would calm everyone down and get the situation, whatever it was, under control. Their partners were panicked for no reason. Helen was either in the area, and they would find out where, or she went somewhere without telling anyone, and there would be nothing further to do but wait for her at the property or go home and wait to hear from her.

Neither of them saw a reason to assume the worst. However, they did admit that if Helen was their mom, they might be more inclined to imagine frightening scenarios, such as kidnapping, especially after hearing about Astrid and getting the ominous text.

Such were their confident assertions as they came to the rescue in Dion's silver sedan.

***

When the cavalry from town walked up to the porch of the barn, they were greeted with hurried hugs followed by an overwhelming ricochet of words. Raven didn't participate in the briefing of Zephyr and Dion. He sat in his chair, waiting for the men and his niece to be brought up to speed and for the excited talk to die down.

Tired of the crosstalk between the couples and wanting to see how her uncle was doing, Persephone came over and sat next to him, understanding that her mom and aunt, amped up on anxiety, needed to spill for a while.

She appreciated her uncle's calm patience. She had spent the last couple of hours with her dad and Dion and knew they wouldn't miss her as they convened with their partners, both listening politely, all the while assuming they knew exactly what was going on.

In the car, she had not shared their certainty about how they would *resolve the situation* as Dion put it, but she saw no point in trying to puncture their male hubris. There was always a chance things would go as they expected and they would get the kudos they hoped for. She had her doubts, though. Her mom had been genuinely shocked by the text, not by the fact that she didn't know who it was from but because of what it said. Something was going on beyond what her dad and her uncle assumed.

Without saying a word, she took out her phone, leaned over, and showed Raven the text, which he looked at in silence, and then got up and went into the barn. He returned to the porch with a compact notebook, something that people might keep a diary in back in Grandma's day before the digital revolution, opened it, and pointed to a sentence. While the others were still engaged in the flurry of talk, he asked her quietly if she thought the sentence in the notebook seemed similar to the one in the text.

"Kind of. I mean, it's short. It has the same tone."

"Always so cryptic, these messages," Raven said, talking to himself, not her, but loud enough for her to hear.

"So presumptive. Is it so hard to write a little more? Give us something to go on?"

Percy couldn't make sense out of what Raven was saying, but she picked up on his frustration.

"Uncle Rav, who wrote this?"

"Which?"

"Both."

"Your grandma is the one who wrote in the journal, but I don't believe she wrote that last sentence. We don't know who or what sent that text. I think whoever wrote in Grandma's journal also sent the text. It is the same person, if it is even a person at all."

Persephone was not tracking what her uncle was saying. *If it is a person?* She could tell it was important to him, which made sense since the text had asked his sisters to listen to him. She assumed what they were supposed to listen to would soon be revealed.

Raven stopped his ruminating and suddenly interrupted the animated discussion that had been going nonstop since the reunion on the porch, asking them why they weren't interested in looking at the text Percy had received.

He passed the phone and the notebook around, telling everyone to compare the sentences. While they were looking back and forth from phone to notebook, Raven announced he believed the author of the text was also the author of the strange sentence imprinted in Helen's journal.

Zephyr asked to see the other sentence, the first one they had encountered in Helen's journals. The entire family then passed around the phone and the two journals and took more time to compare and gather their thoughts.

Not surprisingly, Dion was the first to offer his opinion. He agreed with Ursula that the only explanation that made sense was the simple one: Helen was the author of everything in her journals, including the sentences in ink, and Astrid was the likely source of the text, if only because she was the only suspect they had. Who else could it be? It would have been easy for her to have looked at Helen's phone for the numbers of family numbers. She could have found Percy's number and sent her the message. Simple. Case closed.

"Why is there any debate about any of this?" Dion asked, perplexed. "Or is there?"

"It's just that Mom wrote everything in pencil, and the font is so elaborate... it looks like it was printed by a machine..."

Iris was so clearly unconvinced herself that she was convincing everyone else that Dion and Ursula were right.

Persephone felt sorry for her uncle and wanted to stick up for him, but she couldn't think of any way to counter what did seem the most likely explanation.

"So why would Astrid send this message to Percy?" Raven's tone made it clear just how many fucks he could give any more about convincing anyone of anything.

"Look, I don't expect you all to believe anything else. You, Zephyr, and Percy should read the journals, though. Mom's writing is... he paused and looked up at the porch roof, trying to come up with the right word... "illuminating. Thought provoking."

Though Raven was addressing the men, he was also talking to the air, thinking out loud.

"And we haven't even read them all yet. Who knows what else we'll find out?"

He stopped to take a breath.

"Logical, sensible, likely explanations, I get that's what you want. Why complicate things when it's not necessary?" He was openly mocking them now. "Isn't it time to get in your cars? Activate the GPS. Hit the road. Ring doorbells. That's what you're here for. Time's a wasting."

"Raven, stop."

Iris had her hand on his arm, but he didn't stop.

"Shouldn't you all just get on with it? Dion driving one car and Ursula the other—that's the plan, right?" He brought his eyes down and scanned his family scattered around the porch.

"This is what I'm going to do while you're gone: find out where the vagabond is holed up and warn her that she's a prime suspect in her friend's kidnapping and possible murder."

"Rav, please, just stop."

Ursula gave Dion a knowing glance that communicated *this is what I was warning you about.*

Zephyr cleared his throat and broke into the awkward silence that followed Iris's plea.

"Raven's right. We're here to find Helen. And we should get on with it. The sooner we do, the sooner we can all relax, knowing Mom is OK."

Persephone had something else in mind. She knew what they all needed at the moment.

"I'm hungry. We didn't have breakfast on the way. Uncle Rav, let's go get some eggs. I haven't visited the colony for years. I want to see the chickens."

Raven didn't argue; he jumped up and started walking. He was happy to get away.

***

"Now they can talk about me all they want," Raven said, after he and his niece had walked far enough away from the barn not to be heard.

Persephone didn't say anything, and Raven didn't follow up. He didn't have to. She understood how her uncle was feeling, and he knew she understood.

Raven was her only real uncle, not because they shared genes but because they shared a deep despair about the moral failures of humanity. The insane greed of human beings had doomed countless species of life and had probably doomed the planet. Uncle Dion was an unapologetic capitalist carbon-burning meat-eater. He lived in Birnam Wood and was on the wrong side of almost everything. She refused to consider him a relative.

Standing outside the extensive coop, with chickens pecking at their feet and those on the inside clamoring frenetically at the wire fence for a piece of bread, Persephone asked her uncle if he felt like talking about what was bothering him. Why had he gone off on the family like that? It wasn't like him to be sarcastic and bitter.

"I'm frustrated. I know Mom didn't just walk off and get lost, and I sure as hell know Astrid is not her kidnapper."

"How do you know?"

"I just know. That's what's frustrating. I don't have a rational, *simple* explanation, but I know your grandma did not write those weird messages in her journals, and Astrid did not send that text to you. I don't know who or what did, but since I've been here, I've been sensing... something."

"Sensing what?"

"Whoever or whatever is writing to your grandma, I think, or maybe it's Grandma; other times, it feels like something else..."

"Like what?"

"Not a person, a force, maybe. It's like how you feel when a thunderstorm is about to break. What can I say? I'm not making it up, but I can't say what it is. I have no idea."

"You really think it could be, Grandma?"

"I don't know. I sense her presence and its presence. They're different but the same."

"That's pretty darn vague, Uncle Rav. I sense stuff all the time, and I have no idea what it is. Don't most people?"

"You should read what your grandma wrote."

"I plan to."

Suddenly, the chickens clustered around them on the outside of the coop scattered, squawking anxiously, running away in every direction as fast as their awkward stick-leg gaits would carry them. The chickens inside bolted to the rear of the coop and took to their protected roosts. Raven and Persephone nervously looked around, wondering what spooked them.

It was the fox. It was standing on the trail, looking at them.

Persephone was excited. She'd never seen a fox before, not even in a zoo. Raven stared at the fox, and it stared back. She thought to herself: *they know each other.* They didn't move and didn't speak. The fox seemed content to keep its eyes locked onto Raven's.

Percy let out the breath she'd been holding and whispered, "Have you met? It feels like you know each other."

"I was hoping I'd see him."

"Or her."

"Grandma wrote about seeing a fox, and your mom and aunt saw it in the woods when they were searching for her.

There shouldn't be a fox around here, but there it is."

The fox continued to stand motionless in the trail, it's furry tail swishing slowly, raising dust. It was looking directly at Raven, and he couldn't take his eyes away.

Persephone felt a tingling sensation on her scalp, and then the fox began to shimmer. For a split second, she imagined that it was dematerializing like a Star Trek character beaming down to a planet, and then the fox was gone. It was there, and then it wasn't.

I must have blinked, she thought.

Raven was still staring at the spot where the fox had been.

"You didn't see it go, did you?"

"No, it just disappeared."

"Exactly. I keep trying to tell everyone that something unexplainable is going on around here, but everyone just insists on trying to explain."

Of course, **listen to your brother***. That's what the text was referring to. No one was listening to her uncle.*

"What do you expect, Uncle Rav? I just saw a fox disappear in front of my eyes, and I still don't believe it. If you weren't here as a witness, I would convince myself that it wasn't real, that I didn't see it."

"That's what's frustrating. I don't expect them to believe anything except what they already believe or do anything other than what they're doing, but their searching is pointless, and their paranoia about Astrid is just wrong. They haven't even met her!"

"She made a big impression on you, didn't she?"

"On your grandma, too. Astrid has an otherworldly presence."

Raven paused, remembering how he had felt around Astrid.

"They're not going to find your grandma or talk to anyone who knows where she is. I don't think she wants anyone to know."

After seeing the fox vanish as if it had been the climactic act in a magic show, Persephone had a better understanding of why Raven was frustrated by everyone trying to explain away everything instead of considering what they might not be able to explain; that they might be confronted with a mystery.

She really wanted her uncle to feel heard, but she was starving. They could work it out later.

"I think it's safe to get the eggs now, Uncle Rav. C'mon, let's go back and make breakfast. We can tell everyone we saw the fox."

***

Raven and Persephone, carrying a large bucket of eggs, bustled past everyone still sitting on the porch. The family followed them inside and watched as Raven broke eggs into a bowl.

Tension still lingered from his tirade, and he knew it was up to him to relieve it, so he apologized, acknowledging that he had been taking out his frustrations on them, and that was not OK. Of course, everyone was doing what they thought best, and he understood why they might suspect Astrid sent the text to Persephone, though he was certain that wasn't true.

Iris gave her brother a hug and told him that everyone realized that he had a different perspective than they did. He had been there longer than them. Anyone would be emotionally distraught.

"And you actually met Astrid," she pointed out. "It's probably just as you say: she is Mom's friend and is concerned about her just like us."

"We saw a fox," Persephone announced abruptly.

"*The* fox!" Ursula exclaimed.

"I guess so. Raven told me you and Mom saw it, too."

"We did. It smiled at us."

The fox sighting sparked Dion and Zephyr's attention, and while Ursula related the story of their encounter in the woods while searching for Helen, Iris found the notebook in which her mom had described seeing the fox. She showed it to Zephyr, and Dion read over his shoulder.

"There shouldn't be a fox around here," Zephyr declared as if settling that issue.

"Well, it's here and making itself known to us," Raven asserted while serving the eggs. "Whether or not it's supposed to be here."

"Helen must have been feeding it," Dion said. "A fox wouldn't be coming around otherwise. It's just looking for a handout."

"She wouldn't feed a wild animal human food," Raven said sharply. "And she didn't write about feeding it. She wrote about seeing it for the first time."

As quickly as Dion and Zephyr's interest in the fox was piqued, it died out. The reason the fox had been seen the last two days must be as Dion said: Helen had not been around for a while, and it was showing up, hoping to get a treat.

Persephone, though, after her experience with her uncle and hearing what her grandma had written, was not convinced. She had seen the fox magically vanish.

While everyone was out looking for Helen, she was going to read all of the journals. Her grandmother's words resonated in her mind and provoked a lot of feelings. She had never gotten to know her. Helen had moved to the property when she was a kid, and since then, they had not had much contact. Reading her writing made her come alive. Persephone wanted to know her grandma better; she wanted to feel closer. She wanted to know Helen's history.

This was the first time she had seen something other than a note scribbled on a post-it that was written out in longhand. Cursive.

It's so real. I feel like she's right next to me bent over the page with her pencil when I'm reading it.

While the family ate the scrambled eggs Raven made and finished the last of the coffee, Persephone told them how the fox disappeared in the blink of an eye, just as Helen had described in her journal. Iris added that she and Ursula had had the same experience. One moment it was there, looking at them, and the next moment, it was gone.

"I imagine a fox must be pretty quick," Zephyr remarked.

"It's a trickster in folk tales," Percy added brightly.

"Your grandma doesn't think that tricksters are a myth," Raven said. "I don't know who or what that fox is, but it's trying to tell us something."

Raven knew saying that would make everyone except his niece uncomfortable again, but since he was letting them have their way of seeing things without making a fuss, he was going to have his. He was not going to hide what he believed, and he was definitely not going to deny his feelings and what he knew in his gut. His gut had always been more trustworthy than his mind, and when presented with a choice, he went with the gut.

"What could it be trying to say?" his niece asked, trying to show her support.

"Maybe it's trying to let us know not to worry about Mom, like Astrid said. It was definitely trying to tell me something this morning. It looked right at me and held my eyes for quite a while. I couldn't look away. It wouldn't let me look away."

"So did you get the message?" Dion asked, making it clear by his tone that he thought talk of tricksters and wild animals having some kind of agency in the human world was ludicrous.

"I know the fox has a message—or *is* the message—I'm just not able to decipher it. I don't know how to tune in."

"Maybe you'll be on its wavelength the next time you see it." Dion might as well have said it with a sneer.

The atmosphere on the porch was quickly getting ugly again. Dion tolerated his in-laws as they tolerated him, but whenever the family got together, he and Ursula were outnumbered and put on the defensive. This had been especially true when Kaspar was still alive. Ursula's dad never hid his feelings about those who lived in Birnam Wood and what they represented to him: they were planet killers, selfish hypocrites, capitalist predators, self-righteous, entitled privileged people, etc., etc. His litany of Dion's sins was never exhausted.

Helen was always polite, but that's all the concession she made. She had been instrumental in ceding the library to the ZeroG occupation, and her children were leaders of the neighborhood, whose residents despised the irresponsible, careless lifestyle of Birnam Wood citizens. Dion would complain to Ursula that he was more than willing to live and let live, but his in-laws didn't reciprocate. It was either adopt ZG or be an accessory to the extinction of all living things. There were no compromises to be made, no arguments left to be constructed, no gray area or neutral ground.

Dion considered ZG ideology misguided at best, destructive at worst, and their zealotry obnoxious. The movement was just another religion as far as he was concerned, and he was a committed agnostic. He didn't believe, and he was not going to be browbeaten or shamed into believing. Competent, knowledgeable people all over the world were working on solutions to climatic problems and had been for decades. They would find a way to deal with the effects of climate change, and the world would go on as it always has and always will. The naïve idealism of the ZG movement was a greater danger to the world than those they attacked, the responsible people trying to keep the world's economy viable and find a reasonable solution to the environmental crisis. Zero Growth was not a solution; it was blind faith in a fairy tale. They were actually the privileged ones, able to play their ZG game only because there were still enough people *not* playing it to keep the lights on and the phones working. To keep waste treatment plants operational and their water supply clean. To save their lives when they had a medical emergency.

Ursula listened to his grousing and expressed her empathy, but she could never get over regretting how things had turned out. She had been foolish to believe her family would someday accept Dion and show him respect. He never had a chance.

No one was talking after Dion's snarky comment. Raven's face was frozen in a crooked smile, and Dion looked as if he wanted to be anywhere but on the porch of his in-laws' barn.

"So how are we going to do this?" Zephyr said, clearing his throat loudly. "Maybe decide on a radius for the search? Does 50 miles sound right?"

They all agreed that sounded right, glad to have found something to agree on and cut through the hostility. Ursula would drive her car with Zephyr, and Dion would drive his with Iris. Knocking on doors as a couple seemed like the best approach. Two strange men coming up to a house would be more threatening than a couple, and considering the paranoia of most Americans, they needed to be as unthreatening as possible.

Zephyr joked that they should carry a white flag or have a bouquet of wild flowers in hand. "A plate of cookies would be even better. We'll be lucky if anyone who sees us coming doesn't lock their doors and get their gun."

People would assume that, at best, they were there to scam them or convert them or both at once, and at worst, they were patriots on a deluded mission to subvert the latest conspiracy or drug-addicted psychopaths on a crime spree.

In mid-21st century America, people kept to themselves, living in neighborhoods surrounded by cement walls often topped with razor wire as well as shielding themselves with virtual walls, selecting and exposing themselves only to information that reinforced their beliefs.

There were multiple layers of protection: barriers with steel gates manned by security guards at the entrances to gated neighborhoods, houses equipped with state-of-the-art security systems and CCTV, and the last line of defense, the personal protection provided by electronic devices. People could hide behind their sizable portable screens wherever they went. The closest contact most people had with strangers was passing them on the sidewalk, each person's head safely tucked into the screen of his or her phone. People who might be inclined to say hello in passing thought twice about it. Randomly greeting someone on the street might get you tazed, if not shot.

Even though neither of the couples thought their plan promised success, they felt they had to try, though Dion made it clear that after today, he would be going home. He needed to be back at work, and if he were honest, he confessed, he thought they were on a fool's mission. "I'm here to help however I can," he insisted. "So let's get on with it."

Holding up one of Helen's notebooks, Percy announced, "I want to stay tonight," not really believing anyone was listening or cared, but still, just in case. "Longer, if that's what it takes to finish everything Grandma wrote."

The four members of the search party started planning their routes, examining satellite imagery for buildings in the sizable national forest that extended west, north, and south from the property. There were not many homes within the 50-mile radius they intended to search.

Kaspar and Helen had bought the property decades ago, knowing the wild patch bordered by public land had a good chance of not falling prey to developers. There was only a two-lane highway to the east with a dozen or so dirt and gravel access roads spoking out from it for the search teams to explore.

Dion and Zephyr both insisted that it made no sense to travel out more than 50 miles in either direction down the highway. How far could Helen have wandered on her own? And if she went somewhere with someone, shouldn't they assume she was safe and sound? She could be anywhere.

Zephyr echoed Dion, saying that while he was happy to go along with the attempt to find out what had happened to Helen, he didn't believe she was in any danger, and he was not willing to keep on searching if they struck out that day.

"She's your mom!" he protested. "Her leaving without telling any of you is exactly what she would do. She's fine. She'll be back. What are we going to do if we don't find her? Stay here and wait indefinitely?"

Nobody answered the obviously rhetorical question.

I'm staying, Raven thought.

1.9

The two couples walked the trail back to their cars and drove off in opposite directions down the old highway, engaged in what they felt was due diligence. After fulfilling their duty, they could all go home and feel OK about not knowing what had happened to Helen—unless, of course, by some miracle, they found her. They would be able to rest easy knowing that chances were she was fine and would show up any day. When she returned home and heard about everyone anxiously searching for her for days, of their hysterical suspicions about Astrid, she would laugh and say something along the lines of *I didn't think I needed your permission to leave this place. Sorry!*

Even though he hadn't confided in her, Iris knew Raven would stay after they all left. While she would feel guilty about leaving him there alone, his staying, ironically, would ease her guilt about giving up the search for Helen. If it came to that, at least one of them would be there waiting when their mom eventually came back.

If she comes back.

Iris wouldn't let this thought take root. Zephyr was confident that her mom was fine, and she would be, too. *Besides*, she laughed to herself, *Astrid says it's so! Helen will always be OK. The universe provides.*

While the others searched, as he had announced already to the group, Raven planned to look for the cabin where Astrid said she was staying. They had pored over satellite images of the area and not seen any signs of a building in the vicinity of where she had indicated it should be. He was pretty sure there was no cabin, but he thought there was a chance he'd run into Astrid while he wandered around the property. He wanted to ask her why she had lied about the cabin. What else was she not telling him?

Up the hill, she had said, pointing at nothing in particular, just the slope leading up to the forested ridge. *There is a trail of sorts; nothing more than a deer trail, really. It's hard to follow.*

He could find and follow a deer trail. He was determined to locate the alleged cabin or verify that it didn't exist, and even more determined to find Astrid. He was convinced that she knew more than she let on, though he wasn't clear in his mind what it was that she knew more about.

If he was honest with himself, he would have to admit that finding Astrid had less to do with finding his mom than it had to do with his obsession with finding Astrid herself. Their meeting at the pond had struck some kind of chord in him that wouldn't stop vibrating. Not that he wanted it to.

"So, you'll be OK here alone?" he said to Persephone. "I'll probably be gone all day."

"I'll be reading Grandma's journals. All of them."

"Can you start with the ones we haven't read? That would be helpful."

Raven went into the barn, pulled out the unread notebooks from the chest, and brought them to his niece.

"Anything to do with Astrid is important. She's the key."

"Got it."

Raven stuffed a pack with some food and water and stepped off the porch. Persephone watched him walk across the field. When she lost sight of him in the trees, she began reading.

None of the kids have come by in the last couple of months. They try to keep in touch by phone, but I usually don't know where I left the phone, and if I find it, it usually needs charging. Before long, though, I'm going to have to find my phone, charge it, and ask someone to bring me some rice and flour. And peanut butter! I've been out for weeks.

I choose solitude; I cherish it, but when I'm alone for long periods meditating, spacing out, looking at plants, watching tree limbs sway, listening to the sounds of nature, my mind starts to go on the fritz, as if synaptic connections are decaying.

That description, though, is just my mind using language to try to make sense of what is happening to my mind when I'm alone, so that's an issue. That's always an issue, I suppose, when trying to deconstruct one's consciousness.

Why did I use the word 'decay,' which is definitely a pejorative term? Why say that neural connections are 'decaying,' as in corroding, declining, wearing out? Why do I automatically make a negative value judgement? Why not say that my neural connections are simply changing? That's totally neutral and certainly true. Why does my mind, without stopping to think about it, choose the word 'decay?'

Being alone here, apart from the human world, just me and nature, my only companions chickens and ducks, isn't it likely that my consciousness would change? Isn't it likely that well-established electro-chemical pathways might be altered? But why assume that's a sign of decay? Why characterize the change as fritzing out at all? (because electrical, I suppose). Why not just notice that my consciousness changes and leave it at that?

Everything changes all the time. The natural world changes constantly. My cells die and are replaced. The body I had yesterday is not the body I have today. My consciousness must be changing moment by moment, too. All that's really happening when this 'I,' the observer, thinks, 'oh, my mind is fritzing out,' is that the observer, alone for a long period of time, has noticed that its consciousness has changed, is changing. That's not decay. It's not a perceptual malfunction. It's just what naturally happens.

Maybe I use that language because I'm unconsciously agreeing with Ursula that I am old, and losing my mind is inevitable, that mental decay is unavoidable at my advanced age.

Then again, what does Ursula know? No more than anyone else, which is pretty much nothing.

This is why I write—to discover what I think or what I think about what I think. My writing is a conversation with myself, but if I'm honest, I do have an audience in mind: the kids, and Persephone, who could still have a kid or kids someday. Possible but not probable. I hope they will get something out of my writing, but who can say? What is there to get out of anything anyone writes? It's not like reading compares to experiencing. There's no comparison.

I tell myself they will know me better after reading what I've written, but really? Is the 'me' I construct in what I write somehow more authentic, more the 'real me' than the 'me' they have constructed in their own minds? The me they hang out with in person?

Can we really know anyone, even those we carried for nine months and gave birth to? Can we really know our self? The observer, noticing the constant flux of everything, is in constant flux as well. How can there be an objective reality to analyze, to know, when reality is only what the observer observes? The observer is not omniscient. The observer has to make choices as to what to attend to and what to ignore. As the saying goes, and what Kant concluded: it's all in your head.

I don't think we actually believe that when we say it, but we should: It really is all in the mind. Everything. The so-called objective world is entirely subjective. Without the observer, how can there be something there to be observed? Bishop Berkeley, who was no Buddhist, made this well-known observation. Has it ever been refuted? I don't think so.

So if everything is in my mind, what is outside my mind?

Nothing. The void. The eternal never born, never formed, never made, uncreated, never changing, unknowable reality.

Ouspensky wrote an entire book trying to prove that matter doesn't exist.

The observer, being born, made, created, and ever-changing, dies—the ultimate change—then is born again to go through another cycle of ceaseless changing. The observer can't know reality until it realizes itself to be that reality. Until it sees the light and realizes tat tvam asi, thou art that.

Now I'm really getting nowhere, trying to explain the unexplainable. The fact is reality cannot be explained, only known, only experienced. Language cannot touch it.

Time to get back to what prompted me to say my mind is on the fritz. Does anyone use that old expression anymore? I remember looking it up once, and no one knew where it came from. The best guess was that when wiring shorts out it sounds like 'fritzzing.

Why do I say I'm fritzzing?

Because I see things, hear things, sense things.

I really don't like to use the word 'things,' a meaningless noun that needs an antecedent, but it's impossible not to use it. We use the word when we can't think of what to name the antecedent, or when there are too many antecedents to choose from, when we don't know what the thing is, or the things are, but we know there is a thing or things.

But what things, Helen?

I hear voices saying things (see?!), but I never actually hear what is said. In my mind, the voice is clear enough, and words in English are spoken—or at least words that I think are English and think I should understand—but after the weird shock of hearing an unidentified voice from somewhere saying something, I realize I have no idea what was said.

Now you kids are thinking, whoa, you hear voices in your head? Yeah, I'm thinking that, too, when it happens! Except the experience is not of a voice inside my head; it is a voice outside of my head, outside of me: a voice from the porch if I'm inside the barn or from behind me on the trail I'm walking along, or from the stall next to me as I lie in bed reading. I suppose that is how schizophrenics describe their experience of voices, so I have to wonder if I would be diagnosed if I consulted a psychotherapist. I don't care. I accept the experience without judging myself. It happens; that's all I know.

I see things that I think might be what are called elementals, beings that exist in dimensions we don't usually have access to, the astral realm, to put a name on it, but what is that realm? No one knows, but elementals like fairies and leprechauns are definitely things (no comment) that exist. Where? In realms. Nature spirits. They are described throughout history in stories from cultures all over the world, so why do we insist they are imaginary? We might as well insist that everything is imaginary, which is what literally billions of people believe, except for the materialists who demand empirical proof that a thing exists to believe it exists, even when it's impossible to prove the existence of the thing empirically. Talk about circular reasoning. It's the materialists' go-to logic.

'Whatever cannot be empirically proven is not real,' the materialists confidently assert. Interesting to note that this perspective is relatively new, only a few hundred years old. Science and the technology it engenders may prove how useful and just plain wonderful materialism can be, what with modern conveniences and being able to fly around the world and spend your day streaming audiovisual entertainment to enjoy while eating meals delivered to your door. Considering how perspectives have changed so often over the course of tens of thousands of years of human history, I can confidently predict that this perspective will not be the last. It will not last.

I wonder what the AI programs that do all the writing now would have to say about this? Here's your prompt, robot genius: If something can't be empirically proven, does it exist?

In 500 words or less, please.

What do I see? That's the problem, same as the problem with the voices I hear. I hear snatches of speech that I can't quite make out, and I see glimpses, flashes of unfamiliar forms that I notice out of the corner of my eye that seem recognizable, yet I can't say what they are: animals? birds? fairies? They seem either to be made of light or their appearance alters the light, like a prism. Basically, I see something, and startled, I think, what's that? Then I usually stop moving, if I'm moving, or just stay very still if I'm not, suspended in the moment as if an eerie cloud has passed over that freezes me. I wait motionless until I have to take a breath, but whatever it is, it never appears in full view. In that moment, I believe I may be in touch with this realm where elementals exist, but what do I know?

Am I going crazy? I don't care. So what if I am? People who have tried to describe these experiences to the authorities, those in control of the 'real' world, that is, the material world, have been labeled and judged, tortured and burned at the stake, hung or committed to facilities, or imprisoned or ridiculed or have suffered a number of other terrible consequences. This is how it's always played out. Humans in authority don't want to have to deal with the unknown, the unpredictable. They don't want mystery. They want to explain. They want control, and they'll do anything to gain and maintain it.

That's a concise history of humanity right there.

So, I do cherish my solitude (wouldn't want the authorities to get a hold of me), but I miss my kids after a while.

YOU ARE BLESSED BY GIFT WAVES.

Another message from the ether.

If you kids are reading this someday, I want you to know I am experiencing this right now.

Words have just materialized on the page.

Where have you been, anonymous? Peeking into other old lady diaries?

You're thinking (do you think?): 'So bitter, why?'

Don't you know? You should know.

I am surprised, actually. What a surprise! You're back, mysterious and cryptic as ever. Dropping in without warning, like Astrid, except she, at least, seems to be human and capable of expressing herself in more than one sentence. Plus, she is a friend. She's warm, sweet, and insightful. I don't know who or what you are, but you're not exactly friendly.

Is that your one and only riddle again, anonymous? Are you going to leave me in the dark as usual?

CONSCIOUSNESS IS AN OCEAN
BE A SURFER.

OK, thanks for that! Really!

Much better, anonymous. We're having a conversation now, even though I have no idea what you're talking about. That's OK. I appreciate your attempt to clarify 'gift waves.' I will meditate on the ocean metaphor.

I'm meditating on it now.

My first thought is that you are trying to help me understand how to explore my consciousness. Maybe you mean I should catch a gift wave and ride it as long as I can. Don't overthink, just try to find the sweet spot and stay there. I think surfers call that 'the pocket.'

Am I close?

Please don't disappear! We're just getting to know each other.

I'd like to keep up the dialog. It's interesting.

Look, whoever or whatever you are, this thing we're doing is not like using a phone. I can't hear you breathing at the other end of the line. I can only wait and have faith that you are out there somewhere and will respond.

Do you understand that I need some confirmation here? Otherwise, I will panic and convince myself that you don't exist and that I'm writing to myself, which is not something I want to be convinced of. Is that what you want? Do you want me to question my sanity?

I don't consider what you're doing to be friendly.

Is this what mystics experience when they implore God to speak to them? Am I experiencing anguish similar to theirs when they implore God to speak, and She is silent?

But you're not God.

WHAT COULD POSSIBLY NOT BE GOD?

I need a moment. I'm upset.

I'm crying.

You probably know that.

Do you know what crying is?

Do you have to lurk out there? It's disconcerting. Actually, it's annoying, if I'm being honest, which I don't think I have any choice about with you.

I understand what you're saying, of course. Yes, everything is God, but still, what particular created thing of God are you? What aspect, what particle of the Creation? And do you have a name? I would like to refer to you as something other than anonymous. I would appreciate knowing that I'm not losing my mind and making you up, that when you make words magically appear in front of me, it's your doing and not me writing to myself, that when I'm alone in the forest or by the pond or sitting on the porch looking out on the field that I'm not just hearing and seeing things that are byproducts of a deteriorating mind, but are things that really exist.

IT WILL SOON BE TIME TO MEET

You really don't understand what it is to be friendly, do you? I'm starting to believe you really don't have any idea what it's like to be human.

How am I supposed to sleep after that?

Now I'm getting angry. What the hell is going on? Talk to me. Don't disappear again like you do. I need resolution. Give me a time and a place, at least.

I'm hearing a deep baritone voiceover from a horror movie going through my head: 'Soon, Helen, soon it will be time to meet. Soon… soon… soon.'

Do you care if I sleep? Do you care if you're disturbing the hell out of me…?

***

Good morning. Are you there? I waited up all night for you to reply. I'm not going to put up with this abuse any longer. Today, one way or another, I find out if you are real or if I am psychotic.

The sun is up, and this is what I'm going to do. After breakfast, I'm going to pack some food and water and start walking around the property looking for you. I can't accept this arrangement we seem to have, an arrangement that you have imposed and control. I have never agreed to it. You wrote that we

139

would meet soon. I am insisting that we meet today while I'm out walking around. I expect you to appear. I am demanding that you appear. I am way too agitated to sit still after your last message, too frustrated to write and then wait for a reply that doesn't come, and when it comes makes no sense.

I assume that if you actually exist and are not someone I've made up, then you must know where I am at all times. And truthfully, it's really creepy to imagine that. You should be able to find me and introduce yourself, whatever you are. At least, this is my assumption since you seem to know when I'm writing and what I'm writing. If you know that, you must know what I'm doing and thinking all the time.

Remember, I'm 100 years old and quite vulnerable physically. Maybe you don't know that about humans, but I can't believe that is true, so I would think you would be concerned for my safety. If you are a friend, and I still have a slim hope you are, you should be concerned and make yourself known ASAP since I'm serious (which you should also know) and will keep wandering around the property until you show yourself. Until you're standing or levitating or appearing in some way to me that proves you are an actual entity of some kind separate from me. Otherwise, I may just plop down and stay down and call it a lifetime.

I don't know if I can even write anymore because I'm afraid you'll drop in another maddening koan and then leave me hanging for who knows how long. I am done with that.

At first, I was flattered to be noticed, but now I'm starting to suspect you are teasing me for laughs. It feels less like teasing and more like torture if you want to know.

If you don't show up today, and if I ever do write again, if I don't die from exhaustion today trying to meet you, please stop intruding. You are a psychic trespasser. A voyeur.

Leave me alone.

This was how the entry ended. While reading, Persephone had been visualizing her grandmother writing back to anonymous, all the time wondering as she wrote if she was losing her mind or if she was actually communicating with some unknown entity from another dimension. She couldn't imagine what that would have felt like not to know if anonymous was an actual being of some kind or some aspect of her own personality expressing itself.

There had to be more to this encounter. If she had to, she would read through every last one of the journals strewn around the barn to find out what happened.

Persephone furiously skimmed the beginning of the other notebooks Raven had set aside for her and couldn't find anything that seemed like it was written after the ultimatum her grandma had laid down. She realized then she might have just read the last thing her grandmother wrote, perhaps the last thing she would ever write.

***

It was a brilliant fall day, the sky cloudless and starkly blue, too hot for a September day, but every day now was hotter than it should be—or colder—there was no predicting anymore, and no point in counting on what a day in any month would be like weatherwise. All that could be counted on was the weather would be extreme, as the pendulum of every phenomenon in the world, weather or otherwise, now swung wildly back and forth, the alpha and omega points on the arcs of everything reoccurring so rapidly that moments of rest in between passed without notice, providing no relief from the constant stress of passing from one extreme state to another.

When would everything just collapse? That was the only question left.

Taking a break from reading, Persephone sat on the porch surveying grasses that had been growing in the meadow since the land had first been logged and settled in centuries past, before the industrial revolution of the 19th century had begun the speeding up of the pendulum now swinging out of control. She had a vision of her grandmother on her desperate quest to meet anonymous, walking slowly through the tall shoots as her ancestors might have, her hands gently brushing aside the green blades in front of her until she was swallowed up by the tall brush and disappeared.

Her vision was interrupted suddenly by what appeared to be an actual person walking through the field, not away from her as her grandmother had been, but toward her, and the reality of the person was confirmed when the person waved. Persephone could see it was a woman now that she had snapped to attention.

She gave a hesitant wave back and waited.

The young woman, barely five-foot tall, wearing faded denim cutoffs and a plain white tank top, stopped short of the porch and looked frankly into Persephone's eyes, a smile on her birdlike tanned face.

"Hey, hi... Persephone?"

Surprised at hearing her name, and disconcerted by the woman staring into her eyes, Percy took a while to answer. She finally managed to say *yeah*, thinking to herself, *this must be Astrid.*

Awkward silence followed, the smile never fading from Astrid's face.

Persephone asked, "How do you know my name?"

"Helen told me about you. You're Raven's niece, right?"

"You must be Astrid," she blurted out, releasing her tension.

"That's me. So did Helen ever show up? Raven was so worried about her."

"He and the others are all out looking for her." She didn't want to tell her that Raven was actually looking for her, Astrid the kidnapper.

"And you're not?"

"No, I'm reading my grandma's journals."

Astrid continued looking up at Persephone on the barn porch, her smile never wavering. "Is it OK for me to come up and sit in the shade with you? It's pretty hot out here in the sun."

"Sure."

Astrid sat in Raven's favorite chair and sighed, "That's better."

Persephone realized she was being rude. Astrid was her grandmother's friend. The least she could do was offer her something to drink.

"Water? Beer? I think that's all we have."

"I'd love a beer, thank you!"

Percy went into the barn and returned with a cold home-brewed bottle of beer she had brought with her. Astrid took several long gulps. "Just what I needed, thanks." She beamed sincere appreciation.

"Were you coming by to see about my grandma?"

"Yeah. Also to see how Raven's doing. He was pretty upset when I met him at the pond. I tried to reassure him, but I don't think it helped."

"He told me. He doesn't understand why you're so sure Grandma is OK. Why are you? She is pretty old. She could be in trouble."

"I just know that Helen can take care of herself, and she wouldn't disappear without saying goodbye."

"You mean to you?"

"To all of you. You're her children, her family. And sure, to me, too. We're friends."

Persephone was remembering how Raven had described Astrid's elliptical way of saying things that on the surface seemed reasonable, but at the same time seemed a little off, as if she knew more than she cared to let on, or more than she should.

"They think she might have been kidnapped..." Persephone hesitated, thinking that maybe she shouldn't say more but realizing she had already said too much.

"Really? That's bizarre."

"By you."

"By me? What?" Astrid laughed.

"After Uncle Raven told them about you, they all thought it's possible that you kidnapped her."

Astrid fixed her gaze on Persephone, still quietly laughing. "That's ridiculous? Why would I do that?"

"They jumped to the conclusion, I guess. I don't think they really believe it, though. I agree. It's ridiculous."

"Well, I hope to meet the rest of your family someday after Helen returns. Then we can all have a laugh about it."

Astrid stopped talking and sipped the beer. Persephone wasn't able to come up with anything else to say. Even though she wanted to keep questioning her, she couldn't think of any questions to ask.

"Is there somewhere I should put this bottle?"

"That's OK. I'll take care of it."

Astrid got up from her chair. "Such a pretty name you have, Persephone!"

"Yeah, Queen of the Underworld. My mom's name is Iris, and my dad is Zephyr, so I suppose they felt like they had to make me a mythological figure. I go by Percy, though. I am way more a Percy than a Persephone."

She didn't want Astrid to leave, but she didn't know why. Then it came to her.

"I didn't go out searching with everyone because Uncle Raven wanted me to read what Grandma had been writing. He thought there would be clues."

She didn't add that Raven thought she was the key, whatever that meant.

"Will you read this and give me your thoughts? What she wrote was pretty crazy."

"Sure, as long as you think it's OK with your grandma."

"Did you know she was writing? Have you read any of it?"

"No, I had no idea. Show me."

***

Persephone, sitting on the porch as she had been all afternoon, much of it spent with Astrid, spotted Raven crossing the shadowed field toward her. When he reached the barn, she got up and hugged him.

"The others aren't back?"

"Not yet. Do you want something to drink?"

"Water would be great."

She returned from inside the barn with a glass of water, and once he'd finished with it and set it down, she handed him the notebook with all the messages from anonymous.

"You have to read this. I think it might be the last thing Grandma wrote."

"Really?"

Raven had a story to tell, but he was glad to be spared from telling it right then. When he reached the first message from anonymous, he stopped reading and looked at his niece.

"So you see it, right? She could not have written this. So who did? And how? Why? Your mom and the others just don't want to deal with this. It's too far out for them."

"I get the feeling you describe when looking at it. It's like the words have a life of their own. I expect to hear some voice out of nowhere saying them out loud."

Raven read to the end, where Helen gives anonymous the threatening ultimatum: meet her or else.

Or else what? Did she really believe she would wander around the property until they met or lie down and die?

Percy waited for him to say something. She had assumed he would be convinced that Helen was in danger from anonymous, or at least in danger from her reckless impulse to set out to meet him—or it—but he just sat there quietly, head bowed, the notebook open in his lap.

She couldn't keep silent any longer.

"Well?"

No response.

"Uncle Raven, c'mon, what are you thinking? After I read this, I was really worried. For the first time since we arrived, I thought grandma might be in danger."

Raven didn't look up.

"Or dead."

"I think I might have met anonymous today," Raven said matter-of-factly, his head still bowed. "I want to wait until the others get back to talk about it. I'm tired. I don't want to have to repeat myself."

"Really? You think you met anonymous?"

"Yes, really."

"OK...Fine. I'll keep talking. Guess what? Astrid came by while you were gone."

Raven continued staring at the cement floor of the porch.

"Uncle Raven, what's with you? Do you just want me to shut up?"

He looked up.

"Sorry. So you met Astrid. What did she have to say?"

"She came by to see about Grandma and make sure you were OK. She knew who I was. Seems like Grandma has told her all about our family. I got the same impression you described, like she is so calm and reassuring, but she knows more than she is saying. Anyway, I showed her what Grandma wrote. She said she had no idea that she was writing anything."

"What did she say about that?"

"She said she thought she knows who anonymous might be. She thinks it's someone called 'the Dravidian.'"

"And?"

"She hasn't met this person."

"It's a person?"

"I guess. She called him a 'he.' She said she hasn't met him, but a friend of hers mentioned him when she told him about visiting Grandma. Her friend told her that the Dravidian knows Grandma."

Raven stopped slumping, sat up in his chair, and looked at his niece expectantly.

"That's all she said. I asked her what or who this Dravidian is, and she said it was hard to explain. 'I guess you could say he's a guide,' is all she said."

Raven nodded. Everything that he'd been sensing since he arrived was manifesting. No matter what his sisters and their partners thought, something extraordinary was going on with his mom. She had not just taken a walk and gotten lost.

Persephone put her hand on Raven's shoulder and gently shook him. "Hey, are you there?"

"Yeah, sorry, just thinking about all of the coincidences which are not actually coincidences."

He told her about meeting a mysterious character that day—a man with a weird name and no teeth—Pushan. Raven found the cabin Astrid had mentioned, even though it had not shown up in the satellite imagery they had looked at when preparing to search. Astrid was not there, but Pushan was, along with his donkeys. He thought Pushan might actually be the Dravidian, possibly anonymous, if they were one and the same.

Then suddenly, the search party was back, loudly yelling hello as they approached the barn. Raven and his niece were abruptly thrust back into the world which surrounded the property, the world the others had been driving in and through, hoping to find Helen wherever she might be or find someone who knew where she was or at least was willing to make a guess.

Raven and Persephone gave each other knowing looks. How were they going to explain everything they had experienced while the others had been out searching through that world? They both anticipated the resistance they would face on hearing accounts about characters named Pushan and the Dravidian and about another encounter with Astrid and how all three seemed implicated in Helen's disappearance.

As soon as Astrid was mentioned, they would latch onto their suspicions of her, of how she was the mastermind in the kidnapping plot, and this Pushan and Dravidian must be accomplices or at least colluding with her, aiding and abetting in countless crimes.

To be fair, their cynical view of Astrid would probably not take them that far afield, but they would undoubtedly cling to their vague suspicions and refuse to believe that anyone they had met could possibly be who Helen had dubbed 'anonymous.' They would not be cajoled into considering that something unexplainable, metaphysical, supernatural, preternatural—or whatever word made sense to use—was going on.

Raven and Percy didn't have to share their thoughts with each other to know how their attempts at telling their stories would go, so after hugs all around, they sat down on the porch with the others, and without hesitating, Raven asked them how the search had gone.

"Any luck?"

Let them tell their stories before he and Persephone told theirs.

1.10

Dion and Ursula did most of the talking. Iris and Zephyr didn't mind. They were grateful. They had been talking all day to people who didn't want to talk to them. People who chose, among other reasons, to live in a remote area to avoid talking to other people, especially strangers. Iris and Zephyr were happy to listen to what their partners reported and nodded their confirmation when appropriate to show their support.

As Dion had predicted, none of the people who did agree to talk to them had the slightest idea who Helen was, nor had they noticed an elderly white-haired woman who looked tired and lost wandering around.

Half of the time, when they came to a door and knocked, no one came to the door. Those who opened their doors did not invite them in. Some stood in the doorway to hear them out and then politely said, no, don't know her, didn't see anyone.

They had had no luck at all.

Dion made it clear he was anxious to leave, but when Persephone spoke up and said she'd met Astrid and they had been talking all afternoon, he stopped pacing around like an orienting bee and settled down to listen along with the others.

She told them how Astrid had suddenly shown up, walking across the field, and that she had known her name. She tried to describe how being around Astrid made her feel but could tell no one was interested.

Dion asked the only question that mattered to him.

"Did she tell you what happened to Helen?"

"No, she didn't know where she was."

"You believed her?"

"Sure, why wouldn't I?"

"Because she seems to be lurking around here waiting to meet one of us and talk about Helen. Why doesn't she show up when we're all here?"

"You mean when you're here," Raven said.

Dion ignored him and went on.

"Don't you all wonder why this Astrid—if that's actually her name—who apparently is Helen's closest friend, or only friend, first of all says she has no idea where she is but then assures Raven that she is fine—no, wait, what did she say?—she would *always* be fine—and then while we're all gone searching for her she shows up here to talk to Persephone alone? Why not come and talk to all of us?"

"She said she wanted to see if Grandma had come back. She was concerned about Raven since he had been so worried."

"Right, Astrid is worried about Raven."

"She told me Grandma was fine, too."

"Of course, she did. She doesn't want us to worry. She wants us all to go home."

"You're probably right about that, Dion," Raven said. "She would find our intrusion disturbing."

"Our intrusion! Listen to yourself! 'Our intrusion!' This is your—our—property! It has been for years. This is the first time we've ever encountered Astrid or even heard about her. Who's the intruder? Who's intruding? What is she doing around here? Where does she live? What the hell, Raven?"

Iris piped in, "We haven't heard about her, but Mom has been writing about her."

"I'm sure Mom has her reasons for not mentioning her to us," Raven said.

"Who knows what reasons your mom has?" Dion said with a jeer.

"What are you trying to say, Dion?" Iris did not appreciate his tone.

"How about this? This is what I'm saying. I'm saying what are her reasons for living out here alone? She's 100 years old! Who would do that? Why do you all accept it? And now you're all so worried about what happened to her. Of course, you are! What else can you do but worry? All the time! I know Ursula does. Why does she put you in this position? It's selfish. I don't get it. I'll never get it, but I go along to get along."

Dion's tirade brought with it a simmering, unsettled pause.

"We all know how you feel, Dion," Raven said quietly.

"We go along to get along, too, Uncle Dion, but we don't have to if you don't want us to," Persephone hissed.

She had heard enough from her uncle-in-law, the Birnum Wood banker. Why her Aunt Ursula had married him, she would never understand. Why had she brought a minion of the billionaires, a champion of capital, into the family? And here he was, openly disrespecting her grandma and the rest of them.

A longer, more charged silence.

"What's the plan, then?" Zephyr ventured, hoping to break the tension and get the ball rolling toward home. While he didn't share Dion's antipathy toward the Banis family, he did share his belief that there was no reason for them to be there looking for Helen. He had no doubt she had just gone somewhere with someone and would be back.

"The plan is I'm leaving. Ursula, you have a car, so you're on your own. If it were up to me, I'd call the police and report a missing person, as much good as that would do. Anyway, I don't think she's missing. She just isn't here and didn't bother to let you know her plans."

"Luckily, it's not up to you," Percy spat.

"I'll stay a while longer," Ursula said. "I wish you had kept your thoughts to yourself, Dion."

"Like Raven said, they're not a secret. Isn't it the ZG way to be honest about everything? Transparent? No lying hypocrites allowed in the neighborhood, right? Money-grubbing capitalists not welcome in The Library, I know."

"That's enough, Dion," Ursula said firmly, trying to keep Dion from embarrassing himself and her any further.

Zephyr tried again, "So... is there a plan?"

"I think you all should read what Grandma wrote before deciding anything. It has to do with her disappearance," Percy said.

"We don't know if she has actually disappeared," Zephyr pointed out. "We just know she's not here at the moment."

"You may change your mind after reading this."

Percy opened the notebook and held it up so everyone could stand behind her and read what may have been Helen's last journal entry. When they reached the first message from anonymous, everyone stopped and started to talk, but Persephone urged them to just keep reading. There was more.

***

"So do any of you really believe that this anonymous exists and is actually communicating with your mom by writing these messages in her journals?" Zephyr asked after they had all finished reading over Percy's shoulder.

"She didn't write them," Raven said.

Percy entreated her dad, "Don't you feel the difference? The words make you feel something different than what Grandma wrote."

"I don't *feel* the difference, but I *see* a difference." Zephyr had a shocked look on his face. He couldn't accept that anyone besides Raven would believe that anonymous was an actual person communicating with Helen in this way.

"Percy, are you expecting me to believe there is a mysterious entity communicating with your grandmother by making words magically appear on the pages of her journal? I'm sorry, but I can't go there when there is an obvious explanation. She wrote those words."

Dion nodded, "There's no reason to believe anything else."

"I don't know what to believe," Iris said shakily, "and I don't know what to do, but from what Mom wrote, she may have gone out looking for this anonymous or whoever and may not have come back. She may have wandered around until she was completely exhausted. She could be lying somewhere right now, hurt or dead, and we're arguing about what? What are we arguing about? You are so sure about what you know and what is possible, but what do you really know?"

Iris glared at the two men.

"There's something else," Percy said. "Astrid told me a friend of hers knows anonymous, and this friend thinks he is someone called the Dravidian. She said this Dravidian character has met Grandma."

"I met this friend of Astrid's today while I was out looking for her cabin," Raven added. "His name is Pushan, and I think he may be the Dravidian."

Iris was distraught, "What are we supposed to do now? Start searching for this guy? Go out and knock on doors again asking people if they know someone called Pushan, or maybe the Dravidian? I'm not doing that."

"I know what we should do," Ursula said. "We should contact the police and tell them someone who calls himself the Dravidian may have information about Mom. Show them her writing and tell them we think he has been doctoring her journals to make it seem like he is some kind of supernatural being trying to contact her, that he is preying on an elderly woman for some reason. He might have his eye on this property."

"Please don't do that," Raven implored. "Go home and get on with whatever, but don't tell the cops. They'll bring their dogs and their drones and their arrogant belligerence, and after they're done, the property will be ruined. When she comes back, Mom will never spend another night here."

"I agree, Aunt Ursula," Persephone said.

"Let it go, Ursula," Iris pleaded. "That's a bad idea. You know Mom would never want us to do that."

Ursula didn't respond. Zephyr let out a long, exaggerated sigh and got up from his chair.

"Look, we've done all we can do. Raven, you've been here searching for what? Four days? Five? Today we searched everywhere within fifty miles even though we all know that your mom most likely just went somewhere without telling any of you and will be back."

"What's your point, Dad?"

"We should go home. Your grandma will get in touch eventually, or someone else will."

"You mean like the police or a hospital?"

"Percy, we should go. There's no point in staying."

"I'm staying here with Uncle Raven. I don't know what's going on or what's going to happen, but I know it's not what all of you think."

"Don't speak for me," Iris said. "I don't think anything, and I don't know what to believe."

"I'm leaving," Dion said. "Now. I have things to do tomorrow. Anyone who wants a ride, let's go."

"Iris," Zephyr said gently, "I'm going back with Dion. You should come. Raven and Persephone will be here when your mom gets back."

"*If she gets back*," Iris said somberly. "I'm staying. I don't feel right leaving here after reading about Mom going out to meet someone who may be preying on her."

"You're going to run out of food eventually," Ursula pointed out.

"So come back with some," Persephone said. "We'll let you know when we need it. Anyway, we can live on eggs. They're the perfect food, or so Grandma says."

Dion looked at Ursula. "Coming?"

Ursula hesitated.

"No, I don't think I can leave now. I should stay here with my family. Like Iris said, it doesn't feel right to leave."

PART TWO

JOURNEYS

There is nothing either good or bad, but thinking makes it so.
Hamlet

2.1

Dion and Zephyr left. What a relief! Dion is an ass, but Zephyr is my good friend. We work together all the time on neighborhood projects. We designed and built the prototype coop for Percy and Tristan's chicken campaign, which has been a big morale booster for the neighborhood. The more food we produce—especially protein—the more autonomous we can be. None of us wants to ask Birnum Wood for anything. No one enjoys the humiliation of going through their obnoxious security check on the way to one of their supermarkets.

Zeph is my sister's partner and a brother in spirit, but he is not really in tune with Mom and the property. He and Dion arrived on their rescue mission confident that they would save the day, not understanding that their conventional mindsets were useless here. Rather than save the day, they wasted it.

They wondered why Astrid didn't show herself to them. Why would she? She wouldn't want to be assaulted by irrelevant questions and paranoid suspicions, so she kept her distance. It was no coincidence she made herself known only to Percy and me.

Everyone wonders at amazing, improbable happenings in their lives, and for a moment they may believe in divine intervention or fate, but the moment fades as the engrained refrain of *it's just a coincidence* pops into their minds to explain it all away and leave its significance behind.

It makes sense we default to that convenient explanation; humans like it simple. Believing there are no coincidences requires faith in the unseen and unknowable. Who has that faith? Only kooks who are convinced there is coherence in what looks random to everyone else. The kooks are easily dismissed as silly or crazy, but faithful kooks know that a coincidence always has meaning. It's a message from the source that begs our understanding, but when face to face with mystery, the faithless shrug, say whatever, and return to their phones to enjoy fantasies fabricated just for them.

My sisters are concerned about my emotional health, and Dion thinks I'm a fool, possibly deranged, but I'm not going to forsake what I know to be true because they think I'm distraught or deluded. Everything happening here is connected. I may not be able to explain how to anyone's satisfaction, but I feel it, I know it, and I'm not going to give up trying to understand.

People always want proof. They say, 'show me' and then protest, 'I don't see anything. Where is it?' They have to be able to touch it to believe it's real.

There are reports of yogis who have meditated for years in Himalayan caves, never moving, never leaving. They supposedly lived on the prana in the air.

Prove it.

Everyone trusts their senses to be providing accurate, objective data, but the information the senses provide goes through the brain. So what happens in there? No one really knows. Electrochemical reactions happen, but how do those add up to the consciousness of anything? To emotions and beliefs? To love and convictions? To the experience of beauty?

There are theories. Experiments have been done. Tentative conclusions reached and then abandoned upon further evidence from experiments. But the conclusions rely on observable functions of observable parts of the nervous system.

No unassailable conclusions have been reached regarding the actual nature of self-consciousness, the mysterious observer we are all born with, because the observer cannot observe itself. *The observer is the observed* is how Krishnamurti put it.

Is there anything that has been written about more than the enigma of consciousness? Endless theories on the endless.

Consciousness drives materialists to distraction because nothing about it can be proven or disproven by the senses. The materialists can only conclude that consciousness is a byproduct of the brain's functioning. Self-consciousness is a mirage, an after-image, a story we tell ourselves. Consciousness can't and doesn't exist outside of autonomic physiological operations. All those who believe consciousness is something beyond the mechanical workings of the brain are simply too weak-minded to accept that we humans are soul-less—but smart—big-brained mammals. Clinging to superstition, spiritual mumbo jumbo, and religious dogma out of fear should be forgiven. It's tough to accept that in the end, after a short period of exciting, though ultimately meaningless, sensory stimulation, we just die, forever. It's understandable that people seek what solace they can in fantasies of immortality.

Nothing but this and nothing but that. These are the conclusions the materialists arrive at. The only conclusions possible for their reductionist thinking. Nothing but! Reduce everything down to the smallest observable particle. We are nothing but a swarm of electromagnetic particles that, by some miracle, have life... is life...? Yes, it's a miracle. Miracles happen.

Instead of nothing but, what about all and everything? Look up at the stars on a clear night. Unimaginable immensity. So much space. And they say the space filled with stars started so very long ago and will continue to grow so much larger and for so much longer, and there will be so many more stars and so much more space for an unimaginable, much longer time.

What exactly *is* this matter of the universe that somehow appeared out of nowhere for no reason? An infinitely dense, impossibly tiny black ball of it appeared one day, or was always there, and then for some reason it exploded into smaller bits of the same stuff, the stuff we call *matter*.

What is it? Stupid question, right? It's *matter*! Matter is matter. And it matters because everything is it.

Einstein said that matter times the speed of light squared equals energy, but that begs the question, what is energy? Is matter energy or energy matter? Are they one and the same? But what about the speed of light? How does that fit in? Matter/energy in motion equals time. Does matter/energy need time to exist?

It's all very clear now, right? Everything has been explained except time and gravity, but besides those two ultimate mysteries, there's really nothing much left to discover, nothing much left to learn. Whatever may be left is unimportant. Time just is. It flows. What more do we need to know? Gravity just is. What goes up must come down.

Consciousness, though, we know what that is: nothing, really.

What I, the observer, the subject, knows can't be proven by the senses. No one will ever see what I know. No one will ever hear it, touch it, smell it, or taste it. No one can observe it and replicate it to vouch for its reality, but what I know, I know.

I experience; therefore, I know.

I have consciousness; therefore, I am.

I know that I am because I have consciousness. A = B; therefore, B = A. The question is what is this "I" that thinks it knows?

Why go on and on like this? What a spewage of nonsense.

I am spewing to show why there was no way those two well-meaning men who came to help could understand what is happening here. I don't understand either, but that doesn't keep me from allowing myself to experience what is happening.

At least I got to meet Astrid. If my karma is such, we will meet again. I hope so.

They wanted to explain, not experience. They wanted to close the case, get pats on the back for their help, and go back to their routines. The last thing they wanted was to throw off their cloaks of conventionality and experience something that challenged their assumptions about reality, of what is possible and what is not, something that would force them to acknowledge they had no idea what the hell was going on.

An unknown being somehow making writing appear? Anonymous texts from a supernatural source? A fox that disappears into thin air? A 100-year-old woman who seems to have vanished? Her vagabond friend who shows up to assure us she's fine? Someone known as the Dravidian who is somehow behind it all? Way too much to process, when all they wanted to do, and all they expected to do after driving here and spending a day searching, was to say, *See? I told you she was OK,* and help Helen out of the back seat of their car.

"You're surprised I didn't leave with them," Ursula says, looking at me.

"Why *did* you stay?"

"Someone needs to keep a level head."

"I'm not level-headed?" Iris asks, miffed. "I'm level-headed to a fault, at least according to Mom."

"You're taken in by Raven's woo-woo. You've always been susceptible."

Annoyed, Persephone interrupts, "Your squabbling is getting so old! Does anyone remember why I'm here at all?"

Everyone stops talking, but no one answers her question.

"OK, now that I have managed to get your attention, I'll remind you. Who texted me? And why are you supposed to listen to Uncle Raven?"

"What did Raven say we were supposed to listen to?" Ursula asks. "I must have missed that."

Persephone waits again for a response, and when it doesn't come, presses on. "If no one has a clue about what Uncle Raven said..."

"If anyone should have a clue, it's me," I say, "and I have no idea."

Persephone, looking defeated, nods. "Whatever. What about anonymous? Is it the Dravidian? Is that who texted me?"

"Your grandmother is anonymous," Ursula says dismissively, "and the Dravidian doesn't exist. He is one of her fictional characters or maybe someone she remembers from the cult."

I protest. "Mom was not in a cult. Just because you think her guru was a fake doesn't mean she was in a cult."

"That's debatable."

"Everything's debatable."

"That's debatable."

Persephone, exasperated, butts in. "Will you all stop, please?! Can't we just focus on why we're here?"

"You're right, Percy. We're here to find Mom, not argue about what's debatable and what's not," Iris says.

She entreats her sister, "Do us a favor: will you forget about being level-headed and try to respect everyone's perspective... OK?"

"You mean Raven's."

"I mean everyone's."

"So what's yours then?"

"Mine is to remember I don't really know anything and keep an open mind."

"The thing is, I can't live with not knowing anything. I have to know something. The more I know, the better."

The bickering ends. Nothing is settled, but the atmosphere is refreshed as it is after a sudden shower. The two interlopers from the outside world are gone, and the four of us—blood relations tied to the property and to our matriarch—understand without voicing it that we have a common bond. That bond is what needs respecting more than anything else. Somehow I know this. *Mom is reminding me.*

Iris asks for the third time why I was standing in the field the night they arrived, and I tell her for the second, third, fourth time—I've lost count—I don't know why. I explain once more how I only became aware of standing there when Ursula shined her flashlight in my face. The thought that I was waiting for something—or someone—flashed through my mind.

"That's what you said. You were waiting for something."

"Or someone."

It suddenly occurs to me, and I blurt out, "Maybe Mom is the texter!"

"I don't think so, Uncle Rav."

"Why not?"

"Because... I don't know. It just seems so out there."

"More out there than a mysterious being from another dimension writing to Mom? Sending you a text?"

"I'm trying to stay in touch with reality here, Uncle Rav, despite everything."

Ursula snorts.

Iris asks, "Raven, just how long are we preparing to wait here for Mom to show up?"

"I don't know, Iris... as long as it takes?"

"You know she might be dead."

"She's not dead."

Iris looks down at her feet and mutters, "You don't know that."

"Good question, Iris," Ursula pronounces. "What *are* we going to do tomorrow, anyway? And the day after that, and the day after that? Are we just going to wait? Sit on the porch drinking tea? Meditate at the pond and hope the fox appears again. Who cares if the fox comes?"

Rhetorical questions seem to be the only questions left.

"Honestly, Raven," Ursula continues, "I don't think I can take any more of this. I thought you would be happy I stayed, but you clearly are not, and you're just being a jerk to Iris. She's worried Mom might be dead, and you pretend to know that she's not."

"It's OK, Ursula. I hope Raven does know. Who can say?"

"I'm happy you stayed, Ursula, really I am. Thank you. Mom would be happy, too."

"Possibly."

"Your level head is always needed, especially by me."

Persephone looks up and smiles. "That's right, Aunt Ursula."

Mollified, Ursula says she's tired. Having doors shut in your face all day is not pleasant. She's going to bed.

Iris sighs, "I'm joining you. I haven't spent an entire day in a car for years. I hope I never have to again."

I retreat to my chair on the porch. Mom could be working her way back home right now. Astrid could show up unexpectedly. I realize I'm wishing for both. If asked which wish I would choose—Mom coming across the field in the moonlight or Astrid walking toward me on the porch—I wouldn't be able to answer. It's 50/50.

I haven't told anyone how I feel about Astrid. I'm embarrassed. I'm a 70-year-old teenager, and I am probably lying to myself when I think it's a toss-up about who I really want to see coming toward the barn. When I left her at the pond and turned around to look back, I was hoping I would catch her watching me walk away. I was going to smile and invite her to come and meet the family. Such was my fantasy, but she was gone, and since then, I have not stopped longing to see her again.

So melodramatic, but *longed* is the right word.

When we sat together at the pond, I felt such peace. My mind emptied. Even though we were talking, I was meditating, and it was real meditation. I had no sensations, no thoughts, just an experience of nothingness. She knew everything about me, and everything about me was perfect. I had nothing to prove. Nothing was required; nothing needed doing. As Mom wrote, it's impossible to explain the unexplainable.

Is it so hard to understand that I want to experience that peace again? That I want to feel perfect?

When Astrid shows up, I will tell her how I feel, and she will smile and say, *that's nice,* or *I'm glad,* or she will say nothing. It won't matter. That's the point. Everything we think matters doesn't matter.

Just stop thinking.

2.2

Mom and Aunt Ursula have gone to bed, and Uncle Rav is sitting in his chair on the porch staring into the night. The three of them really seem unable to get their bearings right now. They're regressing back to issues of childhood and acting like children. I suppose it's understandable. Grandma is very old, possibly demented and lost, possibly lying somewhere seriously injured or dead, possibly gone off somewhere with a man or supernatural being called the Dravidian, a possible stalker, a potential kidnapper, someone she possibly met while wandering around this isolated place where she lives alone, off-the-grid, with a phone she doesn't keep charged. Who lives like that when they're 100 years old? My grandma does. Is she crazy? Possibly.

I wonder about her ultimatum to the Dravidian—aka anonymous—does she just want to die? After 100 years of living, a person might be ready to call it quits and might pray before falling asleep that she does not wake up. Did she really believe the secret texter would show him/her/itself if she ordered it to? And then what? Would they go back to the barn for some tea and philosophy? Does she have an unconscious death wish? Did she secretly wish that, exhausted from wandering around looking for her savior in vain, in spiritual despair, she would lie down in the grass for the last time?

I don't know Grandma well enough to speculate—she moved out here when I was a kid, after which I may have visited a half dozen times—but I know her a lot better now that I've been reading her journals, and I can't believe she has a death wish, which is ironic since she claims to be preparing for her death. Who knows what it's like to be 100 years old? Only her.

She's something else. That expression fits her perfectly. She is smart, and she is special, and she is why we're all gathered here. I am getting really irritated with everyone making everything about themselves rather than focusing on their mother, my grandmother, Helen Penelope Banis, and what she has to say in her journals. How can they not feel that what she writes is authentic? Why don't they believe that what she writes is true? She is an eyewitness to the words magically appearing on the page in front of her, but no one except Uncle Rav takes her word for it. Why not? Because she is senile? She sure as hell doesn't seem senile. What she has written should convince anyone that she is far from senile, about as far as you can be.

I'm sticking up for Grandma because I'm a witness now, too, another witness who is disregarded, and it's maddening. It's reverse ageism. I got a text—probably from the Dravidian—that said *listen to your brother*, and yet no one is interested in what that means. No one even bothered to answer me when I asked.

What the fuck? What did Uncle Raven say that they were supposed to listen to? How do they all miss that this is important? Anonymous, the Dravidian, made it a point to text that message to me, presumably because it would draw a lot of attention. I suppose I like to believe it has something to do with me. Maybe he/she/it wanted to get me out here for some reason.

And by the way, I also witnessed the disappearing fox and testified to that, and I met Astrid and talked with her for several hours, many hours longer than Uncle Rav. None of what I've experienced and reported on seems to break through their endless bickering. What am I even here for?

Only the Dravidian knows.

Right. I'm not here because of the text; I'm here because Dad was worried about the latest patriot uprising. I admit I *am* sleeping better out here. The library basement isn't the safest place to be right now, and I was thinking about moving in with Tristan until the trespassers finally got tired of their pathetic cosplay and slunk back to their camps to plot out their next performance.

My mom is pretty much useless about deciding what to do next. Mom seems to have lost her ability to think critically, which is not surprising. Grandma might be lost, hurt, dead, or something else terrible. She might have been kidnapped, though it's hard to imagine how or why. Who knows what might have happened if she actually did meet up with the Dravidian? I wouldn't be able to think straight either if Mom was the one who had vanished, and then I found all the crazy shit she was writing about preparing to die and seeing Lady Godiva when she was tripping.

Aunt Ursula, as always, has to play the adult in the room and stubbornly sticks to an easy explanation that can't be argued with because she must have the last word, even though her plan to call in the Birnum Wood palace guard to investigate would be a disaster.

I haven't told anyone yet that I believe Grandma *did* meet up with the Dravidian, which is why she isn't here. She went somewhere with him/her/it. Like Uncle Raven protesting he can't explain, he just knows, I can't say why I'm convinced of this, but I am. I know.

I did the sensible thing, which seems to elude my elders, and researched *Dravidian* on my phone. I learned that the Dravidians are an ancient people of South India, an interesting twist, considering Grandma's guru was from there. Her guru could actually be Dravidian, possibly *the* Dravidian! Not farfetched at all, although she is dead, so there's that.

I didn't bring this up tonight while they were all reenacting childhood scenes and arguing about nothing. They would have ignored me or immediately discounted it as a coincidence, except for Uncle Raven. When I tell him, he'll be excited. Another connection. Another piece of the puzzle.

I'm excited, too. Astrid said the Dravidian is a kind of guide, and it's no stretch to think, aha! Grandma's spiritual guide—her guru! Look at what he (or she or it) wrote in her journals: *Consciousness is an ocean. What could possibly not be God?* And so on. Typical spiritual pablum. He/she/it said *I will help you*, and I believe anonymous is trying to help her. He/she/it is helping her prepare for her death day. What else could it be?

Uncle Raven understands that the journals are important, but he's the only one who really does. Mom and Aunt Ursula aren't taking them in. They're just words. They don't want to feel what is behind those words, what motivates them. Grandma says plainly that she is preparing for her death, for the actual moment when she dies, but her daughters don't want to accept that. I don't blame them. I wouldn't want to hear that from my mom.

Uncle Rav accepts what Grandma writes as true, but I'm starting to think he is getting a little side-tracked thinking about his own death. He just turned 70, which is pretty old these days, with life expectancy in this country being what it is. Not that many men make it to their 70s anymore.

Since I got here, I've spent most of my time with him, and he's usually pretty far away in his mind. I can see it in his eyes, or rather I don't see anything in his eyes. The recognition isn't there. It's like I need to snap my fingers to get his attention. He's dwelling on something. If not his death, then something else.

It could be Astrid. She is something else, too. She seems to be the only person in this drama who can direct us. I hope she comes around again soon. I think if Mom and Aunt Ursula meet her, they will feel a lot more grounded. Astrid has a way of just making you feel better all around. They would understand Grandma's strong feelings about her, and they might even be convinced by her that Grandma is going to be OK, if only because when she's around, everything seems OK.

There's only one journal left to read, and I'm not ready for bed.

I love hearing her voice in my head.

Pythagoreans worshipped the number 10, the perfect number, the sum of 1 + 2 +3 +4, so having reached the magical age of 100, you could say I am perfection squared!

Dig it!

Ten was a nice age: still a child but barely. Still able to abide in the present. No obligations other than keeping my room clean and doing my homework. And practicing the piano. Not too many memories yet. The oppressive problems of the 21st century still decades away.

100 years old...

Funny, I don't feel 100, ha ha, but it is true that it doesn't matter how old you get; you still feel like you. Like you've always felt. Even when you get to 100.

I do feel grown up. I definitely feel grown all the way up, even though I've shrunk, which is what happens. My body is still functioning well enough, though. I have been blessed with so much, not the least of which is sturdy joints, a strong heart, and hard-working lungs. I don't have a mirror, so I don't have to see what 100-year-old me looks like. I can see how loose my skin is, how my muscles have turned flabby, but I can't see my face, and I don't want to see it. I'm sure I must look exactly like my mother did around the time she died, except way more tanned! My face would be much more weather-beaten than hers.

I didn't anticipate being alive this long, but I'm happy I am. I wanted to live for as long as possible. Death has always frightened me, and it still does. I'm working on that. I have to. When you're 100, death naturally becomes a preoccupation. It is a persistent shadow in your mind. Sometimes I think that it's the only thing on my mind and everything else is a shadow.

As the 20th century came to a close, and the Y2K panic ensued, I started doing the math in my head: if I live to be 80, what year will it be? 90? I knew that if I lived to be 100, I would be alive halfway through the next century. Alive through the final 50 years of one and the first 50 years of another.

I straddle the centuries, the Colossus of Northern California!

I can't help it. The older I get, the more my mind discharges its waste, but nature, abhorring a vacuum as it does, fills the empty spots with random trivia. On the other hand, there are so many nights I lie awake trying to remember some obscure fact, some historical tidbit, or a name. Often a name. The name of someone I knew, someone in a movie I saw, an author. What was that book? 100 Years of Solitude? Written by Gabriel someone. Never read that one. For some reason, I couldn't get into magical realism. I was always more interested in real magic.

I haven't had 100 years of solitude, but I have had about 20. Most people would assume I'm lonely, but I'm not. Given the choice of being alone for a week or being at a weeklong party, I would choose to be alone every time. Every single time. Of course, I look forward to visits from the kids, but I've never considered their offers to live with them. I don't think I would have made the century mark if I'd taken them up on that.

Twenty years of solitude and 100 years of changes. Everything always changing. So much change, from the personal to the planetary. Maybe that's why I enjoy solitary life so much. It's just me and nature. Me in nature. Me on nature's time. Everything is always changing, but it's natural, gradual, slow and easy.

In elementary school, we not only had fire drills, we had nuclear war drills. We would huddle under our desks to protect ourselves from the blast of a hydrogen bomb. Ridiculous, I know, but I guess at the time the authorities felt they had to do something to keep us calm, no matter how pointless. They had to convince us they had everything under control.

Back then, some people built bomb shelters. Now they build bug-out bunkers. We thought nuclear weapons would eventually be outlawed and destroyed—they had to be, didn't they? Surely the leaders of the world would have to agree nuclear war was unthinkable, but instead, almost a century later, just about everyone has at least one nuclear weapon. The countries of the world—big and small—hold doomsday guns to each other's heads, like in a Tarantino movie scene. A scene frozen in time now. By some miracle, the standoff has held up. A testament to the strength of the survival instinct.

Why didn't that instinct kick in as it should have when the existential threat of climate change became imminent? Once again, we little people hoped the prospect of environmental collapse and the possible extinction of life on earth would spur the leaders of the world into action, but no.

Greed trumped survival.

When I was 10, there weren't any billionaires, or maybe a handful, but the 21st century produced a ravenous horde of billionaires. An untold number. A billionaire born every minute. Where did all that money come from? From oil, essentially, and all of its byproducts and applications. Having the money to do it, the billionaires took control of the world. Instead of mounting a last-ditch effort to stop global warming, our masters made it their goal to extract and burn every last drop of fossil fuel so they could make as much money as was possible.

Money trumps life. Life has no value when compared to money.

For a very brief while, until I was maybe 8 or 9, we only had black and white TV. Then color was something even we could afford. Analog home entertainment! Three broadcasting networks subsidized by the tobacco industry.

Then digital everything. High def. Huge flat screens.

The phones got bigger so they could function as mobile TVs.

Desktops gave way to laptops.

Billboards were transformed into colorful, flashing displays.

Now the world is a landscape of screens of all sizes supplying entertainment and advertising, which have become one, in every form in high definition, wherever we might be, whenever it is, whatever we are doing.

Along with the screens came cancer and heart disease. Instead of everyone smoking everywhere, a few people smoked in designated outdoor areas, and that helped, but not that many stopped eating shitty processed food injected with saturated fat and sugar. Vegetables and fruit soaked in pesticides, fish filled with heavy metals, and meat and dairy products laced with hormones and antibiotics were sold in the supermarkets. Microscopic toxic plastic particles polluted the water, laced the soil, and filled the air.

I made it all the way to a master's degree in library science before the Internet. Nothing to browse but the card catalog. I was a librarian when librarians were still valued and needed. Before AI replaced them and almost everyone else.

I had a desk in the middle of the open stacks. People came and asked for my help, which I was happy to give. I was appreciated. Then tragedy: libraries and librarians, books, teachers, education, science, literature, the arts—anything and everything considered liberal, as in a liberal arts education, which in previous centuries had been considered a good and wonderful thing, a most valuable thing, something to be cherished—became passe, devalued, derided and mocked and eventually attacked as evil by the patriots, those loyal minions and clueless marks of the billionaires. A liberal arts education was nothing but elitist devil work, and those who valued it were demonic.

No one was an English major anymore.

The billionaires didn't care what was going on with the people and in the neighborhoods so long as they were making money.

For two-thirds of my life, almost everyone could at least agree on what was fact and what was fiction. Facts were a given. Fiction was something made up. Telling the truth was a virtue. Lying was bad. Bullshitting was not admired.

In the last third, it all flipped. No one really knows why, though there is no end of theories. Basically, civility and common sense suddenly and inexplicably gave way to mass hysteria. Suddenly, almost overnight, it seemed, compassion and goodwill were out, and cruelty and ill will were in. Paranoia usurped hope. Fear ruled over love.

I lived for many decades when political differences were not a matter of life and death. When very few things were considered a matter of life and death, besides life and death.

I remember hiking along a river canyon and marveling at hundreds of salamanders suspended in a crystal-clear pool. I was afraid to jump in, didn't want to bother them, but the water was too inviting on that 90-degree day, so I joined them. They all scattered instantly; not a single one was floating in the pool with me. I got out, and they instantly appeared as if nothing had happened. Maybe in their consciousness nothing had.

I remember having to ask for directions.

I lived for half of my life without a cell phone and half with one I only use for emergencies.

I became a vegetarian when everyone should have.

I have always missed bacon.

I remember walking along the street without worrying about getting shot by someone driving by in a car.

The watershed was the Internet. Everyone knows that. Before dot.com, there was history; after, there was advertising. I have lived a half-life on both sides of that divide, so I have perspective.

Just like anything else, the existence of the World Wide Web has its pros and cons. As a former librarian, I can't deny the wonder of being able to find out anything instantly. That's a definite pro. After that, I struggle to think of another benefit. The enormity of the cons, though, is catastrophic. History no longer exists. Truth is irrelevant. There may not be a future. People spend their waking lives enthralled by their phones, virtually asleep, disconnected from nature and from each other.

I remember when most people had some kind of faith in something.

Am I lucky to be alive after 100 years? No, because luck has nothing to do with anything. There is only karma. Choices and consequences, actions and reactions, causes and effects. The universe is an infinitely long eternal chain reaction. There's no escape. No way to break the chain except to realize there is no chain.

People stopped having kids as the 21st century wore on. Who can argue with that?

I have one granddaughter, and I wonder how she copes, but then we all must cope one way or another. Humans always have to cope, have always had to cope, just like all living things do and have done. Everything and everyone copes. That's life.

Attitude is everything. It's basic physics: positive attracts, negative repulses.

I admire Persephone so much. She has integrity. She doesn't let despair stop her from trying to do something to save the earth. She doesn't embrace nihilism like so many have. She doesn't wallow in bitterness about the betrayal of her generation. How the boomers, once they cashed in on their inheritances—the last of the inheritances—did nothing except line their nests while the world burned. She and many of her generation are doing what they can while their parents and grandparents hide out in gated neighborhoods, still using fossil fuels, still watering their lawns, still eating meat, still using energy frivolously, still shopping online and receiving overnight deliveries.

Is Persephone lucky to be alive?

Luck has nothing to do with anything, including when you're born and to whom. What you do has everything to do with everything. You make choices, and there are consequences. It's not rocket science.

Being a lifelong member of the privileged class, a property owner, I had a chance to escape the world, and I took it. My choice, and there will be a consequence. I can't help wondering if I'm a coward, but I don't regret escaping. The world is too much with me. I am old, aren't I? Really old. Of what use can I be except to do what I'm doing? No carbon footprint to speak of.

I hope Persephone doesn't judge me a coward.

Karma has nothing to do with hope or despair. It just is.

2.3

Ursula is already out of bed when I wake up in what seems to be the middle of the night. I check on Raven and Percy, expecting to find them sleeping, but they aren't there. Something must have woken them all up, and apparently, me, too. They must be out on the porch drinking coffee, waiting for the sun to rise.

Nope.

What is going on? It's too early for anyone to be up, except Raven, who doesn't seem to be sleeping much. Daydreaming, though, is another thing—that he is doing all the time. Ursula and I are concerned about him. Of the three of us, he is by far the most attached to Mom, and she to him, though she would never admit having favorites. Parents are funny that way: they think they can hide their feelings from their kids.

I suppose their attachment to each other shouldn't be surprising as he is the first-born and only son. He would listen with rapt attention from early on to Mom and Dad's theories on life, the universe, and everything, of which they had many. They would start a conversation with a philosophical angle on something or other—it could be anything—and then tease out a string of associations that had no end, in much the same way, it seems to Ursula and me, that Mom creates her journal entries. We take what she writes seriously, but we've heard a lot of it before, if not in exactly the same words. For Raven, though, it's gospel.

Their speculations would invariably wind their way back to where they began. They were the masters of circular reasoning, if you can call that reasoning. They loved Raven for his interest in what they had to say, and he loved them back. He kept traveling with them to commune with the guru and her devotees long after Ursula and I were old enough to make the decision not to go, extricating ourselves from the group's grip. He was the only one of us who got a mantra. I was always too nervous to ask for one and afraid of what it meant to have one. Did it mean I was a devotee for life? That wasn't something I was ready to sign up for.

Ursula should still be sleeping beside me. Where is she? Why am I not still sleeping? Did I have a nightmare? I don't remember dreaming at all since we got here. I just open my eyes and get out of bed.

It's barely dawn, the sky a murky gray, and there is a blanket of dew covering the field that won't burn off for several hours. The birds aren't even up yet.

I'm frightened. Did something just happen? Is that why I woke up? I'm trying not to let fear overcome me, but right now *the Dravidian took them* is racing through my mind. I'm afraid I may have a panic attack if I can't keep the paranoid fantasies at bay. It wouldn't be the first time. While Raven is open and suggestible, I'm defensive and anxious.

I tell myself it's silly to think such things, but how much more ridiculous is it than what we've been reading in Mom's journals? And what we've experienced since we got here? I can't deny that Ursula and I did see that fox, and we did watch it vanish into thin air. Percy did get that text, and Mom apparently believes an ethereal spirit of some sort is communicating to her by magical writing.

Are you that far gone, Mom? How far gone are you? I wish I could be with you to know.

I'm more awake now and able to parse things better. Something must have happened that caused them to leave the barn. They wouldn't necessarily wake me up. They might not have thought of it on the spur of the moment. They might have thought, *just let her sleep; it's nothing.*

Of course, it *is* nothing. There, now I'm calming down. It's barely dawn and I'm all alone, but the sun's light is slowly working its way across the field, gradually illuminating our little valley, as if a curtain is slowly being drawn, and I have had a cup of coffee. All is well. I'll just wait for them to come back.

***

I have a mug in my hand half-filled with cold coffee. I don't remember making coffee.

Maybe I should just go back to bed. When I wake up later, they will be back, sitting on the porch, deciding what to do that day, and I will come out to join them.

∗∗∗

I guess I decided not to go back to bed because I'm walking in the field. Was I sleepwalking and have just snapped out of it? I should have put on Mom's boots because my shoes and socks are soaked. I'm squishing my way to the pond.

I'm remembering what Raven said about not knowing why he was standing in the field the night we arrived. *Now I understand.* I don't know why I'm heading to the pond, but I'm compelled. Has my mind been taken over by the Dravidian? Is this how he captured Mom and the others?

I'm having a really hard time stopping these irrational thoughts. They are flitting around like a flock of disoriented birds. I seem to have lost control of them. My thoughts are no longer under my direction.

Who or what is directing them?

Iris! Stop this train before it runs off the rails. The Dravidian is not the engineer in control of your mind!

For fuck's sake, I'm in bad shape. Why am I so obsessed with someone who my 100-year-old mother probably conjured up in a state of delirium?

Who is the delirious one? Am I projecting?

186

Sitting in Mom's chair at the pond is what I needed to calm down. That must be why I came here. I don't care where everyone went or what happened to them. The Dravidian can have them. He will bring them back or not. They will come back on their own after investigating whatever happened or never come back at all. There's no reason why I should be worrying about them or fearing for them or fearing for myself.

I'm here where I'm supposed to be.

Who is thinking this? I would never think these things!

I've sat in Mom's chair before and tried to meditate as she taught me, but I couldn't stop my mind, until now, when I desperately needed it to stop.

I'm chanting OM, OM, OM under my breath. OM shanti, shanti, shanti, OM shanti, shanti, shanti. OM, OM, OM.

Normally I would have something to say to myself about that, some ironic comment, but my self-critic has been silenced, maybe for the first time. It's nice to have that nag silenced for once.

I keep repeating OM without pause, under my breath, my lips barely moving. I believe I must be chanting OM because Mom is near. I'm sure that's true. Raven has been claiming he can feel her presence and knows she's alive. She must be. Why else would I be at the pond, in her chair, chanting?

The fox is there among the cattails across from me. It's looking at me with its black eyes. I stop chanting and stare back at it.

I notice there's a woman sitting on the ground looking up at me, smiling, and when I meet her eyes, I feel as happy as I've ever felt in my life. I am content to keep looking at her as long as she keeps looking at me. We could do this forever, as far as I'm concerned. It occurs to me that we have been.

I know who it is.

"Astrid? "

"Hi, Iris."

"You know my name."

She laughs. "And you know mine!"

"Do you see the fox?"

"Of course. Did the fox look at you like this when you and Ursula saw him?"

"How do you know about that?"

"I saw you when you were looking for Helen."

"I've seen those black eyes before. I've seen them, and they've seen me. Before Ursula and I saw them. Before seeing them now.

It's staring at me."

"Yes, I can see that."

"What does it want?"

"Why do you think it wants something?"

"I don't know. I feel it."

"I think you're right."

Astrid is suddenly across the pond, standing next to the fox. And Astrid is also sitting on the ground next to me. I'm frantically looking back and forth, trying to stop seeing her in both places at once.

"He wants you to remember your dream."

I'm looking at the Astrid sitting next to me.

"What are you?"

"I am...," she sighs, "... fill in the blank."

She shrugs. "Sorry, I don't know how to answer. What I am is not something your language can describe."

"What... English?"

"No, words."

"Try with words. I need to understand what's happening, or I'm going to have a nervous breakdown."

"It's not possible for you to have a nervous breakdown now.... How about... I'm a helper?... I'm helping. That's true enough."

"Helping how? Why? Do I need help? Do you mean you know where Mom is?"

"You felt her, didn't you?"

"I thought I did."

"You can't see her like you can see me, but you might feel her presence."

"What are you talking about? You're not making sense."

"I'm sorry. I'm not sure I can make sense to you."

A Talking Heads chorus suddenly streams through my mind.

Stop making sense, making sense...

I got a girlfriend that's better than that...

She has the smoke in her eyes...

Astrid eyes are so kind. I can feel how much she cares about me. I give up trying to understand.

"You seem to be able to be in two places at once, which is impossible."

"Not in the 4ᵗʰ dimension."

I had to think about that for a while.

"So we're in the 4ᵗʰ dimension now? Is that what you're saying?"

"Well, it's not possible for anything to *be* in just three dimensions. You can't have what and where without when, so yes, we're in the 4ᵗʰ dimension."

You're right, Astrid; you can't make sense to me.

"You could be in two places at once, too, if you were able to imagine it."

"How am I supposed to do that?"

"Try believing you are across the pond with the fox."

I close my eyes and imagine myself sitting cross-legged next to the fox.

***

I remember being afraid to open my eyes, but they're open now, and I'm walking into the sitting room of an early

20th-century craftsman home. The room is empty except for a woven bassinet. As I walk toward it, my footsteps echo back from a high ceiling supported by thick beams milled from the giant trees of the past. I admire the detailed molding that hides every junction in the room. Those were the days when beauty was valued.

The bassinet cradles what seems to be a hairless, pearly white baby lying on its back. It's looking up at me, motionless and silent. At first, I assume it's tightly swaddled in something white, but then I realize it's not swaddled at all—it has no arms or legs, no mouth or nose, just lidless eyes, two black, bottomless holes.

They have no iris, just pupils.

How strange that a *pupil* can be a part of the eye as well as a student in school. What is the connection? And how weird that my name is Iris.

Raven goes on and on about connections. He picked that up from Mom and Dad. *Everything is connected.* How many times did I hear that from one of them? Yes, everything is connected one way or another since everything comes from the original source of the universe, whatever that is, just like we humans can all be traced back to an original ancestral couple, or perhaps an original divine androgyne, but what is the use of this revelation, if it can even be called that? It's just common sense. It just is. Everything has to come from something.

Raven may not realize how predictable his reaction is to Mom's disappearance. I am more open-minded than Ursula about unknown forces at work behind the scenes. I accept that what we know is virtually nothing compared to all that we don't know, and what we take for granted as fact is still questionable, but I'm with Ursula when she wonders how we are supposed to carry on with our lives when we question everything we think we know.

Raven has always been drawn to the mystery. He craves it. Living in a world without mystery would be hell for him.

I hear something come into the room behind me and turn around. It's the fox. I turn back to the bassinet, but I'm no longer in the room. I'm sitting next to the fox at the edge of the pond.

I think it's telling me to wake up.

2.4

Uncle Raven hands me a cup of coffee. He found me on the porch asleep in a chair with one of Grandma's journals in my lap. He's agitated. When he woke up, Mom and Aunt Ursula were gone.

"Ursula's car is gone, too. Do you think they went out searching again without telling us?"

It takes me a while to come up with a response. I'm barely awake and not prepared for his anxious excitement or even able to make sense of what he's telling me.

"They're gone? So you've already hiked up to the highway looking for them? Why did you go all the way up there?"

"I was up early, and they were gone. No note, nothing, so I walked up there. I'm not sure why I thought I should see if they took the car, but I did. I'm not sure why I'm doing anything anymore."

"I can't imagine them taking the car to start searching again, especially this early. Maybe they just left."

"Without telling us?"

"OK, maybe the car was stolen."

He's pacing up and down the porch, stopping frequently to look out onto the meadow. Aunt Ursula didn't pick up when he called her, and he found Mom's phone ringing in Grandma's bedroom where they had been sleeping. He hadn't thought about the possibility of the car being stolen.

"I'm going to go look for them. I have to do something; I can't relax."

"I suppose I should wait here in case they show up." *As usual.*

He answers me by jumping off the porch and striding across the field toward the woods. The adrenaline must be surging through him. If he didn't have to push his way through shoulder-high canary grass, he'd be running.

I am about to yell at him to wait for me, but I suddenly notice something that stops me from yelling or even thinking, because what I'm seeing is not possible. The forest Raven is headed for is much closer to the barn than it used to be.

I close my eyes and open them again. I still see the same thing: the edge of the forest is closer, and the trees taller. At least, that is my perception. The woods that used to start near the top of the hill and line the ridge have moved down the hill overnight.

I should know. I've been occupying this porch since I got here and have been looking at that hillside constantly. By the time my amazement dies down, and I shift my attention, Uncle Raven has already reached the trees and is out of sight.

What the fuck? Am I actually seeing things now? I look away and talk myself down from the ledge. My perceptions obviously can't be trusted. I've been immersed in Grandma's weird world for days. I've met Astrid. Who knows what that did to me? Uncle Raven just hung out with her at the pond for a little while, and look what happened to him. Every time he mentions her, his voice softens, and his eyes light up. Grandma seems to have fallen in love with her. I just woke up to find out Mom and Aunt Ursula have disappeared. My mind is playing tricks. My mind can't be trusted. None of our minds can be trusted.

I'm staring at the trees, wishing them to dissolve like they might do at the end of a dramatic movie scene. I'm waiting for the lights to come on in our theater and for the forest to go back to where it belongs. I have to stop staring at the trees. I'm feeling more and more disoriented. I can't reconcile what I remember with what I'm seeing. My memory must be deceiving me. The forest was always where it is now. It was always this dense, this dark.

Uncle Raven, how is it that I am supposed to relax? You get to run blindly into the woods without a plan just so you can release your anxiety, and I get to sit here and wait? How can you expect me to sit here waiting for them to come back? I'm just as anxious as you—your sister is my mom! And now I'm being forced to consider that the forest I've been looking at for the last few days has *moved* while we were all sleeping.

Either that or I have to question my memory or doubt my sanity.

Something is seriously off.

Massive understatement.

Why should I always be the one to sit and wait? I get restless, too. I haven't left the barn since I got here except to visit the colony and gather eggs. Why shouldn't I be searching for Mom and Aunt Ursula?

***

The smell of pines is so strong. Like incense. Halfway across the field, all I see is grass. I'm a little boat on a waving green sea. I feel so alone. Everyone has left, and now so have I. When did I step off the porch and start walking? I'm following my uncle into the woods, but why? If I catch up with him, he's just going to be angry and tell me to hurry back.

The forest is inviting me to come. It's telling me that Grandma is in there with the Dravidian. They're waiting for me.

What if the Dravidian turns out to be a bad guy? Instead of a benevolent spirit guide, he may be an evil wizard who has lured Grandma into a trap.

Evil wizard? Trap? Where is that coming from? I've read too many of Mom's fantasy novels. I've lived in a state of paranoia all my life. Fear is so insidious, humanity's default emotional state. I have faith that the Dravidian is not like us. He never doubts. He knows. He is all hope and courage. He's helping Grandma with her doubts and fears.

I have to have faith. In something, anything. If nothing else, faith in myself. Without that, what do I have? Nothing. I live in a world on an existential brink, and every year I live, the world gets closer to it.

Newly arrived from my mother's womb, after wailing to clear out my lungs, I opened my eyes, had the goop washed out of them, and there I was, lying on her chest, searching for her tit, a live human being on a dying planet, the first of the pandemics just getting started. A pandemic that has never ended, the virus morphing as needed to survive. Adapt or die.

Early on, I learned that the billionaires killing the planet don't care if anything or anyone lives or dies. They don't care about life at all. They dream of uploading their consciousness into a chip, which is life enough for them. They believe their personalities will be preserved as long as their orbiting habitats have power. They and their friends can play together forever in a virtual outer space paradise. The rest of us aren't important. We're products and consumers of products. We are all leopards eating our own face.

I don't have money, a house, or a career, but I do have faith in life. I have faith in the planet. Life will prevail no matter how much toxic shit death-eating humans manufacture, consume, and throw into the ocean. Chickens will survive and keep laying eggs wherever they are, no matter what.

If the human race goes by way of the dinosaur, it's not like we weren't given a chance. We were given plenty of warning. We had choices. Well, generations previous had them. By the time I was born, the critical choices had already been made. My generation was left to cling to faith or just say fuck it. It's easy for us to say we would have made better choices, but saying so in hindsight is one thing, doing something in real-time is another.

There's no point in blaming. It is what it is. In the grand geo-cosmological scheme, the earth will survive, and so will life, with or without human beings. Maybe in a million years, or ten million, or a hundred million, another human race will be faced with the same choices. That's karma; right, Grandma?

This is not my first time in these woods, I have been in here with Grandma a few times, but it's my first time in *these* woods, the forest that grew overnight. I feel like a fairytale character: the innocent, trusting girl about to get lost, about to have an encounter with evil. Dark thoughts in a dark place.

I have got to get a hold of myself. The barn is a 10-minute walk away. If I turn around, I can see it, seared by the harsh sunlight of our time.

I remember as a kid when it used to rain in the fall. We would come here to get a pumpkin from Grandma's patch. She has been walking through these woods for years without a worry. There's nothing to fear. Uncle Raven is up ahead on the trail. I'll catch up with him eventually. It's not that dark; slivers of sunlight are breaking through. It's not like I need a flashlight.

What if I really do get lost?

Maybe I should have brought one.

2.5

Someone is banging on the door and yelling my name. I open my eyes, and I see that I'm here in the bed I sleep in whenever I come to the barn. I don't remember getting prepared to go to bed and sleep. I don't remember coming here at all.

Why is there someone out there trying to wake me up? Now I remember: I came to see Mom, and she wasn't here. I've been trying to find her for some time now. We've been trying to find her—the whole family. How many nights has it been? How many days? I've lost count. Each day and every night have been remarkably similar. I've lost track.

"Raven, hey Raven! Get up!"

"Who are you?! What the hell, man! Why are you yelling at me?"

"It doesn't matter. Get out here. It's important."

"Just a second. I'm looking for my shoes."

A man cracks open the door, but not wide enough that I would be able to recognize him.

"Hurry!"

"What's going on?"

"Your nightmare is starting. You need to go with me."

What is he talking about? My nightmare?

I can't find my shoes, and while I'm looking for them all around the barn, I realize I'm alone. Is he saying that something has happened to Mom? My sisters? To Persephone?

Through the open door, I can hear loud combustion engines, multiple engines. Gas-powered vehicles of some kind are coming or are already here. How did they get down the trail? It's not possible. I have to walk my bike the whole way.

Maybe there is another way into the valley I don't know about.

The engine sounds are getting closer, louder. Have my sisters found Mom and called for help? Are they out in the field right now waiting for aid units?

I finally locate my shoes and burst out onto the porch, nearly knocking down the man who told me to hurry. We are face-to-face, and it isn't until I see his toothless smile that I remember him.

"Pushan?"

"Let's get going," he says impatiently.

He's short, stocky, his face dark brown, and his black hair tightly braided. He carries a small axe on his belt and holds a thin bamboo stick in one hand.

"Get going where? Why? Why would I go anywhere with you?"

"If you don't come with me, you're going to regret it."

"Are you threatening me?"

"Look and listen, Raven, but don't take too long."

The roar of the vehicles is getting louder by the second, and I can see dust clouds rising from both ends of the valley. How is it possible that there are motorized vehicles crashing their way through the field? There are no roads. It's barely passable by foot through the thick brush. Are they military?

Pushan is insistent. "Raven, you need to listen to me!"

"What about my sisters? What about Persephone? Where are they?"

"They're not here. All you can do is take care of yourself."

I want to tell Pushan to fuck off and leave me alone, that I need to stay and protect the property, but as the sounds of various combustion engines continue to grow closer and increase in volume, I start to waver. I can make out the outlines of not just a couple of vehicles but more like a dozen. They are heading straight toward the barn from both directions, as if they are playing chicken. Trucks and jeeps. There might be motorcycles. Then I see the flags attached to poles on both sides of every invading machine. I can hear them flapping now.

Fucking patriots!

I realize I just yelled this in Pushan's ear.

"Do you understand now, Raven? You don't want to be here."

"I have to stop them!"

"No, you don't. You have to get out of here."

Pushan strikes me on the back with his stick.

"What the hell!"

"You're worse than a donkey. Get moving."

While I resent getting whacked on the back as if I'm a stray from his herd, it serves its purpose. I start sprinting, as if I'm 20 again, my legs strong and my body light. What a joy to experience that again! *Keep coming, assholes!* I crow like the gingerbread man; *I'll be long gone!* All my proud notions of confronting the intruders are forgotten as I follow Pushan across the field. We reach the forest and keep churning up a trail that leads to the top of the hill.

"Where are we going?" I yell to him from behind.

"We're going to get some perspective. You need it."

My legs are pumping like jackhammers as we make steady progress up the hill. I'm not the slightest bit out of breath. Superstitious, I won't let myself think about it, fearing that I'll break the illusion of being young and tireless again.

The vehicles seem to have stopped. Instead of the sound of revving engines, I hear voices from down below. Many voices, loud and raucous, as if the speakers are in a crowded bar, drunk and yelling over each other to be heard. I have no idea what they are talking about, but whatever it is, excites them. They're slapping each other on the back and whooping it up. Then I hear the unmistakable whomping of a helicopter.

"Pushan, wait. There's a helicopter now."

"All part of your nightmare, is it?"

"What are you talking about?" I am done with his rude, bullshit answers. I stop walking and sit on a fallen nurse log. It's wet.

"This is what you imagined, right?"

I just look at him and wait for him to explain. He sighs and sits on another log on the other side of the trail, facing me.

"You fantasized about what would happen if your sister went back to Birnum Wood and reported your mom missing. Now it's happening."

"How do you know this? Did Ursula call for help? Did she tell you I was afraid this would happen?"

As usual, he doesn't answer my questions. His toothless, leathery face should be ugly, even frightening, but instead, catching his eyes, I feel his compassion for me, as if I'm a child who desperately needs understanding and love.

Maybe that's just what I need.

"What is happening is what you imagined, though the details may be different. Remember why you didn't call your sisters for two days? This is what you were worried about."

"I didn't think patriots would invade the property. I thought Ursula would get Birnum Wood security out here. They would traipse around the property with their dogs. Deploy their drones. Pretend to care. Annoy the hell out of me with their stupid questions and leave their traces everywhere. That was my nightmare."

"You aren't aware of what you actually imagined. This is your true nightmare. What you really fear. Who you truly hate and secretly wish harm. This is what you kept hidden from yourself."

"Sure, I despise these fools. They call people like me hippie vermin, traitors who should be shot. They're the ones who fantasize about killing, not me."

"So you say, but look: they have occupied your property. Their flags are flying in front of your barn. Their trucks are destroying the field. A helicopter is landing on top of the corn your mom raised over the summer."

"It *is* a fucking nightmare, Pushan!"

"Your nightmare."

From where we are sitting, I have a clear view of the barn. There are half a dozen pickup trucks, a few jeeps, and several motorcycles surrounding the building. A least two dozen men and women in black boots, wearing baseball caps and dressed in multiple layers of heavy clothing, are milling around. Some carry rifles and have ammunition belts crisscrossing their jackets.

A man comes out of the barn and onto the porch. He calls for everyone's attention, gives a thumbs-up sign, and then jumps off to join the crowd. The drunken hollering dies down. The man who had been inside motions for everyone standing around to move. They straggle back into the field, following his direction, until he signals for them to stop about 50 yards away from the barn. Another man walks over to one of the trucks, gets a large box from the cab, and puts it down in front of the man who seems to be their leader. A couple of the men in the crowd join him by the box. Each of them reaches inside and takes out something that looks like a pop bottle.

Except the bottles have fuses.

Molotov cocktails.

Can this be happening?

"Pushan, are they really going to burn it down? This isn't part of my nightmare. This is way beyond what I could have imagined!"

He looks at me with sincere regret for what I'm about to witness.

"You had no way of knowing until now. You couldn't acknowledge your hate. Now you have to experience the effects. It's the law."

I can't bear to look, but even as far away as we are, I can feel the heat from the burning barn on my face.

The patriots are cheering.

2.6

The fox, its tail a furry boa wrapped snugly around its body, is lying next to me. I'm looking directly into its black eyes, which are just inches from mine. I can see myself, a miniature person encased in a snow globe without the snow, only darkness.

"What do you see?"

Astrid's question comes from behind me. She's still here. Are we by the pond? I can't tell. I don't see anything except orange fur, black eyes, and a snout dripping with sweat. The fox and I seem to be breathing in unison. My face is flushing hot.

I would lie this way next to Persephone at nap time, exchanging warm breaths. What a relief it was to take a break in the afternoon, to have a couple of hours to ourselves when nothing was required beyond closing our eyes and breathing.

When she was an infant, I was worried about rolling over and suffocating her. No different from any other mom. We moms in The Library share the timeless worries of mothers in any time and place, but we are burdened by something unique to our apocalyptic era: the horrible nagging doubt about our choice to bring children into this world. Were we naïve? Were we selfish? Did we lie to ourselves so we could have what we wanted? What an awful thing to talk about.

But we do talk about it, though never for long. It is too painful. The doubt can never be resolved. When it comes up, we usually just nod our understanding.

I should be wondering what happened to Percy and worrying about if she's OK, but I'm not wondering or worrying. I suppose I have good reason considering the circumstances. This is not the time to indulge in self-recrimination. I need to figure out what the hell is going on with me and this fox I'm lying next to, then possibly move on to concern for my daughter.

I see a reflection of myself in its eyes. There are two of me. We're so tiny.

"How do you feel?"

What kind of a question is that to ask, Astrid?

How should I feel about lying here on the ground with a fox snuggled up next to me, the two of us gazing into each other's eyes? I don't know... I can think of feelings I would expect to have—fear, confusion, amazement, even disgust at having my face practically buried in its smelly fur—but I'm not experiencing those. I'm feeling nothing, really. Like I'm not actually here, so I'm unable to feel anything. I feel as if I've been captured in those two black eyes, that I've become a photograph, not trapped or imprisoned, just fixed like a developed picture, twin portraits of myself, one in each eye. If the fox were to close its eyes, my twin and I would disappear.

Thankfully, I don't think it can close its lidless eyes.

"I get that."

"Get what, Astrid?"

"What you're feeling."

"What do you mean you get what I'm feeling?"

"You're feeling dislocated."

"I can see myself reflected in those eyes. You're right, Astrid. I do feel dislocated. I feel like I have been reduced to a reflection in the eyes of a fox.

"Never mind, Iris, it's not important. Asking you how you feel is a silly question considering the state you're in."

"The state I'm in is not being able to take my eyes off this fox. Will I ever feel normal again? Like I'm not a little figurine trapped inside a magic animal's eye?"

"You're not going to feel normal in the way you hope."

"You're scaring me."

I feel a slight movement behind me, a rustle, and manage to turn my head away from the fox's gaze. Astrid has disappeared. Swiveling my head back around, I find the fox has crept closer. It's tail is longer and now curled completely around me. Somehow, in that instant in which Astrid vanished, the fox grew. Its face looms, the eyes so large it seems I could dive into them and never touch bottom.

I see Mom. I see Persephone. I see myself. We are suspended in a black void, white projections on a black screen, a movie that cuts from one person to the next, from age to age, from infant to teenager to white-haired, bed-ridden senior, back and forth, forward and back, over and over, switching from one to another at different speeds in a random loop from a time-lapse movie. I'm watching the movie, and I'm in the movie. I'm outside and inside the frames. I realize it's not just us—Helen, Iris, and Persephone—but countless others extending through endless time, all recognizable as me and them, them and me...

... I am she as you are she...

... da da... da da... da da... da da...

I can't remember the words.

... I'm...

... I'm crying...

I am the walrus. It makes sense now. I am the coo coo caw ju. I am she as you are me, and we are all together.

I desperately want to keep watching. I don't want the movie to end because I imagine the reel running out and being left alone in the dark with nothing to see, with nothing to hear except the flapping of film spinning around and around an invisible reel. Who will I be then?

What will I be?

I am infant me, I am daughter me, I am mother and grandmother me. Reverse, rewind, fast forward, play and stop.

Play again. I am my daughter, and she is me. I am my mother, and she is me. Granddaughter, mother, daughter, me, grandmother, me, mother, me.

I don't want it to end. I'm afraid I will be edited out, deleted, cut, and left drifting in the void.

The unspooling of endless incarnations freezes on a baby, hardly formed. It looks like one of those large white cannellini beans except for two small dark eyes. Sinewy purplish vines begin sprouting from the eyes, growing quickly, gyrating, twisting higher into the black expanse like Jack's beanstalk and at the same time descending lower, forming impossibly long roots, all the vines multiplying higher and lower—though I have the thought that there is no higher or lower, that my mind must be making sense out of dimensionless space.

The vines become more and more tangled and dense, forming a thicket that completely fills my field of vision. The thicket begins to flower, and what used to be the proto-baby, the white bean, the original seed that I take to be me, them, us, becomes a limitless field of daisies. The shimmering flowers glow like high-def Christmas lights illuminating the black void. I am overcome by the beauty of it. I want the movie to end here; the last frame a shot of me lying down in the middle of this flowering meadow.

Iris, the wind is coming. Let yourself be taken. You'll be OK.

I don't know where I am. I'm floating in a sea of flowers.

There's nothing to worry about. There never is.

Who's talking?

The wind comes from all directions: from above and below and from every side. Not ordinary wind, but a whirlwind that picks me up as if I am a weightless piece of dandelion fluff and carries me up and out of the flowering vines. As instructed, I don't resist, not that I have a choice. I expect to be overcome by fear, but for the first time in my life, I am utterly fearless. Rendered helpless by the wind, I understand there is nothing I can do except go along for the ride. Might as well enjoy it instead of worrying about where I'm going and what's going to happen when I get there.

If I'm actually going anywhere.

It's all an illusion is what Mom's guru would remind her devotees, and how Mom would comfort us when shit got bad, which it often did as the twenty-first century aged. I cling to that belief while riding the whirlwind for what could be weeks or possibly just a moment—time is an illusion, so how would I know for how long, and what does it matter? Nothing matters when you give up the illusion of control, the ultimate illusion. New age spirituality turned the world-is-an-illusion theory into a cliché, but clichés always have some truth.

Flying at hypersonic speed into the stratosphere, I am content to believe my mind is manufacturing a whopper of an illusion that will eventually fade away, like the images of a dream.

How is this comforting?

Because then I know what I'm experiencing right now isn't real.

I'm having trouble following this logic. If comfort, it's cold comfort, because what I'm experiencing feels extraordinarily real. What difference does it make if it is called an illusion or reality?

The whirlwind takes me up to a deep blue sky which immediately (or so it seems) becomes crystal clear, a sheet of flawless glass. I think 'sky' because it seems as if I have been catapulted into the upper reaches of the earth's atmosphere.

The light in this sky has a quality I have never experienced. I'm not just seeing it; I'm feeling it. It has no limits.

What is 'it?'

The light without color...I feel...

I feel...

...loved.

2.7

A dense pall of smoke from the smoldering barn hangs over the field. The cheering has stopped. I can make out the ghostly shapes of the arsonists scattered around the charred skeleton of the old building, a building which had stood there since the 19th century. Still feeling like an invincible 20-year-old, I want to run down from my vantage point on the hill and shame them. I want to stand on the cement porch and scream at them in a righteous fury so powerful they all fall to their knees begging for absolution, understanding at last what grievous sinners and complete assholes they all are. How they defile the universe with their self-pity and infantile narcissistic rage. I want to put the fear of God in them. I want them to realize they are surely going to hell, where they will be chastised without mercy until God, in his infinite mercy, forgives even them.

Pushan, who seems able to read my thoughts, tells me there's nothing I can or should do. Who do I think I am?

Screaming at them like a madman will only make them laugh. It will give them no end of pleasure. After they're done mocking me, one or more of them will shoot me, and after I fall off the porch bleeding from multiple bullet wounds, they will gather around and curse at me, insult me, and kick me with the pointy toes of their boots. After I am left for dead, writhing in pain, all of them will laugh some more.

He reminds me that consequences are doled out in strict accordance with the law, from which law there is no escape for anyone.

"Everyone gets what's coming to them. See?" He points down the hill.

At first, because of the smoke, I can't see what's going on in the valley below, but I can hear very clearly terrified shouting, and what sounds like snarling dogs. I have never heard the gnashing of teeth before, but I have no doubt that is what I'm hearing.

The faint outlines of hideous winged creatures gradually appear, slightly larger than eagles, small dragons perched on top of the truck cabs, some of them gnawing on what could be arms or legs, human drumsticks. Creatures still airborne on their way to the charnel grounds are now whooshing by overhead, flying close enough to where Pushan and I are watching that I catch glimpses of long fangs and reptilian skin that is mostly deep red with slashes of black and burnt orange. As they pass over, I hear them chittering excitedly to each other as they start their dive to the site of the slaughter. The screaming of their victims is horrifying and nearly unbearable as the full host of the bloodthirsty creatures finally lands, and the feasting intensifies.

Thankfully, the attack is over as quickly as it began. An eerie silence follows as the dragons fold their wings, resting on top of truck cabs, surrounded by the remnants of their prey. Some of the satiated monsters hang lazily from the helicopter rotors, slowly spinning around.

"Elementals, I think you call them. Demons. Hate attracts them."

"My hate?"

"All hate. Yours, theirs, everyone's."

"I never dreamed of this. I would never wish this on anyone."

"As you say."

"I didn't do this!"

"So you didn't hate these patriots every time they drove through your neighborhood yelling profanities, throwing trash out their windows, pissing on your sidewalks, shooting their guns off, threatening your friends? Your family?"

"There's hate, and then there's hate, Pushan. I resent them. I'm annoyed by them. I think they're idiots. I…"

"Stop. You're embarrassing yourself."

"I did not cause this to happen!"

"No, you didn't. Hate caused it. You should know this. Your guru taught you that hate is a powerful emotion with terrible consequences. Never trifle with hate."

"My guru?"

"You got a mantra, didn't you?"

"I haven't seen her in years. She died."

"She sees you. You should be grateful, especially now."

The demons have stopped flying overhead. All I hear is the moaning of the wounded, those who are somehow still alive, and the excited chattering of their tormentors. I wanted retribution, but not this. Pushan starts walking again, heading for the ridge.

"Where are you taking me?"

"We need to get out of here. There will be others coming to deal with this mess."

I know by now not to ask. His answers just prompt more questions. I'm pretty sure we must be heading toward his cabin—where else would we be going?—and I can't help thinking—hoping—that Astrid will be there. The thought comforts me.

As we start to hike, I'm fantasizing about how it will be when we meet again. She'll be waiting outside, knowing we're coming. She'll rush over and embrace me, her arms surrounding me, her warm breath on my neck, her soothing voice in my ear.

My soap opera daydream is interrupted by a troop of bizarre and frightening women suddenly passing us on the trail, heading down the hill. They look like women you might see on the cover of a graphic novel or animated creations designed for a video game. Tall, lithe, and barefoot, they are wearing almost nothing, just some tattered cloth. Their skin is dark blue, almost purple, their black hair long and wild, stacked above their heads and surrounding their faces like writhing snakes. Some have belts of skulls wrapped around their waists, and all carry ancient weapons of one kind or another—a spear, a dagger, a trident. Some have what look like lassoes. The expressions on their faces are a startling gestalt: fierce and compassionate at the same time.

They are moving quickly and quietly with a determined purpose, passing us without a word or a glance, not acknowledging us in any way, but as they pass, instead of fear, I feel joy, and I wonder if it was my fantasizing about Astrid that made them appear, just as my hatred of patriots generated the plague of demons.

"Does Astrid wear a belt of skulls?" Pushan mocks. "Does she carry a weapon?"

"For fuck's sake, then, will you just tell me what's going on? Who are those women?"

"They clean up disasters like the one below. Balance has to be restored."

What's the point?

"Stop trying so hard to understand what you can't possibly understand. Your mind is not equipped. Accept it. I'm here to help you, so let me."

The demons, apparently routed almost instantly by the fierce women who have descended upon them, are now, merely moments later, flying over us in haphazard formation, complaining raucously like a band of disgruntled crows. I stop to watch them, praying they take no interest in us.

Pushan doesn't seem to notice and never breaks his stride. I can hear the strange women who chased them off hollering, yodeling even. The sounds they are making are thrilling, cries of triumph that make my heart race. The smoke has cleared off completely, and looking down from the hill, I can see them stomping on the ground in a rhythmic dance. Their legs are so powerful I can feel the vibrations in the ground I'm standing on high above, as if the earth itself is a drum they are playing. Their tangled black hair is flying wildly in all directions as they dance, their faces ecstatic. I feel myself being pulled toward them, down the hill into the valley. I want to join their celebration, exult in their righteous victory.

***

Either I'm getting closer, or they are, because I can clearly hear them singing in time to their earth drumming. The droning of their voices over the stomping of their feet resonates throughout my body, blanking out my thoughts. They're chanting something I have heard before, and I realize I'm chanting along with them and pounding the earth with my feet.

Pushan seems to have disappeared.

I don't care.

**

We're sitting on the ground together, forming a circle close to where the barn used to stand. After the demons had been chased off, the field was somehow cleared of bodies and vehicles. I suppose the women must have supernatural gifts that enable them to accomplish such a miracle, but I never saw them at work.

Since I joined them, there has been nothing but a frenzy of dancing and singing. The revelry over, we're droning the mantra I remember, one we used to chant at retreats with the guru—CHA-MUN-DA-YEA... KAL EE MA... KAL EE MA... KAL EE MA—over and over, creating a hum like that of a massive power line.

A silver bowl, chiseled with intricate spiraling patterns, is making its way around the circle, everyone, in turn, holding the bowl in two hands, taking a drink, and passing it on. Eventually, the woman sitting to my left has her turn and then offers the bowl to me, her face radiating contentment.

The bowl has what's left of the enemy's blood. Dregs from the exorcism. I don't know how I know this. I don't know how any of what I'm experiencing is happening, but it is, and I'm about to drink a blend of demon and patriot blood. In a deep recess of my mind, I'm laughing—a vintage red blend from Northern California!—but I don't dare smile at my joke. I don't think these women appreciate irony, unlike Pushan, whose irony cuts like a knife. I hope they can't read my mind as he can.

Once I swallow some of the warm, sticky liquid, the woman on my right, the last to drink, takes the bowl from me, tilts her head dramatically, black dreads hanging down her back all the way to the ground, and chugs down the rest, completing the ceremony. She turns the bowl over, carefully places it in front of her, and then howls triumphantly. Some of the women in the circle howl back, some nod in satisfaction, and some seem lost in prayer.

A reverent silence follows, broken when the women, having vanquished the demons of hate and restored harmony to this corner of the universe, in unison make a soothing trilling sound. As if on cue, my neighbors to the left and right turn to me. Smiling happily, each takes one of my arms and slides a bracelet made of their hair onto my wrists.

What am I supposed to do? I mumble, *thank you*, having no idea what language they understand. I doubt it's English. They stare at me, not saying anything.

I'm afraid they'll burn holes in my retinas if I look into their eyes, so I keep my head down, sneaking glances at them, wondering if their gifts are just the beginning of another ritual, if I'm expected to do something in exchange. I do understand they have given me a blessing, and I think they must be able to read my mind after all and grasp that I know the meaning of their gift because they abruptly start laughing, pat me on the back, and turn away to face their sisters around the circle.

I wonder if these goddesses, if that's what they are, would consider taking me with them to the next psychic disaster zone. I want to be with them. I've never felt so right.

I've never felt so safe.

Read my mind, please. Grant my wish.

2.8

I should have thought twice about entering an enchanted place. 'Enchanted'—do I think this is Disney World?—but how else would a forest grow overnight if not by magic? The Dravidian must be the magician. He is in charge here. He controls nature. His powers grow in my imagination by the hour.

If my perceptions really are blown, and I'm seeing things, I shouldn't have gone out exploring. If my eyes didn't deceive me, and the forest actually did grow, then I should have checked my hubris because I am asking for trouble walking into a mystery. The Dravidian may practice black magic, not white. Who knows what might be going on in the expanding woods? Why assume I can handle whatever it might be? It's not like I have experience with the supernatural, though Astrid might count. And the fox.

Rationalize all I want, it's obvious that leaving the barn and entering the forest was foolish. I know my mythology— having been named Persephone forced me to get educated—

and I'm pulling an Icarus. Or a Little Red Riding Hood without the red cloak.

Without any cloak or something warm at all. I'm not prepared for anything except a swim, and yet here I am. I walked on these paths with Grandma only once or twice in my life, and when I did walk with her, I wasn't paying attention to where a trail started, what direction we went, where one fork went and another, where we ended up and where we turned around. My eyes were on the ground looking for mushrooms and beetles, or I was scanning the trees for squirrels, or I was picking berries and asking if they were OK to eat. Of course, I would get lost without her as a guide. What is it that I thought I would accomplish *besides* getting lost?

I'm spiraling. I need to stop repeating *stupid, stupid, stupid* to myself. Not helpful, but really, how stupid! I waltzed into the woods and took the first path I saw, not knowing if this was the one that Uncle Rav had taken. How would I have known, and how will I ever know? I'm not a backwoods tracker from some old western who can infer the way to go by the direction a broken branch is pointing.

Are there any trackers left in the world at all? GPS would have ended that profession. Robots and AI ended most of the rest. But new professions have evolved, like mine: I am a proud chicken wrangler. It's only a matter of time before chickens and their eggs are all that stand between us and starvation. Chicken wrangling will become a vital calling. It already is, as far as I'm concerned.

I've been yelling nonstop for Uncle Raven, but he doesn't answer. In between shouts, I don't hear anything at all, not even birds. All I hear is my own breathing, which I notice is ragged. I'm stressed out, breathing through my mouth, wheezing even. And it's getting darker. Did I consider the time when I left? No, I did not, and what little light that has been sneaking in through the forest canopy is disappearing. I'm scared. Forget about catching up to Uncle Raven: I have to find a way back to the field.

***

I've been walking for quite a while in what I think must be the right direction. I can't say for sure how long. The sun keeps the time for me, and it's gone down. Before long it will be the witching hour.

When is that, exactly?

I accept that I'm lost and sit on a mossy, damp log along a path that resembles every other route I've been on since I ventured into this place. I am huddled under a stand of evergreen trees. Pines and firs, I guess, not that I actually know.

If asked, I would say without hesitating, and with great sincerity, that I love nature, but the truth is my love is more a matter of principle derived from my ideals, not my experience. I have never studied or lived in nature like Grandma. I don't know the names of plants and trees, but I love life—at least I can say I am happy to be alive—and what is nature but life? So I think it's fair for me to say I love nature.

I don't need to prove it by naming things. I live in a city, and even though I belong to a ZG neighborhood, it's part of a city, and the remnants of nature left—trees lining the streets, pocket parks, rooftop vegetable gardens—do not really provide city dwellers with an in-depth experience of nature.

I've never even gone camping, but it looks like I'll be camping out tonight, without tent, sleeping bag, food, water, lantern, or warm clothes. Stupid me. All I brought was water, and that's just about gone.

I don't backpack, either. Living hand-to-mouth the ZG way doesn't leave a lot of free time for wilderness vacations. Not that we're starving in The Library, but still, survival requires daily effort. And there is the issue of getting to a trailhead. In what car? With whose money?

I would actually be embarrassed to tell friends that I was going backpacking, it being such an iconic boomer thing to do, posing as a rugged nature lover while tromping through the last remnants of wilderness, carrying the latest in camping tech and a fully charged cell phone just in case, building cairns out of carefully chosen rocks.

Boomers are easy to scorn, but to be fair, nobody has the right to judge with the benefit of hindsight—Oh, yeah, I would have been so different. I wouldn't have done that. I would have done something, something.

Of course, I would have. Goes without saying.

I remember Mom telling me about how when I was born in the 20s, people became paranoid about the dangers of cellular technology: 5G! What is it doing to our minds? Is it altering our genes? It's causing cancer, for sure. Are we being programmed by the Deep State?

Cellular generations are in the double digits now, but those cellular G's that alarmed people are harmless compared to the only G that ever mattered: Economic Growth, with a big G, the one and only G. The first and last G. The Alpha G and Omega G. AG and OG. The economy must grow, so fast and so big everyone will be AGOG!

No one must ever question the primacy of this goal. There is no alternative to the Economy with a big E because billionaires must make more billions, as many billions as it is possible to make, even if it means the earth becomes uninhabitable. Even if it means the mass extinction of life. Why must this be? Because there is only one G! The AGOG!

Insanity: in exchange for billionaires making more billions, we billions with just enough money to survive get a dead planet.

The boomers made their peace with it. They accepted the prime directive to consume or else and didn't stop to consider 'Or else what?' They didn't consider that the 'what' might be a good thing. They didn't complain with any real seriousness when the billionaires took control. They could live out their final years in relative comfort, collecting pensions, harvesting the fruits of investments made with inherited money, the last generation to receive social security before it was phased out. They would be dead before the heat got unbearable, before the beaches they enjoyed strolling on were washed away, before the crops failed and the water was drained out of the last reservoir. They had bucket lists and places to fly to before it was too late.

Then it was too late for everything.

Gen Alpha, my generation, could be called the penniless generation. We don't have pensions, and we won't retire, since we have nothing to retire from, except life. We won't inherit any money—not that we want to have anything to do with money. Money is truly the root of all evil. The mindless pursuit of it is suicidal, as the human race has demonstrated. The proof is in the poisoned pudding. We were left holding an empty bag, but we don't whine about it. If there are histories written—or blogged—about us in the next century, some may call us the hopeless generation, but that would be wrong. All we have is hope. If we lose that, we truly will have nothing.

***

I've never experienced darkness like this. I have a phone with no signal, but it does have a light, which I'm conserving. I really don't want to be out here without a light.

I don't know what to do and have no plan. Maybe that's why I'm in this ugly, bitter doomer mood. I need to snap out of that. Cynicism is not productive and definitely not helpful when lost in the woods.

At least it's not too cold. Yet.

I guess I have no choice but to stay here until the sun comes up. I wonder if I'll be able to fall asleep. Is it safe? I haven't seen or heard a single animal. No snakes crossed my path all day. There's been no sign of the Dravidian. Would I want to encounter anonymous or not? I can't answer that.

Tiny white lights are starting to blink on and off in the trees. I don't think we have fireflies around here, do we? Whatever they are, they are multiplying, filling all of the trees surrounding me. It's scary but also comforting. If they stick around, I won't have to use up my phone battery. God is creating a natural nightlight just for me. It's starting to look like Christmas in here!

Thank you, God.

When was the last time I thanked God?

I'm cold. Shorts and t-shirt are not getting it done any longer. I should probably keep moving, but I'm worried about leaving the fairies.

Yes, the fairies. I'm pretty sure the blinking lights must be fairies since I'm pretty sure we don't have fireflies in California; plus, this place is enchanted. If I leave my rotting log, they might follow me, or they might pop up wherever I go in the forest, but I don't know that for sure, and I don't want to risk losing my light and their company, so I'm not moving.

***

Sitting all alone in the dark for hours sure stimulates the imagination. Senses on alert, straining for information— sounds, sights, smells—that will trigger a fight or flee, and the mind does the rest. A little breeze comes through, rustling the leaves, and I'm holding my breath, waiting for a mountain lion to leap down on top of me. But I trust the fairies will warn me if I'm in danger. They're my friends and will protect me. Or so I tell myself. I am being a mother me to my baby me, trying to keep calm.

I'm cold, and the fairy lights are not warm. I should look around for some tree boughs or gather some moss. Isn't that what characters stranded in the woods at night do to keep warm? Or I could look for a large tree with a trunk that's been hollowed out by a fire and curl up in there.

I don't think so. I haven't seen any bugs, but I'm sure there are bugs in those tree trunks with holes big enough for curled-up me. I will probably have to do jumping jacks or run in place to keep warm. I could do steps up and down on this log I've been sitting on.

You may ask yourself: well, how did I get here?

Songs pop up among the thoughts and memories keeping me awake. It's kind of disturbing to observe just how random the mind becomes when you've got nothing to do except sit alone in the dark for hours.

This is definitely not my beautiful house.

Not that I have a beautiful house. The library is a beautiful building, but the basement of the library, where my bed is pinned between stacks of books, is only beautiful to my arachnid roommates.

***

"Percy!"

Huh? I must have dozed off.

"Hey, it's me."

That confirms it. I'm full-on hearing and seeing things now. Tristan is standing there on the trail. He can't be real.

I'll try talking to him—or it.

"What the hell, Tristan! What are you doing here?"

"Looking for you."

He heard me and answered in his voice. My mind is in overdrive now. Enchantment has reached another level.

"It's the middle of the night!"

"Yeah, it is. I've been worried about you. And I could ask you the same thing: what are you doing out here in the woods in the middle of the night?"

"I got lost. I was trying to find Uncle Raven."

"Why? What's he doing out here? What's going on?"

He doesn't seem up to speed on anything, but he speaks, and he looks like my Tristan, so I am going to hug him.

This will prove if he's real, won't it?

He's so warm.

"That's more like it, Percy. I've been missing you."

I give up trying to understand what's happening.

"I'm cold, Tristan. Just keep hugging me."

The lights are out. The fairies have gone. I can't believe how good it feels to have Tristan here holding me.

Sweet Tristan, my partner in life: I take him for granted. I promise myself to tell him how much he means to me more often. He is a blessing. I love him. I have no idea how he got here and how he found me, or why he doesn't seem to have a clue why I'm here, but I don't care. He's real. His arms are as strong as I remember. His body, familiar and comforting.

"Thanks for coming to my rescue, Tris. I was freezing. I had no idea what to do... There were fairies here in the trees looking after me, but they're gone... I left the barn to catch up to Raven, which was stupid... I got lost... I was hoping I would meet the Dravidian..."

"Percy, stop. You're babbling. I think you might be hypothermic."

"I probably am."

I take a long drink from his water bottle.

"Don't let me go, OK?"

2.9

I'm running faster than I thought possible, possessed by the certainty that I'm being chased by unknown but terrifying creatures that want to kill me. They are braying like hyenas and steadily punctuating the hard-packed dirt with their hoofs. I have no idea why they would be chasing me. I can't even say for sure they are, in fact, chasing me because I'm too afraid to turn my head to take a look. I'm not about to stop running and face them, whatever they are. They are gaining on me, and I can hear them slavering in anticipation...of something. I don't want to find out what they're so worked up about.

Everything on this desert plain populated by these monsters is a dull pewter, including the air. I can't run any faster than I am through the grayness, trying to find a place to hide in what is, at least for me at this moment, a merciless landscape, totally barren and flat. As the predators close in and my fear ramps up to unbearable, the desperate prayer for somewhere to escape that I've been saying to myself suddenly becomes a scream out loud for help from anyone who might be listening.

The scream seems to enrage the monsters, and they howl back at me. At first, I think my Hail Mary for help has just made it worse, but then rock formations begin to materialize in front of me as I run. There are cracks between the giant rocks, and I spot a narrow opening just wide enough for me to knife my way through. I think it must be too small for the monsters to squeeze through. It has to be.

My scream has been answered. I have witnessed a miracle.

I collapse in exhaustion and relief on the gravelly floor of a hollow in the midst of a jumble of stone. The panting beasts have gathered outside. I can hear frustrated bleating between my wheezing gulps for air. Only parts of them are visible through the slit in the rocks—a drooling mouth arrayed with razor-like incisors, a furry shoulder, a hairless paw with three long claws, and bloodshot eyes. The monsters are scuffling with each other, trying to be the first to get in, scratching, yelping, and snorting.

I cower as far away from the entrance as possible, trembling from fear and exhaustion.

***

The awful racket made by frustrated creatures kept from their prey gradually dies down. Is it possible that they are giving up?

I hold my breath as long as I can, listening for a sound.

After inhaling, listening, and exhaling many times without hearing anything, I muster the courage to take a look outside through the slit in the rocks that saved me.

Nothing to see but a gray fog. No movement. No sound. So intent on trying to see outside my fortress without drawing the monsters' attention, I don't notice that the rocks surrounding me have disappeared.

I'm standing again on the featureless plain, alone, peering through rocks that don't exist anymore. I must look really silly.

There is nothing to see in any direction except a gray haze, nothing to hear but my heart thrumming in my ears. For an instant, I wish the monsters would come back because I have never felt so alone and so vulnerable.

Stop thinking that!

Hadn't I desperately screamed for someplace to hide and then manifested it?

Never underestimate the power of thought, Mom always reminded us. At the time, I took her pronouncement with a grain of salt. Not anymore. I should be extra careful about the company I wish for.

How are those creatures even possible? There's nothing here to support life in this forsaken place—not a plant or a tree. Not even lichen. No water. Not even the mirage of an oasis.

I didn't imagine them into existence. Or did I? Am I having a lucid nightmare? Can I wake myself up?

I close my eyes and visualize myself sleeping next to Ursula in the barn, willing myself to wake up, but this is the kind of dream you don't wake up from. It has to run its course. I hope it has.

Like Dorothy, I have been deposited by a tornado in a place that is no place like home, but the monsters chasing me were not winged monkeys with cute bellboy hats charged with picking me up and delivering me to a wicked witch. If those creatures caught me, they intended to do me unspeakable harm. They weren't going to take me anywhere. As soon as they caught me, they were going to dismember me, eat me piece by piece, rip my head off. I have no doubt this was their intention, because once I heard them chuffing behind me, the images of what they were going to do went through my mind like a high-def Halloween PowerPoint, each slide more gruesome than the last. They were going to reduce me to a litter of bones and then gnaw on them.

It's all an illusion. Sure. And it's all real. I'm in a realm or a state of mind (what's the difference?) where those distinctions are meaningless. I'm dreaming, or I'm awake. Pick one. It doesn't matter.

Am I able to make a reality with my thoughts? Is my wish a command?

At this point, Mom would say, Iris, you should meditate. Stop your thoughts, clear your mind, and then reassess.

I don't think that's possible. Random thoughts are racing through my mind, colliding with each other. Driverless bumper cars stuck in high gear. And what about my unconscious? It's not going to stop projecting its wishes, and I have no way of stopping it.

I'm going to try.

Sitting with my legs folded in front of me in a loose meditation pose, one leg folded under another, without thinking about it, I automatically start chanting OM...OM...OM.... I regret now having been afraid to ask the guru for a mantra, though if I am honest about it, it wasn't fear so much as pride. I believed at the time I was above that sort of spiritual hokum, being so smart and well-read, the librarian's daughter and the valedictorian. I was not going to look a fool.

The dread of looking a fool, where does it come from?

The ego, Mom says.

I know, Mom.

Well, do something about it. It's not too late.

OMOMOMOMOMOMOMOM...streams through my mind nonstop. If only I had a mantra from the guru to block all dangerous thoughts and wishes. OM is all I remember. It will have to do.

***

At the horizon line of the gray plain, a mountain rises out of the earth. A perfectly symmetrical triangle of a mountain, like an Egyptian pyramid.

What was I thinking about? Not this. This is something unimaginable. I was thinking of my mom and what she would say to me. I was regretting not having a mantra. I was chanting OM. So why is this mountain being born in front of me?

As the pinnacle of the pyramid mountain rises higher, its base gets broader. It is not exactly a mountain or a pyramid. I think it is something that exists in myth or in fantasy novels: the sacred mountain, the center of the world. Crystal waterfalls flow down from top to bottom on every side. Transfixed by the spectacle, I'm no longer chanting, thinking, or even breathing.

Still rising, the mountain suddenly starts erupting huge orange fireballs, which do not fall back down onto the slopes of the pyramid to harmlessly roll away: they are landing all over the plain as if the mountain is a gargantuan artillery cannon with unlimited range.

The gray air fills with acrid smoke and fiery cinders. A blizzard of hot ash drifts down, covering me with black volcanic soot. At any moment, one of the fireballs could land on me, but what use would it be to run? There is no way to evade the hailstorm of lava bombs.

I want to try to stop the eruption with my thoughts, but it's impossible to concentrate hard and long enough during the barrage of molten boulders. They shake the ground like an earthquake.

A dark rent in the ground as wide as a city block, starts coming toward me faster than a bullet train. It's like the plain itself is opening an underground zipper.

A fissure—it *is* an earthquake!

If I stay where I am, I'm going to be swallowed up, but it's impossible to stand on the buckling earth, much less run.

It's all an illusion.

Now would be the time for me to have faith in the guru. To call on that faith, to stop squirming in fear, huddled up in a fetal position in my mind, trying so hard to figure out what's real and what isn't, what to do, what not to do, what to think, what not to think.

It's time to surrender, as I was advised before the whirlwind took me. After all, the truth is clear: I am totally helpless. I can't do anything to save myself.

I lie down and consciously release my body from my mind. I cut it loose. Now I can't be hurt. I don't have any reason to be afraid.

The earth shakes my untethered body like a rag doll until the runaway fissure speeding directly toward me arrives, and the ground I'm lying on disappears. I plunge into darkness, expecting to be hurled down by gravity to a sudden death, impaled on the point of a jagged rock.

Instead, I'm floating like a feather, weightless. I shouldn't be surprised: I left my body behind.

I can't tell if I'm moving at all. Suspended as I am in an enormous sensory deprivation tank, a pitch-black gash in the earth, I have no way to gauge motion because I can't see a thing.

Time seems to have stopped, or time has stopped, 'seems' and 'is' being the same here.

I smell plowed earth and damp rock. How am I smelling anything without my body? Is my mind creating illusions to keep me from realizing I actually lie dead and broken at the bottom of this crevasse?

I can hear myself breathing but nothing else. My inhalations and exhalations echo back from the bedrock walls of the newly-formed canyon that surround me. This could be proof that I have descended quite a way. If I were still anywhere near the surface, I would be able to hear the loud crashing of lava bombs. At any moment, one or more of them could zero in on me in the dark and take me with it to the bottom, however far that is.

I wonder about the depth of faults created by earthquakes. I studied a lot of things, but not geology.

My breathing, echoed back to me, is rhythmical: a slow, steady beat, like a lullaby. I could fall asleep.

***

Curled up like a hermit crab in a small, circular boat, a ceramic dish the size of one of those aluminum sleds, I'm adrift on a subterranean river.

I guess it's a river, but it could be a sizable underground pool, like a cenote, because there doesn't seem to be a current. I don't seem to be moving.

Mom and Dad didn't take us on too many vacations when we were kids, but they took us to the Yucatan once. We loved it there, especially swimming in the blessedly cool, pristine water of a cenote. The little fish we joined when we swam would nibble at our toes.

It's unbearably hot there now; I wonder if those underground pools in the limestone have all dried up.

I wonder if I'm re-living a memory.

I look down into the water, hoping to see some fish, but it's too dark, even with the ambient light from the iridescent life—lichen? bacteria?—glistening on the smooth granite walls surrounding my little clay boat.

Psychedelic images start to appear, as if someone is operating an array of black light spots and orchestrating an underground light show on the walls of this subterranean river canyon.

A towering, glowing figure of a woman outlined in bright silver comes into view, covering one of the walls. She throws a handful of dice, each about as big as a produce crate, five of them, all of which have sides that are either white or black.

The dice come up 3 white and 2 black. She considers the results of her throw for a moment and then gathers them up and tosses them again: 4 white, 1 black. Again and again, she gathers the dice and throws them, each time pausing to do her mysterious evaluation. I keep score for a while, instinctively knowing that I want to see more white than black, but I lose count, because each time the dice are thrown, I have an emotional reaction that becomes more intense with each roll, making counting impossible. When the dice come up white, I feel relieved and hopeful. When they come up black, I feel remorse and shame.

I am being judged.

As the dice rolls go on, my feelings deepen to the point that when black wins, I want to beg the woman on the wall to forgive me, even though she is just a supernatural two-dimensional projection, even though all I can see is one side of her, a blurry profile, and her two giant hands cupping the five dice, tossing them, and gathering them to do it again.

Even so, I desperately want her to absolve me. If not her, then someone else. Please have mercy, I say to myself, to the woman on the wall, to the universe, to God.

I don't know how much longer I can bear this. I dread seeing black win. Even if there is more white, it doesn't balance out my feelings of remorse and regret. I don't want to look, but I am compelled to look. Whatever it is that creates this scene wants me to look and feel. It wants me to understand.

I want it to be over.

You've always been too hard on yourself, Iris.

Mom?

∗∗∗

It *is* a river, after all. I know because I'm moving now, rapidly pulled by a strong current. If my boat had a prow, I'd be creating a wake, but as it's a circular dish, I'm just getting jostled around, dipping up and down, tilting, spinning. If I weren't so scared, I would probably be getting seasick. The current is intensifying by the moment, and now I can hear the unmistakable sound of cascading water, the roar of a waterfall.

My little round boat is moving so fast that it skips like a flat rock on top of the water, becoming airborne and then touching down, over and over in rapid succession. I have to hang on with both hands to keep from being bounced out into the river each time it lands.

The sound of the waterfall becomes deafening. It's hard to see ahead because of the chaotic motions of the dish and my ever-increasing speed, but I'm able to catch glimpses of a precipice up ahead, like the boundary of an infinity pool, just before my boat and I sail off the edge, awash in a plummeting torrent of water.

Before I've even had time to be terrified, a column of hot air from below—from the center of the earth?—immediately cradles the bowl I'm riding in, heating it up, and keeping me from freefall.

I'm floating in a vaporous cloud. Warm mist from the waterfall surrounds me, and within that mist I can make out what appear to be huge soap bubbles, each with a distinct, colorful sheen, like an aura, swirling all around me within the cloud.

When a bubble gets close, I see people, buildings, and different scenes of what life is like within that bubble, of what life might be like for me if I were somehow there in that tiny universe. Some of the vague feelings, the intuitions I have when gazing at one of these bubbles, are of peace or conflict, happiness or sadness, suffering or ease.

I notice that some of the bubbles in particular attract my attention, while others repel me, though it's impossible to tell if it's not actually the other way around. Which bubbles come near seems to depend on the color of their aura, and I wonder if I'm in my own bubble of a certain color but just can't perceive it.

After some time descending very slowly on the cushion of air, observing the bubbles, preoccupied with the feelings I have of life within them, the mist thickens, becoming soupy. The mysterious ambient light that allows me to see darkens, and I am suddenly overcome by the certainty that I must choose one of the bubbles. It's as though I've been shopping, and now it's time to buy before the store closes. It's time to decide. I know this without a doubt. There is no turning back from this moment. I must choose a life.

A bubble with a yellow aura drifts close, and I feel an overwhelming desire to leave my ceramic boat and enter into the world I sense within. Was I drawn to it, or did I draw it to me?

***

Everything is gone: the canyon, the misty cloud, my boat.

I am something bathed in a warm yellow light.

I am.

2.10

I don't remember dreaming since I arrived here. I wake up with a blank mind, not a single image lingering around the edges. The hours I've been asleep are a clean slate, and I can't shake the feeling I haven't actually slept, like when you are trying to sleep but can't and then lose awareness for a moment. You look at the clock, hopeful that hours have passed, but no, you haven't been asleep. You just dozed for five minutes.

Even though I haven't experienced sleep as I normally would, when I open my eyes in the early morning—and it's always early, always waking with the sun—I'm not tired, just disoriented. My mind is shut down like a computer in battery saver mode until I've made coffee and finished the first cup out on the porch, where I am now, scanning the meadow, as I have every morning, hoping to see Mom alive and well walking toward me through the grass. If not her, then someone who will come up to the porch and tell me where she is, what happened to her. The familiarity of this routine must be what I count on to reboot.

I have enacted this very same script now for many mornings. I don't have a count, but many mornings, not a few, and every one of those mornings, I ask myself if this is how I want to spend the rest of my life.

Should I give up? So then what, Raven? I answer back. Wish your mom good luck, and go back to fixing bikes and building chicken coops? Entertaining the thought of giving up makes me sick to my stomach. This debate with myself and my conclusion to continue my vigil is the final bit of the routine. The last scene of the morning act.

After finishing the second cup of coffee, resigning myself to another day just like the others, on this morning, there actually *is* someone coming across the field: a man driving a small cart with wood wheels pulled by what look like miniature ponies. He has a thin stick he uses to goad them on. I can see him snapping them with it. It's a sight from centuries past. Something I might have seen back in the day when the property was just getting logged and the barn built. When horses were fed in the stalls and a pioneer couple ploughed a corn patch.

Eventually, I can see they're donkeys, not ponies. It has to be Pushan. When I met Astrid that day by the pond, she told me she was taking care of her friend's donkeys, and that friend, Pushan, knew Mom.

It occurred to me at one time I was going to try to find his cabin and talk to him. That time seems so long ago, longer than it possibly could be. The memory is as shadowy as any childhood one. Did I ever do that? Have we already met?

There's no question that my stay here has affected my mind. My short-term memory especially seems to be compromised. I shouldn't be surprised. I'm getting old. I am old. I forget how old since my mother is still alive, and so very much older, making me young by comparison.

He barks something in a language I don't recognize, and the two donkeys stop in front of the porch. They are muscular, sleek animals that look like they could pull the cart at freeway speeds for miles on end.

"Pushan?"

"You don't remember me, do you?"

"Should I?"

He mutters something I can't hear.

"Astrid told me she was looking after your donkeys, so I guessed."

"I can see those banshees did a number on you."

"Huh? Banshees?"

"Never mind. I just call them that sometimes. They're so loud. Singing and screaming all together like an infernal choir."

I have no idea what he's talking about.

"Why am I supposed to remember you?"

He looks at me and smiles. A memory of his toothless grinning face abruptly surfaces.

"No one ever forgets my smile. Maybe that's why I had to lose my teeth."

"The banshees? Who are they?"

"Forget I called them that. I'm being unfair. Familiarity allows me a little license, and even some contempt if it's warranted. When it comes to those I call the banshees, I have no contempt, only respect. They are a band of women who agreed you could join their cosmic circus for a while. They adopted you, like guardian angels might, though you wouldn't recognize them as such. I'm sure it was necessary and beneficial and whatever else as far as your situation is concerned, but now it's time to move on, so let's go."

"My situation? What are you talking about? And what did these women do to me?"

He's not smiling anymore, thankfully. I don't know what he expects, but he's looking at me as if I should know. He seems to believe I will climb into the back of his straw-filled cart and head off with him, no questions asked.

"You wouldn't remember them. That's how it works. You must have done something right to get their blessing, though. They don't just let anyone join their revels."

"I got their blessing?"

"Look at your wrists."

I do as told and find that I have a bracelet woven from black hair on each wrist.

"They gave me these?"

"They don't gift just anyone. As I said, you must have built up a lot of credit to get those."

Every answer to every question just makes me more confused and irritated.

"Pushan, look, I can't go with you. I need to find my mom. That's why I'm here. I can't leave until I know what happened to her. At the very least, I have to know if she's still alive."

"Your mom is fine. Everyone is fine. There's nothing to worry about. All the stuff you are fretting about and have ever fretted about amounts to exactly nothing. If there were any one thing to tell everyone I pick up it would be *stop worrying*."

"You sound like Astrid."

He mutters to himself again.

"Come to speak of her, we're going up the mountain to meet up with your friend Astrid. That's the plan, at least. She's waiting for us. I'm your ride."

"She's my mom's friend, not mine. I only met her once. We didn't talk for more than 10 minutes."

"Are you claiming you don't care that she's waiting for you?" Pushan is unable to keep a grin from spreading.

At that, a riot of memories and emotions breaks out. I do want to see Astrid. I want to see her again so badly that I'm willing to get in the cart with him, someone I have no reason to trust and every reason to dislike, and let him and his donkeys carry me away.

"What is this mountain you're talking about?"

He points across the field. Where there used to be a hill, a gentle rise of the earth covered by trees, there is now a mountain high enough to be ringed by clouds. Tongues of ice and snow drip down from a white top that is exposed now and then as the clouds shift.

My attention was so focused on this strange man and trying to follow what he was saying that I missed this impossible event. This magic. I can't process what I'm seeing. The familiar sight of the hill and its forested ridge that I've looked at for years and have been staring at for so many mornings since I arrived has been replaced by a mountain that seems to have been teleported here from the Himalayas.

"It's a lot, I know," Pushan says, "but it's time to go. You can't stay here forever. There's nothing I can do about that. When it's time, it's time."

I don't understand how, but his eyes, which are locked onto mine, reassure me.

I can't deny I'm ready for a change. I've been searching and waiting for my mom for so long.

There are always these moments when it's time to move on or stay stuck. Transitions are difficult; they are difficult from the time we're born. Moving from one thing to another is so traumatic for children. They live in the moment. Mom says it's time to go home, and they think, *why can't I just stay here in the sandbox and play with my friend? Why do I have to leave?* Angry and frustrated at being taken out of the sandbox for no reason they can understand (It's time for dinner—huh? That's no reason), they throw a fit.

The transitions we face as adults are not any easier, and our frustration and anger is the same, only we may have developed a sophisticated—so-called 'mature'—repertoire of ways to express our rage.

Pushan, who may be afraid that I will resist, puts his arm around me and firmly guides me to his rustic chariot as if I am a child going on a hay ride for the first time. I do feel like a child: cowed, tamed, in the power of a parent, safe and protected.

The sun is high, and the straw bed is warm. In the strange language he uses to communicate with his donkeys, Pushan orders them to move, and I make myself as comfortable as I can as we jostle off across the field. I don't know if we're actually going to summit the mountain in this way or not, but I am done asking questions. From the looks of the mountain, if the plan is to take the donkey cart to the top, I had better make myself a very comfortable nest of straw.

The rhythmic rocking and bucking of the cart as it traverses the field on its wood wheels lulls me into a daze. My eyes slam shut after a sudden bump and then fly open after another. When shut, I mostly daydream about Astrid, imagining her standing outside the cabin or meeting her on the trail on the way. She is smiling. I'm happy.

When my eyes get bounced open, I look around to gauge our progress and become more and more concerned as we don't seem to be making any progress at all, even though I've been getting knocked about for what seems like hours. My eyes have been violently opened and shut hundreds of times, yet we are still in the field, the mountain looming high above but no closer.

"We don't seem to be getting anywhere, Pushan."

"It seems that way to you."

"That's what I said."

"You're right. It seems that way."

When will I learn?

"If we're not actually going anywhere, then please stop and let me out. We're still in the field. I can walk back to the barn."

"Sorry, but you can't do that."

"Do what?"

"Get out."

"So I'm your prisoner?"

"Seemingly."

Pushan bursts into laughter so loud as to put every living creature within miles on alert.

Trying to make myself heard over his cackling, I yell, "Stop! I want out!" at his back. He is still laughing when he calls out to the donkeys to stop. We are in the field, but for some reason, I can't see the barn.

"Where's the barn?"

"We've come a long way... it seems."

He starts quivering with laughter again. I have had enough of the obnoxious riddling and try to stand up to get out of the cart, but my legs are limp and refuse to cooperate.

"What the effing hell, Pushan? What did you do to me? Haul me out then and dump me here until I can walk again. I will be able to, right? My legs must have fallen asleep."

He stops laughing and turns around to face me. "I'm taking you where you need to go. I have to. It's my job."

"So I *am* a prisoner."

Pushan doesn't respond right away. He looks me in the eyes, and I feel his sincere compassion.

"We're all prisoners of karma, son," he says at last and turning back to his donkeys, urges them forward.

Even though I want to know where it is I need to go, I don't ask, finally realizing there is no point. His job seems to be taking me somewhere in this ancient taxi and answering all of my questions with non-sequiturs until I stop asking.

Why? This is the question that underlies all of the questions and the one that Pushan will never answer. Why can't I know why? Am I on a hay ride to hell, tempted into the devil's wagon by his promise that Astrid is expecting me?

Pushan is rude and annoying, but I don't sense an evil purpose. He isn't laughing at me; he is laughing at his own inside jokes, like a kid. I trust that he believes what he's telling me, though it's not clear at all what exactly that is. It's his job to take me somewhere I need to go, and for that I should be grateful is about all I can gather from the few words he's offered in explanation. I know the reason I may be eager to trust him could be my hope of meeting Astrid again, but so what?

Hope is all we really have in the end. I will cling to my hope for a reunion with Astrid.

**

I'm lying on the ground looking up at trees, a forest canopy, and through the boughs, there is a blue sky hosting a great number of birds, but what occupies my mind is not the birds, but a dream. A dream with images and sensations so vivid that I wonder if I am actually remembering something that I experienced rather than dreamed, but what I remember is not something possible, so a bizarre dream it must be.

In the dream, I'm standing in a chariot behind the driver of a classical wooden contraption, a wiry old man with braided hair holding reins harnessed to two donkeys who are pulling us up into the sky. At least, that is what I recall in my mind's eye. How donkeys, however strong—and they do look extremely strong—can provide the power needed to get us airborne and keep us there is unknown, but the driver regularly urges them on with a thin stick in the hand not holding the reins while yelling something in a language I don't recognize or understand.

He seems to believe they are doing what they seem to be doing, which is flying, and he is providing extra motivation. I'm not concerned about whether to believe it or not. I'm just there. It's happening.

We've cleared the tall trees of a forest and are headed up, and I flash on images of Santa behind his reindeer leaving the North Pole. The driver has the reins looped around his forearms to keep himself from falling off the back of the chariot, and I'm holding fast to his waist, the fingers of my hands interlaced tightly together. The gravity of the earth is inexorably strong. I am—no cliché—holding on for dear life. The chariot is not equipped with seatbelts or straps to hang onto. I was not issued a parachute.

We actually pick up speed as we ascend. The roar of air rushing past eclipses all other sounds. An ocean of airwaves crashes against us as we push our way up through the dense atmosphere to... where? The stratosphere, it seems. I want to ask the driver where the hell we're going, but it's pointless. There is no way I can make myself heard.

Maybe the driver read my mind, or maybe he just decided he owed me an explanation because he turns slightly around to get my attention, points at the sun with his stick, and then resumes fiercely goading the donkeys onwards and upwards.

He might have meant, *hey, look at the sun; isn't it amazing?* but the message I got was more like that's where we're going.

We keep that heading, sun straight ahead, and I keep holding on, wondering how long I can possibly maintain my grip around his waist. I wish I was lashed to the chariot like a sailor in a storm. We break through the clouds and eventually level off to cruising altitude. The driver relaxes his hold on the reins, and I relax my grip on his waist as well, but only slightly.

We're gliding now on pure momentum, the thin air offering little resistance. We are practically in outer space and should be completely frozen, but instead, we're basking in the warm, white light of the sun.

I close my eyes, and the brilliant light shines through as if they are still open. I'm afraid my retinas will fry even though my eyes are tightly closed. The light fills my mind and infuses my body. I am so warm....

***

"Raven?"

"Huh?" Someone is talking to me. I was dreaming. It was so real.

"What are you doing here?"

"Here?"

I'm flat on my back. Astrid is hovering over me. In the distance beyond her, above the tree tops, there is a mountain covered in snow. I hear the loud clattering of rocks. A creek. I can smell it: the moss, the rotting wood, the dampness.

She snaps her fingers.

"Hey!"

Her face looms over me.

"Astrid? Is that really you? What's happening?"

She gives my shoulder a shake.

"Snap out of it. You were in la la land."

"I guess I was... am."

I'm content just to look at her welcome face. I need time to regain my senses. Was I unconscious? Neither of us says anything for a while.

"You finally found where I live."

I sputter out, "did I?" then put up my hand to signal I need to talk.

After taking a few deep breaths, I begin to describe my dream, which is still a vivid memory.

I want to remember it. I want to understand it. But what I really want to know is if it was a dream or something I actually experienced or if that even matters. Astrid will be able to tell me. Did I actually reach outer space in the magic flying chariot, fall off, and land here on my back, miraculously unhurt? Considering I was on a supernatural sleigh ride up to the heavens, my falling to earth unscathed seems possible.

After listening to my story, Astrid seems to know exactly what is going on, just as I had hoped.

"Pushan left you here, Raven."

She smiles, and my heart is as warmed by that as it was by the sun before I fell to earth.

"Seems like he has a real soft spot for you."

"Pushan?"

"Yes, the crazy charioteer. He doesn't always stop to let people off. He just keeps going."

"I'm glad he did. I'm so happy to see you. I wanted to meet you again."

I would normally be embarrassed by what I just said, but I'm not my normal self. I don't seem to have control over...over anything. I can't seem to piece together what is happening from day to day anymore. I have lost the thread and dropped a bunch of stitches. All that comes up when I try to reconstruct what's going on is a vague memory of there being a puzzle I was meant to solve, of something I was supposed to do.

"Well, now that you're here, would you like to stay for a while?"

"Yes, I want to, but Astrid..."

I don't know what to say or how to say it.

"It's OK, Raven. You don't need to say anything."

"But I do..." I manage to piece together a question. "Astrid, I do want to be here... but where is here?"

"Where we are has a lot of names. Shangri-La is one you might recognize."

"Shangri-La? No, I don't..."

"But I like Summerland."

2.11

What I last remember is lying on the cold ground with Tristan's arms wrapped around me, pulling me in close, his body molded against my back. Our tightly bound bodies must have kept us warm enough to fall asleep because it is not dark anymore. Light has returned to the forest. The sun is back.

And I'm alone. And cold. Where is he?

He must be scouting around for something to eat. I'm sure there must be plants we could eat if we knew which ones, and berries, but I doubt Tristan would know which are edible and which are poisonous, and I sure as hell don't know. I don't even know if there are fireflies around here or not.

I was content to believe the twinkling lights that kept me company last night were fairies. In the morning light, able to see clearly now what were scary shadows a few hours ago, I feel foolish. The enchanted forest looks very much like a plain old forest with trees and bushes, rotting logs, and mossy rocks. It could be that it is only enchanted at night, but I suspect it is made magical only by my desperate imagination.

I'm am slightly pissed off at being left here alone. I would be more than slightly pissy if Tristan hadn't shown up like he did last night to keep me company, keep me warm, and make me feel safe. Still, what was he thinking when he took off? Did he think I would stay asleep until he got back? Why didn't he wake me up and tell me what his plan was? It isn't like him not to think things through, to be impulsive. To just go off and leave me alone like this is obviously a bad idea, not to mention really inconsiderate, and Tristan is possibly the most considerate person I've ever known.

It doesn't make sense, his leaving.

Maybe he thought we needed water. He would be right about that. It could take a while to find our way back to the barn, even though I'm hoping he knows the way and, when he returns, will be guiding us back. He did find me somehow—and in the dark, no less!

I could use some water. What I brought is almost gone. Sitting here on a rock, waiting, I'm straining to hear something. I should be able to hear him traipsing around in the underbrush, but I don't hear anything. I would welcome any sound. It's too quiet.

Before my phone died, it wasn't keeping time for some reason; it was stuck in roaming mode, which is probably what killed the battery. So the sun is my timepiece, and it has climbed pretty high. I think it must be afternoon, and Tristan has not returned.

I'm trying very hard not to panic, not so much because I'm afraid of being alone, but because I don't know what to do. Do I keep waiting? Do I head out and try to find the way back on my own? I'm paralyzed by too many possibilities. He could be lost, and I could get lost trying to find him, and then we would both be lost. Great. He could have been attacked by an animal, and I might be that animal's second victim, though I haven't seen or heard any animals yet in these woods. He could have hurt himself and is hoping I'll find him. If I do manage to find him and can't help him, then what? He could have fallen into a deep pit, a sinkhole, or an old well. Been snared by some trap set by a hunter long ago. Stumbled over a root and knocked himself out. If I do venture up or down the trail looking for him, I might find him, but what if I don't, and he comes back, and I'm gone? Would he assume I gave up waiting for him and left?

Then there is the most disturbing possibility, one I won't yet admit is possible, though deep in my mind, I know it is entirely possible, even probable: Tristan was never here. I was hypothermic, imagined the whole thing, and passed out in the arms of an apparition.

I have reason to panic, but there is one compelling reason not to: panicking is not going to help me find my way out of this forest before it gets dark again. So must not panic, obviously, but must do something, because the sun is done climbing for the day and heading down. It won't be long before shadows start to form again.

I really don't like shadows. When a little girl, elementary school age, I would have trouble sleeping. Having a bed crammed between tall bookcases in the basement of a musty library built at the turn of the 20th century probably had a lot to do with it—not to mention the periodic incursions of rats—but there was also the turmoil of the times.

Being born in 2020 at the start of the pandemic that has accompanied me every year of my life was auspicious, but not in a good way. It was in the 20s that things really began to turn to shit. The climate crisis was becoming something impossible to ignore mainly because the crazy weather everyone was experiencing couldn't be denied. The billionaires saw trouble on the horizon and got serious about manufacturing a reality for the little people that aligned with their need to be even more obscenely wealthy than they already were. In this reality, there was only one thing that mattered—the economy, their economy, the economy that kept money flowing into their accounts.

We, the people, who they relied on to keep the money flowing to them, mostly fell in line and kept buying their shit, but some didn't. Some resisted.

At the end of the 20s, sea levels began to rise high enough that coastlines were washed away, but in the billionaires' reality, this was just another problem the economy would solve. All faith must be placed in the economy or else disaster. If the people stopped buying the shit they were selling, it would mean the end of civilization. a return to the stone age.

More than a few people had enough insight to point out that civilization was already ending despite their sacred economy. Mother Nature was seeing to that.

As a child, I felt the fear circulating in the air, not consciously, but in my body. I suppose I was anxious, like my parents, but also like everyone else living in a world of increasingly bad news and traumatic cognitive dissonance.

When lying in my basement bed, unable to fall asleep, I would be looking up at the tall shelves of books surrounding me, which in the dark appeared to be black towers ready to topple over and bury me alive. I did my best to convince myself they were just the bookcases I played between during the day, but often I became so afraid that I had to get out of bed and sit on the toilet in the bathroom with all the lights on. Sometimes I would curl up in the bathtub and fall asleep. On the nights I woke my mom up, she would take me back to bed, and I would make her stay.

Worse still were the sleepless nights when I heard frantic whispering on both sides of me as if the tall monoliths surrounding me were inhabited by spirits. I could never make out what they were saying, but I felt their menacing tone. I was sure they were whispering about me and meant to do me harm if given a chance.

I outgrew this period by the time I was in middle school, but shadows in the dark still spark a strong unconscious reaction. An unconscious reaction I'm having right now, just anticipating another night in the woods surrounded by the tall black shadows of trees.

I need to get out of here. I can't wait any longer for Tristan to return.

I yell as loud as I can, TRISTAN, MEET ME AT THE BARN, and start walking down the trail in the direction I hope will lead me out to the field.

***

Trying to find my way out of the forest is just as difficult today as it was yesterday. Each time I commit to a path and a direction, I feel confident it is the right path to be on and the right direction to take. I keep believing that at the next spot where there is a break in the trees, I will be able to see the field and leave this cursed place (I no longer think of it as enchanted), but at each clearing filled with sunlight, all I see beyond are more trees. Every path turns out to be a dead end.

The sun is going down, and I'm scared. Again. I'm not sure I can make it through another night unless Tristan again appears out of nowhere. If he does, I will not question his reality or grill him about where he's been and why he abandoned me. I will grab him and hold him tight. Never let him go. There will be no need to talk at all.

I hope he has water because I'm out. I'm trying not to think about food.

If Tristan doesn't show up in the nick of time like he did last night, I'm going to pray for the fairies to return despite my easy dismissal of them this morning. The light of day swayed me, I plead out loud hoping they can hear me. I understand now that you are creatures of the night.

Without the fairies, I'm in trouble. My phone is kaput. If I don't die of hyperthermia, I may die of fright.

I'm standing at yet another spot on the trail where I should be able to see the field. It suddenly occurs to me that the reason I can't see the field or the barn is that they no longer exist. The enchanted expanding forest may have expanded over all of it last night. The trees may be up to the highway and beyond by now. Maybe I have nowhere to go.

That's not something I should be thinking about. *That way, madness lies*, as they say.

Sometimes I wonder how it is my mind is filled with phrases like that. These sayings must be repeated by so many for so long that they take residence in the collective unconscious and pop up in everyone's mind. Whatever. Why am I thinking about this trivial shit right now?

I have to keep walking and hope I'll find my way out. Even if the forest has grown all the way across the field, it might have made a detour around the barn. I might still have some place to go. I have to believe I have someplace to go.

I turn away from the disappointing view of nothing but more trees and prepare once again to hike in another direction.

There is an animal in the path looking at me.

I freeze before taking a step and hold my breath. It looks like a dog, but it's not a dog. It's a fox. Bushy tail, pointy nose, orangey, reddish fur. All of these signifiers are lodged in my mind, just like random phrases that everyone uses without thinking.

Everyone knows what a fox looks like, but does everyone know if a fox is dangerous? I don't. I don't think I'm food for a fox. It's not that big, and even if its teeth are sharp, it will take a monumental effort to kill me. I think it probably eats rodents and rabbits and such.

It seems relaxed and content just to continue looking at me. Though I don't trust my perceptions anymore, if someone were to ask me right now how the fox looks, I would say the fox looks friendly. I could go so far as to say it's smiling at me. It's definitely not menacing.

Hi, there, I say in the singsong that we use when talking to babies and animals.

It's blocking my way—at least the way I was planning to go. I may have to change direction if it doesn't move. It definitely is not acting like it's rabid. I'm not afraid it's going to attack me, but I'm not going to challenge it, either.

Suddenly, as if answering my greeting, it yips a couple of times, then turns around on the trail and starts to trot. After traveling 10 yards or so, the fox stops and turns around to look at me, just as a dog would, making sure its master is coming. I'm not coming. I'm still standing there. We look at each other again, and after a few moments, the fox turns around and starts off again, only to stop again and look back. There is no doubt in my mind now that the fox expects me to follow, and as soon as I take a couple of tentative steps in its direction, it turns and continues down the trail, stopping again after a few feet to look back again. After a few more check-ins, it seems satisfied that I know what to do and picks up the pace.

Why not follow? Last night the fairies gathered to help me get through the night. Then the miraculous appearance of Tristan. Today, the fox has come to lead me out of these woods. Or so I choose to believe. The forest *is* enchanted. What more proof do I need? The fox materialized at the exact moment I was about to give up, find a log to sit on, and then probably cry. Now instead of sinking into despair, I have hope.

***

I've been following Freya (as I've decided to name her) for quite a while. She never lets me out of her sight. When I need a break, I yell *Freya, I'm stopping for a while,* and she patiently waits for me to get up and start walking again. I was lost when I started following her, and I'm still lost. I may be lost forever.

Though I trust Freya, I have no reason to other than wishful thinking. *She must be trying to help me,* I keep telling myself. What's the point in believing anything else? And if she is under the control of an evil wizard with bad intent, what hope do I have anyway?

Soon I won't even be able to see her ahead on the trail. If she plans to lead me through the night somewhere, she is going to have to be much closer. Close enough that I could grab onto her tail if I needed to.

Freya, I call out, *where are we going? It's getting too dark to hike.* I assume she understands me. She seems to.

I must have sensed at that moment that we had arrived at our destination because she stops about 20 yards ahead, looks back as if to acknowledge she heard me, and then takes a narrow path to the right. Once I catch up to where she left the main trail, I see a huge boulder that must have been deposited there in some prehistoric geological era. It leans at a sharp angle creating a natural stone shelter. Water drips off the tip of the jutting rock and feeds a small pool that Freya eagerly drinks from. I hold my water bottle under the dripping water, fill it up, take a long drink, and fill it up again.

I wonder if the water will make me sick.

What does it matter? For all I know, this is my new home.

I take in where Freya has brought me. Someone has not only been here before but has been here often. There is a small fire pit near the tip of the triangular stone overhang with remnants of many fires. The ground behind the fire pit is swept clear of rocks and forest debris, and further back under the rock is a sleeping pad situated at the base of the protruding triangle to protect the pad from rain. There are candles mounted on flat stones positioned around the perimeter of the area under the stone ceiling. They make their own triangle that mirrors the shape of the stone above. To my utter relief, there is a box of wooden kitchen matches next to one of the candles.

As it does in a forest, night comes swiftly. The matches, thankfully, are dry, and I light every one of the candles. There are charred spots on the stone ceiling above all of them. The flickering candlelight reflecting off crystals embedded in the rock would be romantic if Tristan were here. I still hope he will surprise me.

There's a down sleeping bag rolled up next to the pad, which I gratefully unroll, unzip, and wrap around me like a stole. If I had arrived just a little earlier, I would have had time to gather some wood for a fire. I could have started one with these matches. That is one outdoorsy skill I do have. Backyard bonfires marking special occasions is a guilty pleasure in our neighborhood, but only with dead wood lying on the ground and scrap lumber, of course, and not too much. Just enough for only a couple of hours of smoke, because, as Mom would often repeat, *nothing in excess*.

That was Apollo's creed, she informed us, carved in a stone wall of his temple at Delphi. And thousands of years later, it is the name of Rocky Balboa's arch nemesis.

Mom is always amused by such random absurdities, including the absurd popularity of the Rocky movies.

Typical, she would say, about another absurdity that caught her attention. From the sublime to the ridiculous is how it goes in our absurd time, never the other way around. Maybe when everything has been reduced to the ridiculous, the direction of things will change, and irony will return. Until then, there's nothing to do but laugh.

I know from reading Grandma's journals that Mom inherited her appreciation of irony from her mom, and it has been duly passed on to me. From grandmother to mother to daughter, so many things, material and immaterial, are passed and then passed along again as the daughter becomes a mother and then a grandmother. On and on until...

...until the end of the line, which might be me.

No pressure, right?

Will there even be a Gen Beta?

Tristan, we need to talk. I hope you're out there. I hope you find me. I hope we find each other.

It's totally dark outside this welcome shelter that Freya led me to. No fairies in the trees here. I can see her glowing eyes but nothing else. Is she standing guard? Is there something to guard against? I start talking to her, telling her how thankful I am for her help, what a wonderful place she has brought me to, how much I hope she will be there in the morning, and how incredibly happy she would make me if she could find Tristan and lead us out of the woods to the barn, how she is the most amazing fox in the world, how I wish she would stay with me from now on, guiding me, how we can keep each other company, and on and on basically repeating myself, using the same words in different combinations, until I'm nodding off. The last thing I tell her before I lie down on the pad is that it's OK to join me in the shelter, that I'd like that.

The last thought I have is that Grandma must be the person who comes here, that I'm being kept warm by her sleeping bag. I feel loved, as if the sleeping bag was left just for me. I feel safe. She knew I was coming.

Or was it the Dravidian who knew?

***

Freya is yipping.

"Is everything OK, girl?"

It's light out. Morning.

Her tail is swishing back and forth. She doesn't seem alarmed.

Maybe Tristan showed up.

I unwrap myself from the bag and duck out from under the stone overhang. The sun is up and bright, and my eyes need a moment to adjust. I don't see him.

"Tristan, are you there?"

Nothing.

Freya is on the trail now, looking back at me. She seems impatient.

"Follow you again, girl? Are you going to lead me out of here?" She yips again.

"Great! Just a minute."

I feel like I need to leave Grandma's hideaway just as it was—don't leave a trace—so I roll up the sleeping bag and put it back where I found it. Some of the candles burned all the way down overnight. I will need to replace those someday. I am rested and hopeful. Freya is yipping at me to get up and get going. She knows the way.

I'm thinking that this place might be where Grandma comes to write her journals. I can see her, pencil in hand, leaning over a notebook, writing by candlelight. No wonder she was able to get in touch with someone from another dimension. Her stone shelter is probably a portal. A place where the veil is lifted, and contact is made. Do I even want to leave?

Freya is yipping at me impatiently.

"OK, all right, I'm coming."

I walk toward her, and she practically leaps away down a path I don't remember having seen before, but how would I be able to remember? There have been so many, some traveled multiple times in both directions, but this one seems different. Then I know without a doubt it is different. Not far below I can see the edge of the forest, and beyond that is the field.

I'm as excited as Freya now and actually run past her. I want to see the unobstructed sky again. I want to see the barn. It has to be there, and it is there, just as it should be. I'm whooping as I run into the tall grass, ripping some of it out and tossing it skyward. "Freya! I yell. Thank you! Thank you!"

I look around and don't see her anywhere.

"Freya! Girl, where are you? You saved me!"

I don't see her back on the trail or in the field. I calm myself down and try to hear her yipping. I don't hear anything except a breeze.

One thing is for sure; I'm not going back into the forest to look for her, no matter how much I want her to stay with me. I tell myself she must have fox business to attend to and will show up later at the barn, but I don't believe it, not even a little bit. Why would a fox want to become my companion? She's not a pet. She's a wild animal that lives in an enchanted forest. She may have no existence beyond its boundaries.

The Dravidian may be her master.

I yell as loud as I can:

"IF YOU CAN HEAR ME, FREYA, THANK YOU!"

I hear Tristan yelling back:

"I CAN HEAR YOU LOUD AND CLEAR, PERCY! WHO'S FREYA?"

***

Tristan was waiting for me on that wonderful day when Freya led me out of the darkness into the light. He had no idea why I insisted that he had found me in the forest and then abandoned me, and ever since, I had been trying to find my way out alone. He let me babble on about how relieved I was to see the field, the barn, and him, though it was clear that he thought I was suffering from dehydration or some kind of acute psychological distress, cause unknown. Tristan was, as always, patient, and kindly listened to me without trying to intervene and get me to stop talking about what to him must have sounded like nonsense.

Once my excitement about my salvation died down and I stopped talking, he explained that he had come to the property that morning to visit me and was on the porch of the barn when he heard me yelling for Freya. His story made as little sense to me as mine had to him, but no matter. We were together.

Later, on the porch, I told him the whole amazing story of how I had been on the porch just as we were now and noticed that the forest had expanded down the hill to the field, of how I had felt compelled to go in the woods only to get lost, of the twinkling fairies providing their comforting light, of his surprising arrival in the middle of the night just as I was thinking I might get dangerously cold, and then of waking up the next morning alone, having no idea where he went, of

268

waiting for him, and finally trying again to find the way out of the woods and just getting more lost than ever.

I explained how Freya the fox appeared out of nowhere and convinced me to follow her, of how she led me to Grandma's stone shelter just as it was getting dark, and how Grandma had left a sleeping bag just for me, and then in the morning how Freya had brought me to the edge of the forest at last and then disappeared.

"I know," I said, when I finally finished my fairytale. "It's a lot to believe."

"I think you must have been a little out of your mind, Percy," was all he had to say. "But I'm glad you're here now, safe and sound."

Realizing that, for whatever reason—and clearly, reason had become something very relative and perhaps irrelevant—in his mind, he had just arrived to visit me, I stopped trying to convince him otherwise.

I stuck to the promise I made to myself when still lost: no looking back; just grab him and don't let go, which I had done more than once since our reunion. No recriminations, no questions, no being right or wrong, no trying to explain or trying to make him understand. Just accept, surrender to the flow, and live in the moment. Tristan is here, and I am here. The sun is shining. We have a chicken colony to attend to and all the eggs we can eat. There is clean spring water to drink and a pond to bathe in. We have Grandma's vegetable garden to keep alive and to keep us alive. We have everything we need and nothing more we could want.

Except maybe a baby, I thought.

I need to ask him how he feels about that.

PART THREE

THE LAST ENTRY

After your death, you will be what you were before your birth.
Arthur Schopenhauer

3.1

Everyone was sure the patriots were responsible. For weeks they had been terrorizing the neighborhood, and the explosion which leveled the library and broke every window within several blocks was assumed to be a bomb.

The impossibly loud BOOM in the middle of the night instantly woke everyone in the neighborhood. People fled their homes and gathered in the streets, where they clustered in groups, small and large, some with broken glass stuck to their shirts or nested in their hair. Some were bleeding, but no one noticed, not even those bleeding.

The confused and terrified citizens were at once mesmerized by a massive plume of fire that jetted up into the night sky higher than any structure still standing in the vicinity of the blast. The flame instantly incinerated anything within its white-hot aura.

The spectators gazed at the inferno in awe and dread. It seemed to be coming straight out of the center of the earth, straight from hell.

The venerable Carnegie library, the center of the neighborhood, had been reduced to a glowing red pile of bricks. The flame, drawing everyone to it, roared out of the rubble. If people had been able to look at the column of fire dispassionately, instead of with fearful wonder, they might have remarked that it looked exactly like what it was: a great quantity of natural gas on fire. In an instant, when the gas had been lit, the old edifice had been blown apart and transformed into a giant stove top with all its burners turned up as high as they could go.

A gas line that ran under the library had sprung a tiny leak where it had been capped years ago, a tiny part of infrastructure long abandoned and forgotten. Gas had been accumulating under the building for who knows how long.

After investigation, it became clear that the explosion had not been caused by a bomb manufactured and planted by patriots. The most widely accepted theory then became that no one had known about the gas leak, and the explosion had been caused by a random person walking by tossing aside a still-burning cigarette which ignited the fumes trapped under the library.

No matter the lack of evidence, the most paranoid in the neighborhood remained stubbornly convinced the disaster had been orchestrated by the patriots, who, knowing about the leak—or worse, creating it—waited for their chance at a moment of insane glory in the 100 years war, and then took it.

There was no way to prove anything, so the event eventually became known as The Accident.

3.2

Ursula couldn't contain her irritation over the ever-annoying confusion between The Library as neighborhood and the library as building when she heard her husband trying to tell her something, and all she heard was the word 'library.'

Disoriented and groggy, she snapped at him. "Which fucking library? What are you saying, Dion?"

He was on the phone with someone. Ursula glanced at the alarm clock: 2:15 am, the middle of the night.

"Both, Ursula. The building and the neighborhood. It's a disaster. You can see the fire from here. I think if you went outside, you would feel the heat. It's huge."

"Who are you talking to?"

"It's Zephyr. There was an explosion at the library. He thinks patriots set off a bomb."

"A bomb? What?"

Dion handed his phone over. Zephyr was screaming in her ear.

"Ursula, they've bombed the library! It's horrible! It's..."

Even though Zephyr was shouting, she could barely hear him over the commotion in the background. It sounded as if the entire neighborhood was there with him, loudly talking all at once, yelling, running back and forth past him.

Everyone sounded scared. Sirens were strobing in and out nonstop. She could hear the first responders attempting to gain control of the chaos shouting through megaphones, yelling at people to get back, to move away, to stop.

Ursula was wide awake now and shouting back at him. "What about Iris and Persephone?! Zephyr!! Are they OK?! Zephyr!!

All she could hear was the swelling sound of the crowd in the background, an ocean of noise, as if she had a shell, not a phone, next to her ear.

"Zephyr... Are you there?! Are they OK?! Please... Zephyr!" He wasn't answering. He must have dropped his phone.

She grabbed the car keys and ran out the door.

**

In shock, Ursula stood with Zephyr and Tristan, watching the gas-fueled flame erupting from the ruins of the library. It was a macabre fountain of fire that cruelly taunted them with its irony. The occupation of the library had been the inspirational beginning of their ZeroG neighborhood. The old building was the neighborhood's heart, and it was being destroyed by an uncontrollable conflagration of gas.

They stood together, saying nothing, sobbing, taking shaky breaths, and then sobbing again, not able to think, waiting for a reason not to stand there. Not even the sunrise prompted them to move. What reason could there be to move? Move where? To do what?

They would have to move, though. The damage would have to be dealt with. Work crews would arrive during the day to begin the long process of reclamation. They wouldn't be allowed to just stand in the street indefinitely, staring at the site of the tragedy. They would be in the way. They would be in danger from buildings threatening to collapse.

Just about everyone who had watched with them through the night had filed away, many whispering their condolences as they passed by. Condolences that didn't register and wouldn't for some time. They would be forced to file away, too, but thankfully, they wouldn't have to think in order to move. Thinking would induce overwhelming, paralyzing emotions. Thinking and feeling would have to be carefully calibrated over time. Doled out in manageable interludes.

They knew this without thinking.

The firefighters eventually located the source of the gas leak, and the burning fountain was turned off, drained of its fuel. Fire in the surrounding area was contained for the most part. What remained in that terrible morning after was a gaping wound, an entire block reduced to ashes and bricks. Windows were shattered up and down the streets of the neighborhood, a neighborhood that might have to be renamed now, if it still existed.

Ursula was the first to move. She turned away from the smoldering wound, took Zephyr by his arm, and pulled him to her. Tristan followed, and the three of them held each other for a long time, their foreheads meeting in the huddle, helping to keep them upright. They were sharing the beginning of a profound grief they would endure for the rest of their lives.

It was not only Iris and Persephone who had been trapped in the basement of the library. Raven had been there, too.

When they felt able to stand on their own and broke from the embrace, Ursula was the first to say something, the first words any of them had spoken since they had come together as witnesses the night before.

I will tell Mom.

Zephyr and Tristan nodded, and each of them walked away in a different direction, to where their beds were, to try to sleep, the only way to escape the pain that threatened to overwhelm them.

When she finally came home late the next morning, Dion didn't say anything. What could he say that would make sense, that would somehow help? He put his arms around his wife and guided her to the couch. Leaning back against a cushion, eyes closed, Ursula let out a long, strangled sigh. She had nothing to say either.

Before long, she was asleep, her tear-stained face a mask from an ancient Greek play. Dion stayed with her until she was deeply unconscious, then stretched her limp body out and covered her with a blanket.

She woke up many hours later, sometime in the night, and saw Dion across from her, asleep in his favorite recliner, keeping vigil. She didn't want to wake up then or ever. Waking up meant thinking and feeling.

She closed her eyes and wished for oblivion.

3.3

A phone call would not do, and her mom wouldn't answer anyway, so Ursula drove alone to the property to tell her the terrible news in person. Her survivor's guilt, on top of the grief at losing her siblings and niece, the last of their family's line, was almost unbearable.

She needed her mom more than she thought she would ever need her, considering they were practically estranged. As only children can know, Ursula had always been aware she was the least favorite child; then, after grown-up Ursula married Dion and moved to Birnum Wood, her mom joined with the rest of the family in judging her decision a betrayal.

Marrying him made her a pariah. She begrudged them all for turning against her and Dion for what she considered nothing but petty political reasons, but her mom's rejection was what broke her heart. She had never forgiven her for refusing to honor her choice, a choice made freely as an adult. It was as if her mom's love for her was based on what side she took in the 100 years civil war. Unconditional love it was not.

If she had ever confronted her parents or her siblings with her feelings, she had no doubt they would have self-righteously protested, claiming their rejection of Dion was not just politics, it was principle, as if they occupied some moral high ground that conferred on them the right to judge, to which she would have said, *Bullshit, you never even tried to get to know him. You didn't give him a chance, just like you never gave me a chance because I was different. I didn't think like you. I wasn't keen on joining the ZG revolution. I didn't think it was right to demonize people who didn't have the same perspective and beliefs as you. People who just wanted to live their lives in whatever comfort they could manage. People like me. I guess family doesn't have the same meaning for you as it does for me.*

She never gave herself a chance to say those lines. Once or twice she had mustered the courage to challenge them but then backed off. Her cowardice was just another thing to regret now, along with all the other regrets—the *why didn't I's?* and *I should have's*—that started piling up after The Accident. Oppressed by the weight of regret, she felt like she might implode at any moment. She would blink and be gone forever.

"I'm ready," she had told Dion, standing at the door, car keys in hand. "My mom needs to know what happened, and I need to be with her."

While driving to the property and then walking the trail from the highway to the barn, Ursula obsessively rehearsed what she would say, trying various combinations of words, imagining the scene with her mom over and over again. None of the words she practiced in her head seemed right, and the scenes she visualized all ended with her feeling worse than she already felt, her mom looking at her as if she was somehow to blame for the tragedy.

She found it impossible to imagine her mother giving her the comfort she craved because her guilt wouldn't let her imagine it. The guilt which tormented her insisted she didn't deserve comfort—she should have died with everyone else. Her mom would agree, of course. Why was she, Ursula, of all the children, the one to be spared?

Survivor's guilt means torturing yourself with that pointless, unanswerable question.

Her feelings were a clusterfuck of intense emotions from sadness to anger to guilt and resentment. Each took its turn being the dominant emotion of the hour. She'd had enough therapy over the years to know she had to give herself a break, or she might never recover from the grief.

She had to forgive herself. Emotions were obviously going to be intense, the guilt excruciating, and there was nothing she could do about it. All she could count on was time doing its healing magic. She wasn't exactly young anymore. She hoped there was enough time left in her life for the magic to work.

A little smile formed as she remembered talking with her sibs about how their perceptions of age were distorted by their mom being so old. Pushing 70 for her and her sibs was like pushing 50 for all the other people who didn't have a century-old parent. They had not been given the opportunity to live their lives without parents, to consider their own mortality, so long as their mom continued to live on, seemingly immortal.

It felt strange to smile, but that was another thing she would need to do besides forgive herself: she would need to allow herself to smile, even laugh in time.

And then she was there at the property, looking at the side of the barn.

She had imagined in the car and then on the trail the beginning of the scene that she anticipated was about to occur: her mom sitting in her chair on the porch, surprised to see her, springing up and rushing over to hug her, saying how glad she was that she had come—just her, Ursula—how wonderful that she had come on her own...

...but Helen wasn't there, and she instantly felt relieved that the moment of truth had been postponed. She plopped down in the porch chair that her mom was supposed to have been sitting in.

It was a sunny afternoon. Chances were her mom was outside, but she pushed open the heavy door built long ago to keep horses corralled and poked her head inside. The barn felt abandoned. Cold and still. Quiet.

"Mom?" No answer. "It's Ursula…"

She went back out to the porch and looked up and down the field. There was nothing to see but tall grass and a few birds pecking for seeds.

She cupped her hands and yelled MAW… UM a few times and only got a faint echo back.

The pond was the logical spot to check next. On the well-worn path there, she remembered walking with her siblings to go swimming on a day just like today. They had all come in Ursula's car to visit. They knew Helen didn't like surprises, but they had surprised her on her 85th birthday, and she seemed sincerely happy they had. That day, unlike most days, she had been in the mood to be social, to party with her family. They knew it could easily have gone the other way, so they were in great spirits, relieved they had made their mom happy on her birthday instead of annoyed.

But Helen wasn't at the pond floating on her back as she liked to do.

Ursula sat in her mom's green plastic meditation chair and watched the ducks like living pendulums dipping their beaks in the water without cease: down, up, down, up, gulp, shake a tail feather, repeat. She realized she was again glad not to have encountered her mom because no matter how many times she had run lines, she still had no idea what she would end up saying in the moment, if anything at all.

Sitting there by the pond, in her mom's meditation chair, she was getting increasingly anxious about the reception she would get when Helen returned and encountered her daughter, the messenger tasked with reporting that the entire family had died in a terrible accident.

Everyone, that is, except for her, Ursula, the traitor.

She feared that her anxiety would render her speechless when face to face with her mom.

Don't shoot the messenger, OK, Mom? It's not my fault that I'm the only one left. I wish I could trade places with any one of them.

She really did wish that.

There was nothing else to do but go back to the barn, but Ursula stayed in the chair, stalling, afraid to go back. What if Helen's reaction was as she imagined? Her mom bitter and angry, blaming her for being the sole survivor. She didn't think she could cope with that. She might break down and either let loose a lifetime of resentment and recriminations in a burst of passive aggression or run away back to her car, crying her eyes out.

C'mon, Ursula. Your mom is waiting. You have no right to keep the truth from her, no matter how painful for her and for you. You know she can take it. You're the one who's struggling. Give her a chance to help you. She's your mom. She loves you in her own way. Get your shit together.

282

She knew deep down that her mom loved her, but all her life, she had struggled to believe it, convincing herself that she loved Raven and Iris so much that there was little, if any, love left over for her.

It was mid-afternoon when she returned to the barn. She didn't encounter Helen on the way back, and she wasn't on the porch. Ursula stopped to survey the field one more time and then went inside for some water. She had tried Helen's phone multiple times, and it was either dead or turned off, as usual.

Where could she be?

Sitting at the old picnic table wedged in between two stalls, drinking a glass of water, she saw a letter, or what looked like a letter, a white legal envelope with something written on it in a ridiculously fancy font:

FOR MY CHILDREN

She hadn't noticed it when she had opened the door before, but then she hadn't taken the time to look around. She picked up the envelope. She could feel the folded paper inside.

It must be a note from Mom telling us where she is.

Helen might very well have expected a visit because none of them had been out to see her in at least two months. Not even Raven, who tried to check in on her once a month, had made the trip out on his bike.

Still, it was weird. Why not just leave a short note stuck to the door? It wasn't like her mom to be so formal. The tone of **for my children** was not her style. When had she ever addressed them as 'my children?'

The weird vibes she was getting from the letter began to make her nervous. She had searched for her mom for several hours, sure that at some point she would have found her, and now here, suddenly, was this strange letter that she was increasingly convinced had not been there when she first arrived.

What was going on?

She was afraid to open it. She was afraid, even, to touch it.

For my children...what the hell?

She had actually never visited her mom by herself. She had never been alone in the barn, alone on the property, walking around, just her and the creatures who live there, whatever they were. She knew there were the usual rodents and birds. The chickens at the colony, the ducks on the pond. Probably snakes and spiders. No one had ever seen a bear. Coyotes roamed through now and then. Deer were rarely sighted. There was nothing to be afraid of.

Get a fucking grip, Ursula! Mom left a note. What is your problem?

The day was moving along, the sun was going down, and her mom was not there. Only the envelope was there, the phrase 'for my children' now practically throbbing whenever she glanced at it. Each time she looked, the words seemed to get larger, and somehow brighter, even though they were written in deep black ink.

That letter is going to start talking to me. It's going to start chanting, 'read me.'

Nothing was going as expected. Nothing. Sitting there by herself at the picnic table in her mom's dimly lit barn, she felt like she was floating in space, completely untethered, destination the nearest black hole.

I need to calm down.

She called Dion, but he didn't pick up. Then she called Zephyr, who did answer. Did he know where Helen might be?

No, he didn't.

She told him about the mysterious letter and asked him what he thought she should do. He said, "Read it, of course. Why are you even calling me about this?"

Talking to Zephyr helped. He was a sensible man. She trusted his judgement. He didn't seem at all mystified that there would be a letter addressed to 'my children'—two of whom had just died in a horrible accident—waiting for her at the barn.

He had said matter-of-factly, "Just see what it's about. What else can you do?" And she had told him, "Thanks, Zeph. I'll let you know how it goes with Mom when she shows up, and I've given her the terrible news."

He's right. Just see what it's about. It's not like I have a choice. Mom wrote this for us to read. I'm one of her children, the only one living. I'm here, so it's up to me.

She carefully opened the envelope without causing even the tiniest of rips and gingerly took the letter out, the folded page clamped between her thumb and index finger. She couldn't remember ever having received a handwritten letter from anyone. No one wrote letters anymore to anyone.

DEAR KIDS,

… is how it started. How could anyone even write something in this font? It was like calligraphy. The letter actually didn't seem handwritten. Each written line had a blank line after it. All the words were perfectly formed and looked as if they had been stamped on the page by a machine.

I'M SORRY I'M NOT HERE.

I'M ON A MOUNTAIN IN INDIA. A SACRED PLACE.

I CAME HERE TO DIE. THE GURU IS GOING TO GUIDE ME.

PLEASE DON'T WORRY, AND PLEASE FORGIVE ME.

THIS IS SOMETHING I NEEDED TO DO.

YOU MAY UNDERSTAND WHEN THE TIME COMES.

IT'S MY KARMA TO DIE HERE.

IT'S YOUR KARMA TO HAVE A MOM WHO HAS THAT KARMA.

WE ALL SHARE THE KARMA WE ALL CREATE.

IT'S ALL ONE.

NOW I HAVE A BIG REQUEST.

I WANT THE PROPERTY BEQUEATHED TO TRISTAN AND PERCY.

THEY ARE THE FUTURE. PLEASE GIVE THEM A CHANCE FOR A GOOD LIFE.

THE PROPERTY IS PROTECTED. THEY WILL BE PROTECTED.

YOU PROBABLY THINK I'M CRAZY.

FORGIVE MY CRAZINESS.

BETTER YET, APPRECIATE MY CRAZINESS.

I LOVE YOU.

MOM

This was not how she had imagined it was going to go when she was rehearsing her lines on the way there.

She couldn't remember the last time her mom had said 'I love you' to her. She needed to hear it, even if it was only printed on a piece of paper as the closing of a letter. When she read it, she could hear Helen saying it inside her head. It was nice to hear, but after replaying in her mind several times the sound of her mother saying, 'I love you,' her customary bitterness kicked in.

Karma, yeah. Don't you think we know, Mom? You dragged us kids to meet with your guru as long as you could, and we heard all about karma from her. Then we heard about it from you and Dad, and then from Raven. And all things considered, I have to say it does make sense. More sense than heaven and hell. So what? Just because it's plausible doesn't make it a reality. I don't believe in karma and reincarnation. I don't believe that karma is the law of the universe. I believe the law is simple: you live, and then you die. That's it. It's always all about you, isn't it, Mom? Run away to the property to live by yourself after Dad dies, and then run away to some exotic place to die and excuse your selfishness by invoking karma. Nice.

In a perverse way, it actually *was* comforting reading this letter from her mom, hearing her voice in her head, and she, Ursula, reacting in her usual way. She was experiencing once more her part in their well-established mother-daughter relationship, and she had the disquieting thought that she was probably more comforted by this letter than she would have been if she had had a live conversation with her mom about The Accident. That could have easily gone sideways. And quickly.

At least the anxiety that had built up over the day was gone.

If her mom was still alive and had somehow heard about The Accident up on her holy mountain, would she have even blinked an eye? When she learned her daughter and granddaughter had died, and Raven, too, buried under the books and bricks of the library, would she have interrupted her meditation to mourn them? Would she have thought of her lone surviving daughter and how she was doing?

She knew why her mom hadn't told them her plans and left this letter instead. She was afraid they would try to stop her. She made sure not to give them any details about where she'd gone so they wouldn't try to rescue her from whatever cult she had joined. A death cult, from the sounds of it.

No doubt there would be some grand ceremony upon her mom's death with drums and gongs and dancing while her body burned at the top of a flaming pyre. The guru would be there lost in some ecstatic state, possessed by the spirit, eyes wide, chanting prayers or spells or instructions or whatever it was he did to play his part in providing his help, bestowing guidance to the soul now released from its body.

How was it possible that dying like this would be the karma of a white woman librarian born in the 1950s in a small town in America?

One thing Ursula saw very clearly is that if karma indeed is a thing, it often has bizarre results.

Raven and Iris might have accepted their mom's decision, but she wouldn't have. She would have gone to India with Dion to try to bring her home. They would have found out where all the sacred mountains are and traveled to each one. And who is *the guru*, anyway? Her guru had died years ago, around the time Kaspar had had his stroke. Could she actually be referring to her old guru back from the dead coming to help her die? It was all too much to process, and besides, a waste of time. There was no way to make sense of it because it was nonsense.

She could hear her mom telling her it was her karma to have to deal with a mother like her. She imagined her mom mounting the pyre where her body would be immolated, turning around and saying to her: *See, you are supposed to learn from this. That's the whole point of karma. You learn. You grow. You get closer to the goal.*

And she bitterly replying: *It really sucks that I didn't get to say goodbye to my brother, my sister, and my niece. Now I don't get to say goodbye to you, either. And what, exactly, am I supposed to learn from that? That karma is a bitch?*

Fully agitated now by the letter, every line of it, one after another, running through her mind, Ursula went out to the porch and sat in one of the Adirondack chairs. What now? She hadn't expected having to deal with this. She couldn't even put together in her mind what this was. Her mom had gone to India to die under the guidance of the guru of a death cult. How the hell had she traveled there? Where did she get the money for a plane ticket to India? Who took her to the airport?

Was she surprised by any of it? Not really. It would only be surprising to those who didn't know her mother. At least it wasn't a suicide note, though, in a way, it read like one.

Now that she was outside in the light of the afternoon and had some distance from the letter, she thought for the first time about its authenticity. Was it really a letter from her mom? The font was bizarre. What had her mom used to write it? She wondered if the letter could serve as a will and be considered legally binding. It wasn't signed and dated. Would the property actually go to Tristan now?

The tone of it was familiar, though, and the narcissism all too familiar: *I love you, kids, but I'm not going to give you the satisfaction of providing care for your old mother in her last years. I'm not going to give you a chance to work out your feelings, to say goodbye, to bury (or burn) me because I've decided to go to India to die under the direction of the guru. And I'm so grateful, but not to you, to him (or her). I wouldn't want to give you the opportunity to feel wanted or needed. To benefit from the healing you might experience from that—Oh, and by the way, even if some of you are interested in the family property, will you please give it to Percy and Tristan? It's my dying wish.*

One good thing resulted from the letter: she was angry, and that meant progress in the steps to overcome grief. What else could she expect from a *Dear Kids* letter from her mom?

No reason to be surprised but every reason to be hurt.

For all she knew, her mom had already died.

I wonder what she thinks she'll be reborn as? she snarked to herself.

3.4

"You're not alone, Ursula."

Startled, she scrambles up from her chair on the barn porch. A young woman, Persephone's age, is sitting in the chair next to her, looking at her, smiling openly as if they already know each other.

"Who...? What did you say?"

"I said you're not alone."

"Well, yeah. I was, but now you're here."

The woman laughs. "What I mean is, you're never alone."

Ursula gives her the once-over. "I don't know how you managed to sneak up on me like that, but I don't appreciate it."

"Sorry. I guess I don't make much noise." The woman is still smiling despite Ursula's rude reception.

"I'm Astrid..." she offers, "a friend of Helen's. She asked me to look after the place."

"Then you know where my mom went."

Ursula is meeting Astrid's eyes now that she has settled back down in the chair and is looking directly at her visitor.

She's pretty. Those hazel eyes.

"Not exactly. I couldn't point it out on a map, if that's what you mean...

...You're angry," Astrid adds abruptly.

"Yeah, I am. I just learned my mom went to India to die."

"You feel betrayed."

"Who wouldn't?" Ursula spits out. "And would you mind not telling me how I feel? Who are you to tell me what I'm feeling? You have no idea! What are you doing here, anyway?"

Astrid gets up from her chair and stands facing Ursula. She's so short. She can't be more than five feet tall. She looks like a middle-school girl with those pigtails.

"Can I give you a hug?"

Ursula coughs out a nervous laugh. "You want to give me a hug?"

"It will do you good, Ursula. Trust me."

Ursula realizes she has not introduced herself. How does this woman know her name? Had her mom been talking about the family with her? Then inexplicably, her habitual suspicions are overwritten by an overwhelming wish to be hugged by this mysterious pixie standing in front of her. She has perhaps never wanted anything more in her life.

"OK... Sure... Why not?"

She gets back up from her chair and holds her arms open as if to say, now what?

Astrid walks into them, circles her arms around Ursula, and rests her head on her chest. The hug evolves quickly from a tentative exploration of just how tight would be appropriate to full-on squeezing each other as if they are old friends who hadn't seen each other in years.

Ursula is happy to stay in the embrace as long as Astrid is willing. Her hair has a pleasant smell of pine that complements the warm current of energy flowing between them. Each moment that goes by dissolves a bit of Ursula's anger and relieves some of her pain. Ursula sighs. When was the last time she felt contentment?

Astrid gradually releases her grip enough to pull back slightly and look up at Ursula.

"See? You aren't alone. All you need is a hug from someone you've never met to realize that."

Astrid smiles cheerfully while looking into Ursula's eyes. Ursula mumbles, "thank you."

With their arms still loosely around each other, resting on each other's hips, they stand together, feeling an intimate glow that normally would have made Ursula nervous, but in that moment is welcome. Since The Accident, she had withdrawn from life. Pulled the plug and disconnected. She had been sleeping 12 hours a day and dreading the 12 hours she forced herself to be awake. It feels good to be close to someone, to feel something positive instead of the negative emotions the black hole of grief tears out of her in the waking hours.

Eventually, they let go of each other and sit back down in the porch chairs. Ursula's initial paranoia gone, she now regards Astrid as a guest—even a friend—rather than as an intruder. She wonders if she should say something...

"Thanks, again, Astrid," she stammers. "You were right about the hug."

"Feel better?"

"Much better...I've been a mess."

"Of course, you have! You have every reason to be. Give yourself a break."

"That's what I tell myself."

Astrid must know what happened. How does she know about The Accident?

***

The sun is going down, and Ursula knows that before long she will need to start hiking back to the car to drive home to Birnum Wood; either that or spend the night at the property.

She doesn't want to leave Astrid's comforting presence only to return to the scene of her grief.

"It's getting late, Astrid. I really need to get going," she offers hesitantly.

Ursula is looking at Astrid, expecting a response that doesn't come, and if she were able at the moment to understand what she wanted, she would realize she is hoping that Astrid will suggest they spend the night together in the barn.

"I hope I'll see you next time I come."

"I'll be around. I promised your mom."

Ursula continues to stall, waiting for Astrid to suggest she just stay...

"You and Mom are...close?"

Astrid suddenly looks very concerned.

"Ursula, I'm so sorry. I thought you knew."

"Knew what?"

"Your mom..."

✱✱✱

"It's dark and getting cold. We should go inside."

Astrid offers her hand to Ursula and leads her into the barn to the couch.

"Tea?"

She starts a fire in the stove, and though Ursula has not said yes or no, she makes some herbal tea and brings it over to her.

Ursula is sniffling, taking deep breaths, and exhaling slowly.

"I'll sit here with you, all right?"

Ursula sips the tea and nods. "I have to let Dion know I'm spending the night," she mumbles.

✱✱✱

"It's OK to lie down," Astrid says, sliding to the end of the couch to make room.

Ursula puts her head down on a pillow next to Astrid and curls her legs up to fit on the couch. Astrid covers her with a blanket and gently rubs her back. Ursula feels like a child whose only need is to feel loved, and Astrid seems to understand that, patiently caring for her, not expecting or asking for anything.

"Do you want to sleep?"

"I don't think I can."

"How about if I talk then? Would that be all right?"

"Sure."

"If you want me to stop, just say 'stop.'"

"OK."

"You just lost your family. Who wouldn't be feeling alone and abandoned?"

Yes, who wouldn't?

She replays in her mind Astrid telling her that Helen had died.

"How do you know what happened to my mom?"

"A friend in India."

This is the moment of absolute loneliness for her. A friend in India had told Astrid that Helen had died, and she, the only surviving daughter, was just now finding out.

"You're never alone, Ursula. You're a bead connected to an infinite string of human beads."

By now Ursula is not surprised by Astrid's insight into what she is feeling, but instead of crying, she has to laugh.

"You mean 'beings.'"

"Well, yes and no. I meant to use the word beads. Our human souls are beads connected by the eternal string of time, OK?"

Astrid laughs and admits, "You're right. It's pretty funny."

Ursula realizes how familiar it feels to be lectured like this—tortured metaphors always a feature not a bug. It is almost as if Astrid is a member of her family, a long-lost sister. No wonder she and her mom were friends.

The human bead string evokes in her imagination a comical image of beads with faces, the string of faces stretching out to the end of the universe and back, some smiling, some frowning, some excited, some bored. The possible expressions are... well, infinite.

"You're laughing, Ursula."

"I know. It feels strange...It's just that image of the human beads. Mom and Raven should be here for this. They love this shit. You all could make a night of it just by working out all the nuances of this metaphor."

Ursula smiles. "Sorry, Astrid, no offense."

"Do you want me to keep on with this shit, or does it annoy you?"

"It's fine. It feels good to laugh, so keep going, please. This is the kind of conversation we all used to have right here on this couch, drinking tea. It's nostalgic. It's almost heartwarming. The family would go on and on about something or other that no one but them would ever think about, much less talk about, and they'd come up with metaphors just like yours."

"Which made you laugh like now?"

"Not laugh laugh like human beads does."

Ursula, remembering, laughed again. "I didn't laugh so much as put on a self-satisfied, I-know-better smirk. I thought their speculating was silly, and sometimes annoying if they were trying extra hard to get me to understand something I had no interest in understanding."

"If you're using words, all you have to work with are metaphors."

"I suppose so."

"Should I go on?"

"Go ahead, but don't say you weren't warned if I smirk."

"Forgive me, OK, if this is not the right time to bring this up, but why be devasted by death? I don't mean just you. Everyone. If there's life, there has to be death. Can't have one without the other, but death is not an end. It's a transition... ...Should I stop?"

Ursula shakes her head.

"When you're born, the light comes on. When you die, the light goes out. On to off to on to off, forever, a never-ending toggle switch. Death and birth are just the positions between on and off."

"Yeah, I've heard this before, but how I see it is I get turned on, my light shines for a while, and then my bulb burns out. It does not come back on. It's toast."

"Who flips the switch? What is the bulb? What shines?"

"Stop....I have to tell you something. I used to hate it when everyone in the family but me got all wrapped up in this nonsense. I was always the odd one out—practical, mundane, unimaginative Ursula—but I have to admit that with you right now, I'm kind of enjoying it. Kind of. My enjoyment may not last, though."

"A welcome distraction..."

"Maybe."

"Maybe it's just that you're willing to accept the nonsense from me but not from them."

"Could be. After we hugged, I felt so much trust between us. And it went both ways, right? At least, that's what it felt like."

"Imagine feeling that trust with your mom and the rest of your family."

"I don't know if I can."

"Do it now. Imagine one of these nonsensical conversations you used to have with your family, but you're feeling this trust."

After some false starts, Ursula manages to do as suggested. She is surprised by the warm feelings it brings up.

"I do feel different."

"Because you're not separating yourself from them. It feels good because, in reality, you aren't separate. You never were."

Ursula doesn't say anything, but she understands. She experienced the difference in her imagination.

"Can you imagine believing your mom loved you without having to qualify it with she loved you the least?"

"That's probably not possible."

"Can you forgive her for all the things you blame her for?"

"Stop."

***

After that first night, when she found out her mom had died, Ursula never called Dion again. When she was with Astrid, it seemed as if it didn't matter if Dion was worried or even if she never saw him again. An attitude like that should have been unthinkable, but sequestered in the barn with Astrid, Ursula was entertaining many previously unthinkable thoughts and imagining what used to be unimaginable.

She would open her eyes after another dreamless sleep and be lying on the couch, her head on Astrid's lap. Other times, she might be in Helen's bed, and Astrid would be standing there with a cup of coffee ready for her. Or tea. Or even scrambled eggs. She would be sprawled in a chair on the porch with a blanket around her, and she would hear Astrid in the barn singing to herself in a language she didn't recognize. They would sit together at the pond or under one of the old-growth trees in the woods. They would talk, and their conversation was like call and response, Astrid doing the calling and Ursula the responding.

During this time with Astrid, she came to forgive her mom for all the times she had felt ignored by her, slighted and dismissed. For not living up to her expectations of who a mom should be, of how a mom should act. For not being that interested in family ties and obligations. For countless other things that now seemed entirely unimportant. She climbed the mountain of her personal regrets and neurotic self-doubts and, once at the top, managed to forgive herself for everything without exception. She gained an understanding of the true nature of love, which is simply that it has no conditions. At all.

Ursula sometimes was concerned about not being able to remember how she had even come to be there with Astrid, how it was that Astrid was there every time she woke up, and how it was that they both stayed at the barn together without ever discussing it, but that concern faded away. Ursula was satisfied with telling herself that it had just happened.

She had no desire to leave as long as Astrid was there every time she opened her eyes and every time she closed them.

Astrid said one day, "Your mom was very brave."

This was how their last conversation began.

"How so?"

"She wasn't afraid to do what she needed to do. She wasn't afraid to commit. She had faith."

"Like, get away from all of us and live like a hermit?"

"Just so," Astrid said, smiling.

"She wouldn't even keep her phone charged. It was so annoying!"

"You know your mom. She was not interested in compromising or giving in, even when it came to her death. She was afraid of death, but she didn't let fear stop her from making the most of it."

"The most of what?"

"The moment of death. There's no moment in life more important."

"That's pretty hard to grasp, since death is the end of life."

"Maybe I should say it's just as important as the moment of birth."

"Stop....I can tell that you're about to talk about karma and reincarnation now."

Astrid didn't respond.

"No one ever explained it to me. Why must there be karma?"

"There's free will, so there has to be karma. If everything is preordained, there's no need for karma."

"Keep talking."

"Free will means having a choice. But in order to have a choice, there has to be a consequence; otherwise, the choice doesn't matter. It's meaningless. If a choice doesn't matter, then it's not really a choice. It's just a random action that results in nothing. Without karma, there is no reason for any action, no reason for anything at all. There is no reason, period."

"It seems to me that a lot of our choices are just random, but still, we make them freely. We're free to be random."

"Sure. True. And the karmic consequence is we keep on dying and getting reborn to try again to realize what we are born to do and what the reason is. Why we have been blessed with consciousness and free will. In an eternal universe, there's always another chance, another choice. No matter how many random choices are made, in the end, because of karma, they result in something. So, again, like karma and free will, another bound pair: if there is karma, there has to be reincarnation."

"OK, I'll bite. So what are we born to do?"

"Realize who we are."

"I knew it! This dead end is where so many family talks would end, and I would always say, *why does realizing who we are matter at all? Who actually cares who we are?* How would realizing who we are change the fact that there's nothing after death? When I die, that's it. Lights out. Toggle switch off forever. The end, fade to black."

"When you die, Ursula, what dies?"

"I die."

"What is this 'I?'"

"Me."

"Who is me?"

"Stop."

Ursula had been down this road before so many times with her family, especially her mom. She didn't want to go there again. She was surprised and disconcerted that Astrid was challenging her like this.

"Honestly, Astrid, your questions are pointless, and your answers are really nothing but cliches now. Can we please change the subject?"

"If not who, then what is me?"

"Stop....How about, what the hell *are* you, Astrid? A supernatural therapist who works for free? My dream mother and perfect friend?"

"I am what you are."

"No, you're not."

"I am who you are. We are all one, not separate."

"Stop. Just stop."

Astrid seemed determined to disturb her. She was threatening the soothing idyll they had enjoyed for so long. Ursula did not want it to end. Why was Astrid trying to end it?

"I'm sorry, Ursula, but everything changes, even here."

"Here? The barn?"

"Here, where you've had a well-deserved rest before moving on."

***

Ursula opens her eyes. She is lying next to Iris in her mom's bed in the barn. She feels a pleasant wave of affection for Iris wash over her as she watches her twitch in her sleep, dreaming about something. She can hear Persephone and Raven talking outside the stall while they get the coffee going.

"It's time to wake up the sleepyheads," her mom announces, standing at the stall door, holding a basket.

"I've got eggs."

3.5

While leaving the library the night of The Accident, after the long meeting with her siblings about what to do about mom, Ursula was caught in the white-hot blast as she was crossing the street to her car.

She suffered multiple internal injuries and severe brain damage. She never regained consciousness and passed away in the hospital ICU where Zephyr and Dion kept a constant vigil for several days.

Even though Zephyr was not 'family'—at least on paper—he felt he owed it to Iris and Persephone to step up and take responsibility for informing Helen about the tragedy since Dion had made it clear that as far as he was concerned, he was done with the Banis family.

Someone needed to travel to the property and tell Helen what had happened.

Legally speaking, as Ursula's widow, Dion was the only living member of the family besides Helen, but he was not going to get involved with issues concerning care for his mother-in-law and the ultimate fate of the family property unless forced to.

He thought the family had cursed him and Ursula. *If she had just left that god-damned library two seconds earlier,* he bitterly lamented to Zephyr. *And hell if I know why she was there so late. They must have been drinking some of that horrible*

Library homebrew. They asked her to come over there for dinner to talk about Helen. They were worried about her. They thought the three of them should set up more frequent visits. Make a plan. Get out a calendar and commit to dates. That woman is so selfish. All she has to do is keep her fucking phone charged and answer it, but no, she won't even do that. She would rather let them worry about her, force them to devise ways to provide care for her, make them take the trip out to see her. She doesn't give a shit about them.

Zephyr didn't share Dion's extreme animus toward Helen, but he empathized. She did follow the beat of her own drum, there was no question about that, and he couldn't deny it was maddening not to be able to reach Helen by phone, but Dion was wrong about her not loving her children. Dion didn't have a clue about the love a mother feels for her children.

She hates me. They all did. I don't want anything to do with her, he ranted to Zephyr. Go ahead and take Ursula's car out there to tell her what happened. I can't do it. I won't. As far as I'm concerned, she's to blame.

***

Zephyr felt a little spooked as he drove to the property in Ursula's car and extremely nervous about bringing Helen the horrific news. There was no good way to deliver such a blow. Every way would be equally bad. He had his defenses built up to protect him from the debilitating grief of losing Iris and Percy, not to mention his best friend. He was afraid that seeing Helen and talking about what happened would destroy those much-needed defenses. Like in a Jenga game, the defenses would have to come down slowly and in carefully chosen pieces. He knew there was a good chance they would remain in place for the rest of his life. He might not have the courage to remove even one piece.

His heart was beating double-time as he walked up onto the barn porch and pushed open the door.

"Helen? Helen, are you here?"

He could already tell she wasn't, but he still had to go through the motions of calling for her. There were no obvious signs of anyone having been in the barn recently, and he was now not just a little spooked. He was feeling outright dread.

Helen was 100 years old. No one in the family had been out to see her for a long time, which was what had prompted the fateful meeting at the library. He didn't want to imagine how he might feel if he found her lying dead somewhere.

Then he saw the envelope on the table.

By the time he had finished reading the letter, slowly, line by line, Zephyr's heart had sunk to the bottom of his stomach. He felt sick. The phrase *a sickness unto death* came to mind. He had no idea where it came from—the depths of his unconscious, he supposed—but he felt the sickness unto death in the pit of his stomach, the pit that was occupied by his weary heart, and he knew what it was, this sickness. It was despair.

Lose all hope ye who enter here. His unconscious was serving up material for his blank mind. He knew this famous line was about entering hell, or a description of what hell actually was: the place where there is no hope, the place of despair. The world was going to hell, the neighborhood destroyed, and his loved ones were dead: What was left but despair?

Hope was left, and he knew he must not lose it. Helen's dying request expressed her hope for the future. Tristan and Persephone *were* the future she had written.

Now just Tristan. He wondered how Tristan would feel about fulfilling Helen's wish without Percy.

The thought of Tristan making a life here did give him hope. Helen said the property was protected and would be protected. He had no idea what she meant, but he believed her. Or he wanted to believe her because he had a vision of the rebirth of The Library. A new beginning in a new place with a new generation. He laughed to himself about channeling Star Wars mythology.

The Library neighborhood was not coming back. That was a fact. Many of its buildings were destroyed and would not be rebuilt, and the spirit of its citizens was broken. The library they had witnessed burning to the ground was more than a symbol to them. It *was* the neighborhood. The neighbors they had lost in the explosion weren't just any neighbors; they were the Banis family, the mother librarian's kin. They had made the neighborhood possible. Iris was fated to be the last librarian. The books could not be replaced.

He had lost track of time. It was too late to hike back to the car and drive home. Not really, but he didn't have the motivation it would take. He didn't have the energy after finding out that Helen, the very last of the Banis family, was dead, or at least planning to be soon. The letter made it clear she was not returning.

He texted Dion that he wouldn't be back until the next day.

Would he even be able to sleep? Would the barn be haunted by the family ghosts?

He stood on the porch, not knowing what else to do. It was very dark outside and very quiet. The dark quiet of night in the countryside. He heard some owls hooting at each other. He half expected to see Helen walking through the grass toward him.

Hey, Zeph. I tried to die, but it seems I'm actually immortal.

Eventually, he had the wherewithal to go inside and inspect the barn. It was Tristan's property now, or it would be if her letter had any legal weight, and even if it didn't, who would care? Not Dion, and he was the only person who had a claim. He should come back with a report on the state of the property. Tristan would appreciate it. It would help him decide if he wanted to live there as Helen had hoped.

Zephyr found himself invested in his vision of the neighborhood reborn, and he hoped to convince Tristan. Helen had been the mother of The Library, and in death she would be the mother of the new neighborhood, the goddess of The Property, or whatever it would be named. It wouldn't be up to him.

Karmically speaking, it all made sense, if not practically speaking, since the only building was the barn. Where else could people live?

Where there's a will, there's a way. It would be up to Tristan to have the will. He realized his grief was talking, but so what? He would dream of something good, something hopeful. He would have faith in the future.

He made his way around the barn, looking through every stall and the common areas, noting what Helen had left behind. There wasn't much. She had lived beyond simply. She had lived as a hermit with almost nothing. If Tristan were to move out here, he would be able to use everything, because everything Helen had was useful in some way. Everything she had, she used.

He opened a chest at the end of her bed, assuming it held an extra blanket or two, which it did, but under the blankets, there was a surprise: Helen's journals, or what he assumed were her journals.

There were maybe two dozen notebooks. He opened one, and it was filled with writing. He quickly closed it, feeling as if he were violating her privacy. She had left the notebooks for her kids to find; that was obvious. Did he have the right to read them?

If not him, who? Dion would say burn them. He realized it was pointless for him to pretend he might resist on some moral pretense, and now he didn't have to worry anymore about whether or not he would be able to sleep. There was a nighttime of reading ahead.

3.6

Zephyr didn't have to convince Tristan of anything. After reading the letter Helen had left, and then all of the journals Zephyr had brought back with him, he said with serious conviction, *we'll do the old lady proud.*

Tristan couldn't decide if Helen had lost her mind in the end or if her mysterious friend Astrid and the ethereal messages from anonymous were real, but he agreed with Zephyr that it didn't matter. As Helen argued at length in her philosophical ramblings: reality is a construct. What is real depends on the constructor. Who can say what is real and what isn't?

After getting to know Helen through her journals, he was inspired, but by what?

Her faith in the invisible.

That was true.

Her courage to act on that faith.

That was truer.

He was grateful to Percy's grandmother—the librarian turned hermetic mystic who at 100 years old had, it seemed, traveled to India to die at the direction of a supernatural being who wrote messages to her in her diaries—grateful for the opportunity to have faith in something and act on it. She had the faith to challenge anonymous and declare *I'm coming to find you whether you like it or not. Take me or leave me.* She had walked out into the field that morning, having no idea what would happen to her, prepared never to return.

He was inspired by such a badass old woman to be a badass himself and accept the challenge she had presented to him and Persephone in her letter: be the future. Represent. Percy would have been just as eager to accept the challenge.

He missed his partner and best friend. The ache would never disappear entirely, but resurrecting the neighborhood would help soothe the pain. Persephone would be proud.

But no one knew, and no one had any way of knowing, if Helen had actually died, and they would never know unless Helen posted another note, or the Dravidian did exist and appeared to tell them, or Astrid showed up one day bearing news of her friend.

There was a distinct chance Helen would return someday without warning, and by then he and who knows how many others would be living in her barn, making themselves at home.

After reading her journals, he knew Helen wouldn't mind. She would welcome them.

He must have banked some good karma. Trying to start a new ZG community at the Banis family's property was probably the only project that could have lifted him out of his depression after The Accident. He had a purpose now and a way to honor Percy. He had been gifted an opportunity and a responsibility to create something worthwhile, something good, something new. He was not going to let Helen down.

***

It's up to us to be the future, Tristan told the first four people who told him they wanted to live at the property. He insisted they all read their benefactor's journals for insight into what he meant.

After they were done reading, he asked them: What is this future that their benefactor referred to in her letter? Over many conversations, they arrived at a consensus, a shared dream they devoted themselves to. A vision they hoped Helen shared with them.

In the barn there were several books, one about using cob as a building material. There was plenty of clay soil on the property, and they learned how to make cob and mold it into simple living spaces. In time, the property began to look like a hobbit settlement. She also had a book about permaculture, and they created swales for growing food near the pond and the spring that fed it. They learned about how to capture methane gas from the pit toilets they dug and use it to create electricity. A sympathetic neighbor living off-grid on the edge of the property gave them a pair of goats. There were plenty of chickens living at the colony.

Once there were a couple dozen residents, they chose a name: The Egg. The little valley was shaped like an egg, and their community was growing inside it.

An egg holds a future yet to be born.

3.7

Tristan had a secret.

In the early days of The Egg, wanting to be familiar with every inch of the property, he spent many hours exploring. He traversed the field multiple times and walked the length of every path Helen had made in the forest.

When he was walking in the woods, he couldn't shake the feeling he was being observed, even followed. Sometimes the sensation was strong enough to stop him in his tracks. He'd hold his breath and listen for any sound, however faint. Peer into the forest until his eyes hurt. Sometimes, exasperated, he would even shout HEY, YOU! Or HELLOOO, WHOEVER YOU ARE, or some other such phrase.

After a while, he more or less got used to the feeling and stopped focusing on it. Like a tiny pebble in his shoe, he could feel it, but he was able to put it out of his mind. He decided that it must be Helen's vibrations lingering along the paths she had walked for years. She haunted the forest.

Over the years, he continued his jaunts through the woods, and on one of these walks, not long after the birth of his twins, Percy and Iris, on a trail he'd taken dozens of times, he noticed a faint path, one of those spurs off the main line that usually ends up in a dead end at a fallen tree or the edge of a ravine.

He couldn't remember having seen it before and was deciding whether or not to take it when he caught a glimpse of something moving some 20 yards away down this narrow detour. It looked like a dog.

Could belong to a neighbor, he thought. He followed as it trotted away. *Then again, it could be the fox Helen saw.*

Tristan hoped every time he went out exploring, he might meet the fox Helen had described in one of her journals. If the fox was real, it would be some corroboration for everything she had written. Seeing the fox would at least ease some doubt about the existence of Astrid and anonymous, not to mention the integrity of Helen's mind.

He lost sight of the animal when it took a quick turn to the right onto what wasn't something you could call a path anymore. Just a narrow slash of space through the brush. He walked to where the animal had disappeared from view and looked around. Nothing was moving, but he could hear water plopping in slow drips into what must be a pool. He moved through the trees in the direction of the sound, pushing branches away from his face as he went.

The water was dripping off a sharp ledge jutting out from an imposing rock covered in moss, ferns, and tiny cedar seedlings. The ledge formed a natural shelter, a protected stone hollow that could just about be called a shallow cave. The dripping water fed a small pool in the sandy earth, big enough for one person to sit in.

There were candles on the ground under the ledge, and in the back of the hollow, far enough to be protected from rain, there was a sleeping pad and down bag. There were even dry matches which he used to light some of the candles.

He sat on the pad and felt tremendous peace. He had no doubt this was where Helen had come to meditate—and sleep, from the looks of it—while listening to the steady beat of water that had been dripping like that for how long? Before the barn was built? Before the field had been cleared? For ages, possibly eons. For centuries.

Sitting in that hallowed space he thought about what she had written, words he had been over so many times himself and with others, and with those words filling his mind, he realized how absurd it was to question anything she had written as somehow demented, somehow compromised by her advanced age.

Under that rock, resting on Helen's pad, he was in the timeless space where Helen had lived for 20 years. He realized her words had just been a sideline, a hobby, something to do. Something for her kids to remember her by.

Those words didn't exist in this space where she lived. They didn't mean anything. They were nothing more than candle smoke. Take them seriously or consider them nonsense; it didn't matter. Question the reality of something she wrote, reject it, or accept it—irrelevant. This space was her life. She may have come to believe it was where she would live forever. Or where she would die.

He laughed to himself, thinking about Helen's antipathy toward her cell phone. How jarring its sounds notifying her of nothing would be as they echoed back from the stone walls. Alien sounds. The stuff of horror.

As his eyes got used to the candlelight, he saw there was one more thing on the ground near the back wall. It looked like an ice bucket.

It was an unadorned metal container, not much bigger than a toaster. It had a tight lid. Nothing moved or rattled inside when he picked it up and shook it. It weighed about as much as a fresh loaf of sourdough bread.

His hands and face were sweaty and his heart was racing. He was pretty sure he knew what it was and what it held. Because he was sure, he was afraid to find out. He sat down on the pad with the container in front of him and stared at it for quite a while, keeping his mind blank.

Eventually, Tristan slowly worked the lid loose. When he pulled it free, there was a poof of dust.

Ashes. Helen's ashes. What else could they be?

There was a note resting on top of the ashes. Even in the candlelight, he could see it was written in the same weird font used in the letter left in the barn, the same font Helen attributed to anonymous.

Tristan gasped in recognition of what that meant.

Anonymous must be real.

Whatever 'real' means.

Was she or was anonymous the author of the letter left for her kids? Did she even go to India? Were these really her ashes? Was the whole thing an elaborate prank?

He realized he could ask question after question and be left only with more questions. All he could do was choose what to believe. He thought that's all anyone can ever do.

He clung to his conviction that he had seen the fox. The fox had led him here to make this discovery. Not even the most committed pranksters could have orchestrated that.

Holding a candle up for light, careful not to drip wax on the ashes, he read the short note:

HELEN PENELOPE BANIS

BLESSED BY DIVINE GRACE

RECOGNIZED THE CLEAR LIGHT OF REALITY

THEREBY ESCAPING THE WORLD OF KARMA

OM SHANTI OM

Tristan didn't fully understand what the words of this epitaph specifically signified, but he did understand they were a tribute to Helen.

He read the note several times, each time opening himself up to the feelings the words evoked in him. The words resonating in his mind made him extremely happy.

Before leaving the shelter, he found a cleft in the rock where he could hide the urn. When they were old enough, he would bring the twins to the sanctuary and share the secret with them. It would be their secret to pass on to their kids, or so he hoped.

The secret belonged to Persephone and her family. His family would keep it safe.

Printed in the USA
CPSIA information can be obtained
at www.ICGtesting.com
LVHW012122291123
765059LV00012B/627